THE
DRUIDS' KEEP

THE DRUIDS' KEEP

Volume Two of
THE SWORD OF SHANNARA

Terry Brooks

www.atombooks.co.uk

An *Atom* Book

First published in Great Britain as part of The Sword of Shannara by
Futura Publications Limited in 1978
Reprinted 1983 (twice), 1985, 1986, 1987, 1988, 1989, 1990
Reprinted by Orbit 1992 (twice), 1993, 1995, 1996, 1997, 1998,
1999, 2000

First published in this edition by Atom 2004

A CIP catalogue record for this book is available from the British Library.

ISBN 1 904233 341 4

Printed and bound in Great Britain
by Bookmarque Ltd, Croydon, Surrey

Atom
An imprint of
Time Warner Books UK
Brettenham House
Lancaster Place
London WC2E 7EN

CHAPTER

1

D awn hung above the sweeping ridges and peaks of the Dragon's Teeth with a cold, gray determination that was neither cheerful nor welcome. The warmth and brightness of the rising sun was entirely screened away by low cloud banks and heavy mist that settled into the ominous heights and did not stir. The winds blew with vicious force over the barren rocks, whipping through canyons and craggy drops, across slopes and ridges, cutti ng into the scant vegetation and bending it close to the point of breaking, yet slipping through the mixture of clouds and mist with elusive quickness, leaving it unexplainably and strangely motionless. The sound of the wind was like the deep roar of the ocean breaking on an open beach, heavy and rolling, blanketing the empty peaks in a peculiar drone that, when one had been enveloped for a while, created its own level of silence. Birds rose and fell with the wind, their cries scattered and muffled. There were few animals at this height – isolated herds of a particularly tough breed of mountain goat and small, furry mice that inhabited the innermost recesses of the rocks. The air was more than chill; it was bitterly cold. Snow covered the upper reaches of the Dragon's Teeth, and changes in the seasons had little effect at this altitude on a temperature that seldom reached thirty degrees.

These were treacherous mountains, vast, towering and

incredibly massive. On this morning they seemed shrouded with a strange expectancy, and the eight men who comprised the little company from Culhaven could not ignore the feeling of uneasiness that preoccupied their thoughts as they trudged deeper into the cold and the gray. It was more than the disturbing prophecy of Bremen or even the knowledge that they would soon attempt to pass through the forbidden Hall of Kings. Something was waiting for them, something that had patience and cunning, a life force that lay hidden in the barren, rocky terrain they were passing through, filled with vindictive hatred of them, watching as they struggled deeper into the giant mountains that shut away the ancient kingdom of Paranor. They trudged northward in a ragged line, strung out against the misty skyline, their bodies wrapped tightly in woolen cloaks for protection against the cold, their faces bent before the wind. The slopes and canyons were covered with loose rock and split by hidden crevices that made the footing extremely hazardous. More than once, a member of the little band went down in a shower of loose rock and dirt. But still the thing concealed in the land chose not to show itself, content merely to let its presence be known and to wait for the effect of that knowledge to wear away at the resistance of the eight men. The hunters would then become the hunted.

It did not take long. Doubts began to gnaw quietly, persistently at their tired minds – doubts that rose phantomlike from the fears and secrets the men concealed deep within. Locked away from each other by the cold and the roar of the rising wind, each man was cut off from his companions, and the inability to communicate only heightened the growing feeling of uneasiness. Only Hendel was immune. His taciturn, solitary nature had hardened him against self-doubt, and his harrowing escape from the maddened Gnomes in the Pass of Jade had drained him at least temporarily of any fear of death. He had come close to dying, so close that in the end only instinct had saved him.

The Gnomes had come at him from every direction, swarming up the slope in reckless disregard, enraged to the point where only bloodshed would quiet their hatred. He had been quick, slipping back into the fringes of the Wolfsktaag, motionless in the brush, coolly letting the Gnomes overextend themselves until one had come within reach. It had taken only seconds to stun the unsuspecting hunter, to cloak his captive in his own distinctive Dwarf habit, and then yell for assistance. In the darkness, flushed with the excitement of the hunt, the Gnomes were unable to recognize anything except the cloak. They tore their own brother to pieces without realizing it. Hendel had stayed hidden and slipped through the pass the following day. He had survived once again.

The Valemen and the Elves did not possess Hendel's strong sense of self-reliance. The prophecy of the Shade of Bremen had left them stunned. The words seemed to repeat themselves over and over in the howl of the mountain winds. One of them was going to die. Oh, the words of the prophecy had phrased it differently than that, but the implication was unmistakable. It was a bitter prospect to face, and none of them could really accept it. Somehow they would find a way to prove the prediction wrong.

Far in the lead, his great frame bent against the driving force of the mountain winds, Allanon was mulling over the events that had transpired in the Valley of Shale. He considered for the hundredth time his strange confrontation with the Shade of Bremen, the aged Druid doomed to wander in limbo until the Warlock Lord was finally destroyed. Yet it was not the appearance of the driven wraith that so disturbed him now. It was the terrible knowledge which he carried, buried deep among his blackest truths. His foot struck a projecting rock, causing him to stumble slightly, and he fought to keep his balance. A wheeling hawk screamed shrilly in the grayness and shot down out of the sky over a distant ridge. The Druid turned slightly as the thin line following struggled to keep pace. He had learned more from the Shade than the words of the prophecy. But he had not told the others, those who had trusted him, the whole truth, just as he had not told them the whole story behind the legendary Sword of Shannara. His deep-set eyes blazed with inner fury at the predicament in which he had placed himself in not telling them everything, and for a moment he even considered doing so. They had given so much of themselves, and the giving had only begun . . . But a moment later, he wrenched the idea from his thoughts. Necessity was a higher god than truth.

The grayness of dawn passed slowly into the grayness of midday, and the march into the Dragon's Teeth wore on. The ridges and slopes appeared and faded with a dreary sameness that created the impression in the minds of the laboring travelers that no progress was being made. Ahead, a vast, towering line of peaks rose bleakly against the misty northern horizon, and it appeared that they were moving directly into a wall of impenetrable stone. Then they entered a broad canyon which wound sharply downward into a narrow, twisting path that broke between two huge cliffs and faded into the heavy mist. Allanon led them into the swirling grayness as the horizon disappeared and the wind died into stillness. The silence was abrupt and unexpected, sounding almost like a soft whisper through the towering mass of rock, speaking in hushed, cautious words in the ears of the groping travelers. Then the pass widened slightly and the mist cleared to a faint haze, revealing a high, cavernous opening in the cliff face where the winding passage ended.

The entrance to the Hall of Kings.

It was awesome, majestic, frightening. On either side of the rectangular black entryway stood two monstrous stone statues carved into the rock and rising well over a hundred feet against the dark cliff face. The stone sentries had been fashioned in the shape of armor-clad warriors, standing watchfully in the deep gloom, hands gripping the pommels of huge swords which rested blade downward at their feet. Their weathered, bearded faces were scarred by time and the wind, yet the eyes seemed almost alive, fixed carefully on the eight mortals who stood at the threshold of the ancient hall they guarded. Above the great entryway, scrolled into the rock, three words of a language centuries old and long forgotten served as a warning to those who would enter that this was the tomb of the dead. Beyond the vast opening, all was blackness and silence.

Allanon gathered them closely around him.

'Years ago, before the First War of the Races, a cult of men whose origins have been lost in time, served as priests for the gods of death. Within these caverns, they buried the monarchs of the four lands along with their families, servants, favorite possessions and much of their wealth. The legend grew that only the dead could survive within these chambers, and only the priests were permitted to see that the dead rulers were interred. All others who entered were never seen again. In time, the cult died out, but the evil instilled in the Hall of Kings continued to exist, blindly to serve the priests whose bones had years before returned to the earth. Few men have ever passed . . .'

He caught himself, seeing in the eyes of his listeners the unasked question.

'I have been through the Hall of Kings – I alone from this age, and now you. I am a Druid, the last to walk this earth. Like Bremen, like Brona before him, I have studied the black arts, and I am a sorcerer. I do not possess the power of the Dark Lord – but I can get us safely through these caverns to the other side of the Dragon's Teeth.'

'And then?' Balinor's question came softly out of the mist.

'A narrow cliff-trail men call the Dragon's Crease leads downward out of the mountains. Once there, we will be within sight of Paranor.'

There was a long, awkward silence. Allanon knew what they were thinking; disregarding it, he continued.

'Beyond this entrance, there are a number of passages and chambers, a maze to one who does not know the way. Some of these are dangerous, some are not. Soon after we enter, we will reach the tunnel of the Sphinxes, giant statues like these sentries, but carved as half man, half beast. If you look into their eyes, you will be turned to stone instantly. So you must be blindfolded. In addition you will be roped to one another. You must concentrate on me, think only of me, for their will, their mental command, is strong enough to force you to tear off the blindfolds and gaze into their eyes.'

The seven men looked at one another doubtfully. Already they were beginning to question the soundness of this whole approach.

'Once past the Sphinxes, there are several harmless passages leading to the Corridor of the Winds, a tunnel inhabited by invisible beings called Banshees after the legendary astral spirits. They are no more than voices, but those voices will drive mortal men insane. Your ears will be bound for protection, but again the important thing for you to do is to concentrate on me, let my mind blanket yours to prevent it from receiving the full force of those voices. You must relax; do not fight me. Do you understand?'

He counted seven barely perceptible nods.

'Once beyond the Corridor of the Winds, we will be in the Tomb of the Kings. Then there will be only one more obstacle . . .'

He stopped talking, his eyes turned warily to the cavern entrance. For a moment it seemed he might finish the sentence, but instead he motioned them toward the dark entryway. They stood uneasily between the stone giants, the graying mist clouding the high cliff walls surrounding them, the black, yawning opening before them waiting like the open maw of some great beast of prey. Allanon produced a number of wide cloth strips and gave one to each man. Utilizing a heavy length of climbing rope, the little group bound themselves to one another, the surefooted Durin taking the lead position, the Prince of Callahorn again assuming his post as rear guard. The blindfolds were securely fastened in place and hands were joined to form a chain. A moment later, the line moved cautiously through the entrance to the Hall of Kings.

There was a deep, hushed stillness in the caverns, magnified by the sudden dying of the winds and the echoing of their footfalls along the rocky passageway. The tunnel floor was strangely smooth and level, but the cold that had settled into the aged stone from centuries of constant temperatures seeped quickly through their tensed bodies and left them chill and shaking. No one spoke, each man trying to relax as Allanon led them carefully through a series of gently winding turns. In the middle of the groping line, Shea felt Flick's hand grip his own tightly in the blackness that surrounded them. They had drawn closer to each other since their flight from the Vale, bound now by ties of experiences shared more than by kinship. Whatever happened to them, Shea felt they would never lose that closeness. Nor would he forget what Menion had done for him. He thought about the Prince of Leah for a moment and found himself smiling. The highlander had changed so much during the past few days that he was almost a different person. The old Menion was still in evidence, but there was a new dimension to him that Shea found difficult to define. But then all of them, Menion, Flick and himself, had changed in little ways that could not be readily detected until each man was considered as a whole. He wondered if Allanon had seen the changes in him – Allanon, who had always treated him somehow as less than a man, more a boy.

They came to an unsteady halt, and in the deep silence that followed the commanding voice of the Druid leader whispered soundlessly in the mind of each man: *Remember my warning, let your thoughts turn to me, concentrate only on me*. Then the line moved forward, the booted feet echoing hollowly on the cavern floor. Immediately the blindfolded men could sense the presence of something waiting ahead of them, watching silently, patiently. The seconds fitted away as the company moved deeper into the cavern. The men became aware of huge, still forms rising up on either side – images carved of stone with faces that were human, but attached to the crouched bodies of indescribable beasts. The Sphinxes. In their minds the men could see those eyes, burning past the fading image of Allanon, and they began to feel the strain of trying to concentrate on the giant Druid. The insistent will of the stone monsters pushed into their brains, weaving and tangling into their scattered thoughts, working tenaciously toward the moment when human eyes would meet their own lifeless gaze. Each man began to feel a rapidly growing urge to rip away the restraining cloth which shackled his sight, to strip away the darkness and gaze freely on the wondrous creatures staring silently down on him.

But just when it seemed that the probing whisper of the Sphinxes must at last break through the waning resolve of the beleaguered men and draw their thoughts completely away from the fading image of Allanon, his iron thought cut through to them with the sharpness of a knife, soundlessly calling to them. *Think only of me*. Their minds obeyed instinctively, wrenching free of the almost overpowering urge to gaze upward into the watching stone faces. The strange battle wore on without respite as the line of men, sweating and breathing harshly in the stillness, groped its way through the tangled maze of unseen images, bound together by the rope about their waists, the chain of tightly clenched hands, and the commanding voice of Allanon. No one lost his grip. The Druid led them steadily down the row of Sphinxes, his own eyes locked onto the cavern floor, his indomitable will fighting to hold the minds of his sightless charges. Then at last the faces of the stone creatures began to fade and fall away, leaving the mortals alone in the silence and darkness.

They kept moving, winding through a long series of twisting passages. Then once again the line stopped, and Allanon's low voice cut through the blackness, ordering them to remove the blindfolds. They did so hesitantly and found themselves in a narrow tunnel where the rough stone gave off a peculiar greenish light. Their drawn faces bathed in the strange glow, the men glanced quickly at one another to reassure themselves that they were all present. The dark figure of the Druid passed noiselessly down the line, testing the rope that bound their waists and warning them that the Corridor of the Winds still lay ahead. Stuffing bits of cloth in their ears and binding them with the loosened blindfolds to mask the sounds of the invisible beings Allanon had named Banshees, the men joined hands once more.

The line wound slowly through the faint green light of the narrow tunnel, their footsteps barely perceptible to their tightly covered ears. This section of the caverns ran for more than a mile, then faded abruptly as the passage widened and grew into a towering corridor that was totally black. The rock walls drew away and the ceiling rose until both had disappeared altogether, leaving the company alone in a strange limbo of darkness where only the smooth cavern floor offered any reassurance that the earth had not dissolved entirely. Allanon led them into the blackness, showing no signs of hesitancy.

Then abruptly, the sound began. Its incredible fury caught them completely unprepared, and for a moment there was panic. The initial shock grew to an enormous roar like the sound of a thousand winds combined in fury and biting force. But beneath this was the horrifying cry of souls screaming in anguish, voices scraping and twisting their tortured way through all the imaginable horrors of inhumanity in utter despair of any hope for salvation. The roar climbed to a shriek, reaching a pitch so far beyond the comprehension of the mortals' stunned minds that their sanity began to break apart. The terrible sounds washed over them, mirroring their own growing despair, driving relentlessly inward and stripping away the tattered nerve ends like layers of skin until the very bone was laid bare.

It had taken only an instant. In another instant, they would have been lost. But for the second time the hopelessly numbed humans were saved, this time from complete madness, as the powerful will of Allanon broke through the crazed sound to cloak them with protective reassurance. The screams and the roar seemed to lessen and fade into a strange buzzing as the grim, dark face projected itself into the seven feverish minds and the iron thoughts spoke soothingly, commandingly: *Let your minds relax – think only of me.* The men stumbled mechanically through the heavy darkness of the tunnel, their minds groping at the safety line of coherence and calm that the Druid held out to them. The walls of the corridor reverberated with the still-audible shrieks, and the massive stone of the cavern rumbled frighteningly. One final time the voices of the Banshees rose in feverish pitch, screeching violently in a desperate effort to break through the subconscious wall erected by the Druid's powerful mind, but the wall would not yield and the power of the voices spent itself and faded into a deathly whisper. A moment later, the passageway narrowed once more, and the company was clear of the Corridor of the Winds.

Visibly shaken, their faces streaked with sweat, the men stood dumbly as Allanon brought the line to a halt. Shaking their scattered thoughts into some semblance of order, they removed the rope about their waists and the cloth binding their ears. They were in a small cave, facing toward two huge stone doors laced by iron bindings. The rock walls around them emitted the same peculiar greenish light. Allanon waited patiently until everyone had fully recovered, then beckoned them forward. He paused before the stone portals. With only a slight shove from the lean hand, the massive doors swung silently open. The Druid's deep voice was only a whisper in the stillness.

'The Hall of Kings.'

For over a thousand years, none but Allanon had entered the forbidden tomb. All that time it had remained otherwise undisturbed – a mammoth, circular cavern, the great walls smooth and polished, the ceiling shimmering in a green glow similar to that reflected by the tunnels they had already passed through. Along the circular wall of the giant rotunda, standing with the same proud defiance they presumably had exhibited in life, were stone statues of the dead rulers, each facing toward the center of the chamber and the strange alter that rose upward in the shape of a coiled serpent. Before each statue was piled the wealth of the dead, casks and trunks of precious metals and jewels, furs, weapons, all the favorite possessions of the deceased. In the walls immediately behind each statue were the sealed, rectangular openings in which rested the remains of the dead – kings, their families, their servants. Inscriptions above the sealed crypts gave the history of the rulers interred there, frequently in languages unfamiliar to any of the wondering members of the company. The entire chamber was bathed in the deep green light. The metal and stone seemed to absorb the color. Dust covered everything, a deep rock powder that had settled over the centuries and now rose in small clouds as the footsteps of the men disturbed its long rest. For over a thousand years, no one had violated the peace of this ancient chamber. No one had tampered with its secrets nor attempted to unlock the doors that guarded the dead and their possessions. No one but Allanon. And now . . .

Shea shivered violently, unexplainably. He shouldn't be here; he could feel a small, distant voice telling him he shouldn't be here. It wasn't that the Hall of Kings was sacred or forbidden. But it was a tomb – it was a tomb for the ancient dead. It was no place for the living. Something gripped him, and with a start he realized it was Allanon's hand touching his shoulder. The Druid frowned darkly at him, then called softly to the others. They huddled silently in the greenish light as he addressed them in hushed tones.

'Through those doors at the far end of the Hall is the Assembly.' He directed their gaze to the other end of the rotunda where a second set of huge stone doors stood closed. 'A wide set of stone stairs leads downward to a long pool fed by a spring somewhere deep beneath the mountain. At the foot of the stairs, directly before the pool, stands the Pyre of the Dead, where the monarchs buried here lay in state for a certain number of days, depending on their rank and wealth, presumably so that their souls could escape to the life beyond. We must pass through that chamber in order to reach the passageway that will take us to the Dragon's Crease on the other side of the mountains.'

He paused and breathed deeply.

'When I traveled through these caverns before, I was able to hide myself from the eyes of the creatures put here to destroy intruders. I cannot do this for you. There is something in the Assembly, something whose power may prove to be greater than my own. Though it could not sense my presence, I was conscious of it hidden beneath the deep waters of the pool. Below the stairs, to either side of the pool, are narrow walkways leading to the other end of the chamber and the opening to the passages beyond. These walkways are the only way past the pool. Whatever it is that guards the Pyre of the Dead will strike at us there. When we get into the room, Balinor, Menion, and I will move onto the walkway to the left. That should draw the creature out from his hiding place. When we are attacked, Hendel will take the rest of you along the right walkway through the opening at the far end. Don't stop until you reach the Dragon's Crease. Do you understand?'

They nodded slowly. Shea felt strangely trapped, but

there was nothing to be gained by talking about it now. Allanon straightened to his full seven-foot height and grinned menacingly, his strong teeth gleaming. The little Valeman felt a chill run through him that made him glad ten times over he was not the enemy of the mystic. In one effortless motion, Balinor drew forth his great sword, the metal blade ringing sharply as it cleared the sheath. Hendel was already moving across the Hall, the heavy mace held tightly in one hand. Menion started to follow, then hesitated, gazing doubtfully on the stores of treasure heaped about the tombs. Would it hurt to take a few? The Valeman and Elves were moving after Hendel and Balinor. Allanon stood watching the highlander, his long arms folded into the black cloak. Menion turned and looked questioningly at the mystic.

'I wouldn't if I were you,' the other warned shortly. 'It's all coated with a substance poisonous to the skin of living things. Touch it and you will be dead in less than a minute.'

Menion stared at him incredulously for a moment, shot a quick glance back at the treasure, then shook his head resignedly. He was halfway across the chamber when, on sudden inspiration, he whipped out two long black arrows and walked over to an open chest of gold pieces. Carefully, he rubbed the metal tips in the precious metal, making certain that his hands did not touch anything but the feathered ends. Grinning with perverse satisfaction, he rejoined the others across the room. Whatever waited beyond the stone doors was going to be given the opportunity to test its resistance to this poison that would supposedly kill any living creature. In a tight cluster, the company gathered around Allanon, their metal weapons glinting coldly. A stillness settled over the great room, broken only by the expectant breathing of the eight men huddled about the closed doors. Shea glanced back for just a moment at the Hall of Kings. The tomb seemed undisturbed save for the ragged trail of footprints in the dust leading across the chamber. A deep haze of this dust hung swirling in the greenish light, stirred by the intruders' footsteps, but settling slowly back to the ancient cavern floor. In time, all evidence of their passing would be erased as the tracks were covered over entirely.

At Allanon's touch, the stone portals swung open and the company moved noiselessly into the Assembly. They were on a high platform that ran forward into a wide alcove and then descended in a series of broad stairs. The cavern beyond was enormous, a vast, towering cave that still exhibited the full, unaltered splendor of its rough, natural creation by nature's careful hands. From the high ceiling hung jagged stalactites, stone icicles formed by water and mineral deposits over thousands of years. Beneath these sculptured stone spears lay a long, rectangular pool of deep green water, the surface smooth and glasslike. When a single drop of water fell heavily from an overhanging stone projection, the placid surface rippled outward once and was still. The wary men moved forward to the edge of the platform and looked down on the high stone altar set at the foot of the stairs before the pool, its ancient surface scarred and pocked and in places almost crumbling. The cavern was dimly lit by streaks of phosphorescence that ran brokenly through its rocky walls, giving an eerie, fluorescent glow to the ancient chamber.

Slowly the men moved down the stairway, their eyes picking out a single word inscribed in the stone surface of the altar. A few knew its meaning. *Valg* – a word taken from the ancient Gnome tongue. It meant Death. Their footsteps reverberated in muffled echoes through the vast cavern. Nothing moved. Everything was shrouded in age and silence. On reaching the foot of the long stairway, they hesitated for a second, eyes fastened on the silent pool. Impatiently, Allanon motioned Hendel and his charges to the right; then with Menion and Balinor following, he moved quickly onto the left walkway. A misstep now would prove fatal. From across the pool, Shea watched the three figures edge their way silently along the rough stone wall, keeping well to the rear of the open walkway. There was no movement in the placid waters. They were about midway now, and Shea breathed for the first time.

Then the still surface of the dark pool surged upward and from out of the depths emerged a nightmare. Serpentine in appearance, the loathsome monster seemed to fill the cavern, its slime-covered bulk raising skyward, shattering the ancient stalactites. Its shriek of fury boomed through the Assembly. The massive body twisted and flexed as it reared out of the water. Long front legs tipped with deadly hooked claws clutched the empty air, and the great jaws clashed sharply, grinding together the blackened, pointed teeth that lined the edges. The wide, staring eyes burned red amid a cluster of bumps and stunted horns that covered the misshapen head. The entire bulk of the creature was covered with a reptilian skin that dripped with scum and waste that must have been carried from the nether world's blackest pits. The mouth oozed venom that fell into the water and rose with faint traces of steam. The monstrous thing glared at the three humans on the walkway and hissed with unbridled hatred. Jaws wide, screeching in anticipation of the kill, it attacked.

Everyone reacted instantly. Menion Leah's great ash bow sounded in staccato pings as the poisoned arrows flew with deadly accuracy, burying themselves deeply within the unprotected inner flesh of the serpent's gaping mouth. The creature reared back in pain, and Balinor quickly seized the initiative. Moving to the edge of the walkway, the giant borderman struck powerfully at the exposed forearm of the monster. But to his shock, the great sword only barely scratched the scaly hide, glancing off the heavy coating of slime. The second forearm made a quick swipe at the attacker, missing by inches as the intended victim dove to one side. On the opposite walkway, Hendel made a rush for the open passage at the far end of the pool, shoving the Valemen and the Elven brothers before him. But one of them triggered a hidden release, and a heavy stone slab collapsed in the opening, sealing off the escape route. In desperation, Hendel threw his powerful body against the stone barricade, but it refused to budge.

The serpent had been attracted by the sound of the falling stone. Turning away from its battle with Menion and Balinor, it moved eagerly toward these smaller foes. That would have been the finish if not for the quick reactions of the battle-hardened Dwarf. Forgetting the stone slab and disregarding his own safety entirely, Hendel charged at the huge monster bearing down on him and drove the heavy iron mace directly into the closest burning eye. The weapon struck with such force that it smashed the glowing orb. The serpent reared upward in excruciating pain, crashing heavily into the jagged stalactites as it whipped its bulk from side to side. Deadly rock fragments showered the entire chamber. Flick went down with a sharp blow to the head. At the edge of the pool, Hendel was buried under a cascade of crumbling stone and lay motionless. The other three fell back against the blocked entryway as the massive attacker loomed above them.

At last Allanon joined the unequal battle. Raising both arms, he extended his lean hands, and his fingers seemed to light up like small glowing balls. Streaks of blinding, blue flame shot out of the tips and struck the head of the raging creature. The force of this new attack completely stunned the unprepared serpent, who thrashed wildly above the boiling water of the pool, shrieking in pain and fury. Moving quickly ahead on the walkway, the Druid struck a second time, the blue flames flashing against the head of the enraged beast, twisting it completely around. This second strike threw the great scaled body backward against the cavern wall where, thrashing in an uncontrollable frenzy, it jarred loose the stone slab that blocked the passageway out. Shea and the Elven brothers had barely managed to drag the unconscious Flick out of the way in time to avoid being crushed by the massive body. They heard the stone slab drop forward with an audible thud and, spying the open passage, yelled wildly to the other fighters. Balinor had reattacked the writhing monster as it again came within reach, striking vainly for the head as it swung down at him, still stunned by the force of Allanon's bolts. Allanon had his eyes fixed on the serpent, and only Menion saw what the others were yelling about and waved them madly toward the opening. Dayel and Shea picked up the fallen Flick and carried him into the tunnel beyond. Durin started to follow, but then hesitated as he caught sight of the unconscious Hendel, still buried beneath the shattered stone rubble. Turning back, he rushed to the pool's edge, grasped the Dwarf's limp arm and vainly attempted to pull him clear of the debris.

'Get out!' roared Allanon, who had suddenly spotted the Elf near the opening.

Choosing this moment of distraction, the serpent struck back. With one mighty sweep of its clawed arm it brushed Balinor aside, knocking him with crushing force against the chamber wall. Menion leaped in front of the monster, but its sudden rush bowled the Prince of Leah over, and he was knocked from sight. The serpent, still in great pain from its multiple wounds, could think only of reaching the tall figure in the black robes and crushing the life out of him. The beast had one more weapon in its arsenal, and it used it now. The venom-tipped jaws gaped wide at the sight of the intended victim, standing alone and unprotected, and great sheets of flame shot forth, completely encasing the Druid. Durin, who was in position to see everything happening on the walkway, gave an audible gasp of dismay. Shea and Dayel, standing just beyond the entrance to the tunnel leading from the Assembly, watched in mute horror as the flames covered the tall mystic. But

17

a second later the fire died, and Allanon stood untouched before the astonished onlookers. His hands raised and the blue streaks of flame shot out of his extended fingers, striking the head of the serpent with terrific force, sending the scaled body reeling back once again. Steam rose in great clouds from the thrashing waters of the pool, mingling in a heavy mist with the dust and smoke stirred by the battle until everything was obscured from view.

Then, from out of the haze, Balinor appeared at Durin's side, his cloak torn and shredded, the shining chain mail chipped and battered, the familiar face streaked with sweat and blood. Together they pulled Hendel from beneath the rocks. With one great arm, the Prince of Callahorn lifted the silent form over his shoulder and motioned Durin ahead of him into the passage where Dayel and Shea still lingered with the unconscious Flick. The giant borderman ordered them to pick up the fallen Valeman, and without waiting to see if they obeyed, disappeared down the darkened corridor, Hendel over one shoulder, the great broad sword held tightly in his free hand. The Elven brothers quickly did as they were told, but Shea hesitated, searching worriedly for some sign of Menion. The Assembly was a shambles, the long rows of stalactites smashed, the walkways a mass of rubble, the walls cracked and shattered, and everything obscured by dust and steam from the boiling pool. To one side of the cavern, the massive form of the serpent was still visible, thrashing in agony against the broken wall, its great bulk a writhing mass of scales and blood. Neither Menion nor Allanon was in view. But a moment later both appeared from out of the thick haze, Menion limping slightly, but still clutching the ash bow and the sword of Leah, Allanon's dark form tattered and layered with dust and ash. Without speaking, the Druid waved the Valeman ahead of them, and together the three stumbled through the partially blocked opening.

What happened after was vague in everyone's mind.

Numbly, the battered group hurried along the tunnel, carrying the two wounded and unconscious men. Time dragged agonizingly away, then abruptly they were outside, blinking in the bright light of the afternoon sun, standing at the edge of a dangerously steep cliff face. To their right, the Dragon's Crease wound its way downward to the open hill country below. Suddenly the whole mountain began to rumble menacingly, shaking in short tremors beneath their feet. With a sharp command, Allanon ordered them down the narrow trail. Balinor led the way, carrying the still form of Hendel, Menion Leah a couple of steps behind. Durin and Dayel followed, carrying Flick. Behind them came Shea and finally Allanon. The sinister rumbling continued somewhere deep within the mountain. Slowly the little group moved along the narrow pathway. The trail wound unevenly amid jagged overhangs and sudden drops, and the men were forced to flatten themselves against the cliff face at regular intervals to avoid losing their balance and falling to the rocks hundreds of feet below. The Dragon's Crease was well named. The continual twists and turns in the path required concentrated skill and caution to navigate successfully, and the recurring tremors made the task doubly hazardous.

They had progressed only a short distance along the treacherous pathway when a new sound became audible, a deep roar that quickly drowned out the rumblings in the mountain. Shea, last in line with Allanon, was unable to define the source of the roar until he was almost on top of its origin. Rounding a sharp cut in the side of the mountain, which brought him onto a ledge facing northward, he discovered an enormous waterfall directly across from their position on the mountainside. Tons of cascading water crashed with a deafening roar into a great river hundreds of feet below that swept between the mountain ranges and poured into a series of rapids than ran eastward to the Rabb Plains. The mighty river swept directly below the ledge on which he stood and the narrow trail ahead, its white waters churning and slapping against the confining sides of the two peaks that hemmed it in. Shea looked at it for a moment, and then hastened on down the trail at Allanon's command. The rest of the company had gone a good distance ahead of them and for a moment were lost from view in the rocks.

Shea had gone about a hundred feet past the ledge when a sudden tremor, more violent than the others, shook the mountain to its core. Without warning the section of the trail on which he was standing broke away and slid steadily down the mountainside, carrying the hapless Valeman with it. He gave a cry of dismay, fighting to break his fall as he saw himself sliding toward a steep overhang which dropped off sharply into a long, long fall to the raging river on the valley floor. Allanon rushed forward as the Valeman slid wildly in a cloud of dust and rock toward the waiting overhang.

'Grab something!' roared the Druid. 'Catch yourself!'

Shea clutched vainly, clawing at the sheer face of the cliff, and just at the edge of the drop-off caught himself on a projecting rock. He lay flat against the nearly vertical surface, not daring to try to climb back up, his arms nearly breaking from the exertion.

'Hold on, Shea!' Allanon encouraged him. 'I'll get a rope. Don't move an inch!'

Allanon called down the trail for the others, but whether they could have helped, Shea never discovered. As the Druid shouted for assistance, a second tremor shook the mountain and jarred loose the unfortunate Valeman from his precarious perch, sending him sliding out beyond the overhang before he could even think to catch himself. Arms and legs flying madly, he fell headlong into the swiftly flowing waters of the river below. Allanon watched helplessly as the Valeman struck with crushing force, bobbed to the surface, and was swept away eastward toward the plains beyond, tossing and turning in the boiling river like a small cork until he was lost from sight.

CHAPTER

2

Flick Ohmsford stood quietly at the foot of the Dragon's Teeth and stared into space. The fading rays of the late afternoon sun crossed his stocky frame in faint glimmers, casting his shadow onto the cooling rocks of the giant mountain at his back. He listened for a moment to the sounds about him, the muffled voices of somebody from the company off to his left, the chirping cries of the birds in the forest ahead. In his own mind he heard Shea's determined voice for an instant, and he recalled his brother's great courage in the face of the countless dangers they had encountered together. Now Shea was gone, probably dead, washed out by that unknown river to the plains on the other side of the mountains they had battled so hard to cross through. He rubbed his head gently, feeling the bump and the dull pain from the blow of the rock fragment that had knocked him senseless, preventing him from being able to help when his brother had needed him the most. They had been ready to face death at the hands of the Skull Bearers, ready to perish by the swords of the roving Gnomes, and even ready to succumb to the terrors of the Hall of Kings. But for it all to be ended by a fluke of nature on a narrow cliff ledge, when they were so close to escaping, was too much for anyone to accept. Flick felt such biting hurt inside that he wanted to cry out his bitterness. But even now, he could not. His insides knotted at the anger he could not manage, and he felt instead only a great sense of waste.

Menion Leah seemed in marked contrast as he paced in furious desperation several yards away from the Valeman, his lean figure bent in what could only be described as a wounded crouch. His own thoughts burned deep with anger, the kind of futile rage that a caged beast displays when there is no hope of escape, and only its pride and its hatred of what has happened to it remain. There was nothing he could have done to help Shea, he knew. But that did little to ease the sense of guilt he felt at not having been there when the cliff ledge gave way and the Valeman was thrown to the churning waters of the rapids below. Something might have been done to prevent it had he not left Shea alone with the Druid. Yet he knew it was not Allanon's fault; he had done everything possible to protect Shea. Menion moved with long, angry strides, digging into the ground with the sharp heels of his boots. He refused to admit that the quest was ended, that they would be forced to admit defeat when the Sword of Shannara was so nearly within their grasp. He paused and considered for a moment the object of their search. It still didn't make any sense to the highlander. Even if they got the Sword, what could a man, not yet more than a grown boy, hope to do against the power of a creature like the Warlock Lord? Now they would never know, for Shea was probably dead; even if he wasn't dead, he was lost to them. Nothing seemed to make much sense anymore, and Menion Leah realized suddenly how very much that causal, relaxed friendship between them had meant. They had never spoken of it, never really openly acknowledged it, but it had been there all the same, and it had been dear to him. Now it was ended. Menion bit down on his lip in helpless anger and continued to pace.

The others in the company were gathered near the foot of the Dragon's Crease, which ended just yards behind them. Durin and Dayel spoke to each other in hushed tones, their fine Elven features wrinkled with concern, their eyes lowered, looking at each other only occasionally. Close at hand, his solid frame propped against a massive boulder, rested Hendel, who, while always closemouthed, was now moody and unapproachable. His shoulder and leg were bandaged, his stolid face scarred and bruised from the battle with the serpent. He thought briefly of his homeland, his waiting family, and for an instant wished he could see the green of Culhaven once more before the end. He knew that without the Sword of Shannara, and without Shea to wield it, his land would be overrun by the Northland armies. Hendel was not alone in his thoughts. Balinor was thinking much the same thing, his eyes on the solitary giant standing motionless in a small grove of trees some distance away from the others. He knew that they now faced an impossible decision. Either they must give up the quest and turn back in an effort to reach their homelands and perhaps locate Shea, or they must continue on to Paranor and seize the Sword of Shannara without the courageous Valeman. It was a difficult choice to make, and no one would be very pleased either way. He shook his head sadly as the memory of the bitter quarrel between his brother and himself passed momentarily through his mind. He had his own decision to make when he returned to the city of Tyrsis – and it would not be pleasant. He had not spoken to the others about it, and at the moment, his personal problems were of secondary importance.

Suddenly the Druid wheeled about and started back to them, his own mind evidently decided. They watched him approach, the black robe flowing gently as he came, the fierce dark face resolute even in this moment of bitter defeat. Menion had frozen in his tracks, his heart beating madly as he awaited the confrontation he knew must come between them, for the highlander had chosen his own course of action, and he suspected it would not be that of

Allanon. Flick caught the hint of fear in the face of the Prince of Leah, but saw there, too, a strange courage as the man braced himself. All of them rose hesitantly and came together as the dark form drew closer, their tired, discouraged minds suddenly regenerated with a fierce determination not to admit defeat. They could not know what Allanon would command, but they knew they had come too far and sacrificed too much to give up now.

He stood before them, the deep eyes burning with mixed feelings, the shadowed face a granite wall of strength, worn and scarred. When he spoke, the words were frosted and sharp in the silence.

'It may be that we are beaten, but to turn back would be to dishonor ourselves in our own eyes as much as in the yes of those who depend on us. If we are to be defeated by the evil in the Northland, by things born of the spirit world, then we must turn and face it. We cannot back away and hope for some elusive miracle to stand between us and what most surely moves even now to enslave and destroy us. If death comes, it should find us with weapons drawn and the Sword of Shannara in our hands!'

He bit off the last sentence with such icy determination that even Balinor felt a slight shiver of excitement course through him. All stood in mute admiration of the Druid's unflagging strength, and they felt a sudden pride in being with him, being a part of the little group he had chosen for this dangerous and costly quest.

'What about Shea?' Menion spoke out suddenly, perhaps a bit sharply, as the Druid's penetrating eyes turned on him. 'What has become of Shea, who was the reason for this expedition in the first place?'

Allanon shook his head slowly, considering once again the Valeman's fate.

'I cannot guess any better than you. He was washed out to the plains by that mountain river. Perhaps he lives, perhaps not, but we can do nothing for him now.'

24

'What you are proposing is that we forget him and go after the Sword – a useless piece of metal without the rightful bearer!' Menion shouted in anger, his pent-up frustration coming to the fore at last. 'Well, I go no farther until I know what has happened to Shea, even if it means giving up the quest and searching until I find him. I will not desert my friend!'

'Watch yourself, highlander,' warned the slow, mocking voice of the mystic. 'Do not be foolish. To blame me for the loss of Shea is pointless, for I most of all would wish him no harm. What you suggest lacks any resemblance to reason.'

'Enough wise words, Druid!' stormed Menion, stepping forward in absolute disregard for what might happen next, his hot temper driven to the brink by the tall wanderer's impassive acceptance of the loss of the Valeman. 'We have followed you for weeks, through a hundred lands and perils without once questioning what you ordered. But this is too much for me. I am a Prince of Leah, not some beggar who does what he is told without question, caring for no one but himself! My friendship with Shea was nothing to you, but it was more to me than a hundred Swords of Shannara. Now stand aside! I will go my own way!'

'Fool, you are less a prince and more a clown to speak like this!' Allanon raged, his face tightening into a mask of anger, the great hands balling into fists and clenching before him. The others paled as the two opponents lashed verbally at each other in unbridled fury. Then sensing the physical combat that was about to ensue, they stepped between them, talking quickly, trying to calm them with reason, fearful that a split in the company now would mark the end of any chance for success. Flick alone had made no move, his own thoughts still on his brother, disgusted by the helplessness he felt at being powerless to do anything but feel inadequate. The minute Menion had spoken, he knew that the highlander had expressed his own

25

feelings, and he would not leave here without knowing what had befallen Shea. But it always seemed that Allanon knew so much more than the rest of them, that his decisions were always the right ones. To disregard the Druid's words completely now seemed somehow wrong. He struggled within his own mind for a moment, trying to think what Shea would do in this situation, what he might suggest to the others. Then almost without realizing it, he knew the answer.

'Allanon, there is a way,' he declared abruptly, shouting to be heard above the noise. They all looked over at him at once, surprised by the determined look on the stocky Valeman's face. Allanon nodded to indicate he was listening.

'You have the power to speak to the dead. We saw you do it back in the valley. Can you not tell if Shea lives? Your power is great enough to seek out the living if you can raise the dead. You can tell where he is, can't you?'

Everyone looked back at the Druid, waiting to see what he would do. Allanon sighed heavily and looked downward, his anger for Menion forgotten as he pondered the Valeman's question.

'I could do this,' he responded to everyone's amazement and general relief, 'but I will not. If I use my power to find out where Shea is, whether he is dead or alive, I will most certainly reveal our presence to the Warlock Lord and to the Skull Bearers. They would be alerted and waiting for us at Paranor.'

'If we go to Paranor,' Menion cut in darkly, whereupon Allanon wheeled on him in fury, his lagging anger revived. Again everyone leaped to separate them.

'Stop it, stop it!' Flick ordered angrily. 'This is helping no one, least of all Shea. Allanon, I have asked for nothing during this entire trip. I had no right to ask; I came by my own choice. But I have the right now because Shea is my brother, perhaps not by blood or race, but by stronger bonds still. If you will not use your power to find out where he is and what has happened to him, then I will go with Menion and search until Shea is found.'

'He is right, Allanon.' Balinor nodded slowly, one great hand coming to rest lightly on the little Valeman's shoulder. 'Whatever befalls us, these two have a right to know whether there is any chance for Shea. I know what it means if we are discovered, but I say we must take that chance.'

Durin and Dayel nodded vigorously in agreement. The Druid mystic looked aside to Hendel for his opinion, but the taciturn Dwarf made no movement, staring into the other's black eyes. Allanon looked at them one by one, perhaps assessing their true feelings as he thought of the risk involved, weighing the worth of the Sword against the loss of two of the company. He stared absently at the fading sun as the twilight of early evening settled into the mountains with slow ripples of darkness blending into the red and purple of the passing day. It had been a long, hard trip, and they had nothing to show for it – only the loss of the man for whom the whole journey had been made. It seemed so wrong, and he could appreciate their reluctance to continue now. He nodded to himself in understanding, then looked back at the others and saw their eyes turn suddenly bright, believing him to be nodding his agreement to Flick's demand. Without even a small smile of acquiescence, the tall wanderer shook his head firmly.

'The choice is yours. I will do as you ask. Stand back and do not speak to me or approach me until I tell you.'

The members of the company backed away while he remained quietly in place, head bent in concentration, the long arms clasped before him with the great hands buried in the long cloak. Only the distant sounds of evening were audible in the deepening gloom. Then the Druid stiffened and a white glow spread out from his tensed body, a blinding aura of light that caused the others to squint, then shield their eyes protectively. One moment the glow was everywhere and the dark form of Allanon was lost from sight, and in the next it flashed brilliantly and was gone. Allanon stood as he had before, motionless against the darkness, then slowly slumped to the ground, one lean hand pressed tightly to his forehead. The others hesitated for only a moment, then disregarded his earlier command and rushed forward, afraid that he had been injured. Allanon looked up in disapproval, angered that they had disobeyed him. Then he saw in the bent faces their deep concern. He stared in disbelief and with sudden understanding as they gathered about in silence. He was deeply touched, a strange warmth spreading through him as he realized the loyalty these six men of different races, different lands, different lives felt for him, even after all that had happened. For the first time since the loss of Shea, Allanon felt a sense of relief. He climbed shakily to his feet, leaning slightly on the strong arm of Balinor, still weak from the strain of seeking Shea. He stood quietly for a moment and then smiled faintly.

'Our young friend is indeed alive, though it's a miracle I cannot explain. I located his life-force on the other side of these mountains, probably somewhere near the river that carried him out to the east plains. There were others with him, but I could not determine what their purpose was without an extensive mind probe. That would surely give our position away and weaken me to the point of uselessness.'

'But he is alive, you're certain?' Flick demanded eagerly.

Allanon nodded his assurance. The entire group broke into broad smiles of relief. Menion slapped the elated Flick on his broad back and did a small dance step and leap.

'Then the problem has resolved itself,' the Prince of Leah exulted. 'We have to go back over the Dragon's Teeth and find him, then continue the trip to Paranor to get the Sword.'

His smiling face fell abruptly and the slow burn of anger replaced it as Allanon shook his head negatively. The others stared in astonishment, certain that his was what the Druid himself would have suggested.

'Shea is in the hands of a Gnome patrol,' the mystic stated pointedly. 'He is being taken northward, more than likely to Paranor. We could not reach him without fighting our way back through the guarded passes of the Dragon's Teeth and trailing him over those Gnome-infested plains. We would be diverted for days, perhaps longer, and our presence would be detected in no time.'

'There's no guarantee they don't already know about us,' Menion shouted irately. 'You said that yourself. What good will we be to Shea if he falls into the hands of the Warlock Lord? What good will the Sword do us without the bearer?'

'We cannot desert him,' pleaded Flick, stepping forward once more.

The others said nothing, but stood mutely, waiting to hear Allanon's explanation. Darkness had completely enfolded the high mountain country, and the men could barely make out one another's faces in the dim light; the moon was hidden from view by the monstrous peaks that rose behind them.

'You have forgotten the prophecy,' admonished Allanon patiently. 'The last part promised that one of us would not see the other side of the Dragon's Teeth, but that he would be first to place hands on the Sword of Shannara. That one we now know to be Shea. Furthermore, the prophecy said that we who reached the other side of the mountains would view the Sword before the passing of two nights. It would seem that fate will bring us all together.'

'That may be good enough for you, but not for me,' stated Menion flatly, with Flick nodding in vigorous agreement. 'How can we place our trust in some crazy promise made by a ghost? You're asking us to risk Shea's life!'

Allanon seemed to smolder in fury for a moment, fighting to control his quick temper, then calmly he looked at the two and shook his head in disappointment.

'Have you not believed in a legend from the very start?' he asked quietly. 'Have you not yourself seen the foothold that the spirit world has secured in your world of flesh and blood, earth and stone? Have we not from the beginning been fighting against beings born of this other existence, beings who possess powers that surely do not belong to mortal men? You have witnessed the potency of the Elfstones. Why would you now turn your back on all that, in favor of what your common sense tells you – a reasoning process that relies on fact and stimuli accumulated in this world, your material world, unable to transpose itself to an existence where even your most basic understandings have no meaning.'

They stared at him wordlessly, realizing that he was right, but unwilling to abandon their plan to find Shea. The whole journey had been premised on half dreams and old legends, not on common sense, and suddenly to decide it was time to be practical once again was indeed a ludicrous idea. Flick had given up being practical the day he had first run in fear from Shady Vale.

'I would not be concerned, my young friends,' Allanon soothed, suddenly next to them, a lean hand on each shoulder, strangely comforting even now. 'Shea still carries the Elfstones, and their power will give him great protection. They may also guide him toward the Sword, since they are attuned to it. With luck, we will find him when we find the Sword at Paranor. All roads now lead to the Druid's Keep, and we must be certain we are there to give what aid we can to Shea.'

The other members of the company had gathered up their weapons and small packs and stood ready, their silhouettes shadowlike in the dim starlight, finely etched pencil lines against the blackness of the mountains. Flick gazed northward to the dark forest that blanketed the low country beyond the Dragon's Teeth. In its midst, rising upward like an obelisk, were the cliffs of Paranor, and there at the apex, the Druid's Keep and the Sword of Shannara. The end of the quest. Flick looked quietly for a few moments at the solitary pinnacle, then turned to Menion. The highlander nodded reluctantly.

'We'll go with you.' Flick's voice was a hushed whisper in the stillness.

The swirling waters of the rushing river dashed madly against the confining walls of their mountain channel, beating and raging their way eastward, dragging with them stray debris and driftwood that had fallen into their restless grasp. They rushed down out of the mountains in heavy rapids that churned fiercely around smooth-surfaced rocks and sudden bends, winding slowly toward the calm of the quiet rivers that branched into the hilly lowlands above the Rabb Plains. It was in one of these small, quiet tributaries that the man, still bound to the splintered log by his leather belt, finally washed up on a mud riverbank, unconscious and nearly drowned. The clothes he wore were ripped and shredded, the leather boots lost, the damp face ashen and bloodied from the beating sustained when he had been swept through the series of rapids down the river that had carried him to this place. He awakened, realizing that he had at last reached land. Feebly untying himself from the beached log, he dragged himself on hands and knees farther onto the shore and into the deep grass of a low hill. As if by reflex, his battered hands felt for the small leather pouch at his waist, and to his relief it was still there, securely bound by the leather thongs. A moment later, the last of his remaining strength exhausted, he fell into a deep, welcome sleep.

He slept soundly in the warmth and quiet of the day until late afternoon, when the cooling grass whipping against his face in a building breeze caused him to stir slightly. There was something else as well, something in his now-rested mind that warned him suddenly that he was in danger. But he could barely rouse his sluggish body to a half-sitting position as a group of ten or twelve figures appeared at the crest of the hill above him, paused in astonishment as they saw his raised figure, then hastened down the hill to reach him. Instead of carefully turning his battered body to check for injuries, they flung him flat once again, gripping his helpless arms behind his back and tying them securely with leather thongs that bit into the unprotected skin. His feet were bound as well, and at last he was turned face up where he could finally focus on his captors. His worst fears were immediately confirmed. The gnarled yellow frames, clothed in forest garb and armed with short swords, were easily recognizable after Menion's description of the incident that had taken place only days before in the Pass of Jade. He looked fearfully into the sharp Gnome eyes as they gazed with some amazement at his half-man, half-Elf features and at the remnants of his unusual Southland garb. Finally, the leader reached down and began to search him thoroughly. Shea struggled, but was slapped hard several times and at last lay motionless as the Gnome removed the small leather pouch containing the precious Elfstones.

The Gnomes gathered around curiously as the three blue stones, shining brightly in the warm sunlight, were emptied into the hand of the leader. There was a brief discussion, none of which the captive was able to follow, concerning what he was doing with the stones and where he could have found them. At last it was decided that both the captive and the stones should be taken to the main encampment at Paranor where higher authorities could be consulted. The Gnomes dragged their captive to his feet, cutting the thongs that bound his legs, and proceeded to march him northward, pushing him from time to time when he slowed from exhaustion. They were still moving northward at sunset when, on the other side of the mountain barrier known as the Dragon's Teeth, the Druid leader of a small band of determined seekers struggled within his own mind to pinpoint the missing Shea Ohmsford.

It was in the early-morning hours, wrapped with the blanket silence of darkness and hidden by the shadows of the heavy forests that so completely shut out he reassuring light of the moon and stars, that the company stood at last before the cliffs of Paranor. It was a moment that would last forever in their minds, as expectant eyes traveled upward over the steep rock walls, unbroken by trail or ledge, upward past the dwarfed height of the tall pines and oaks, which ended abruptly as the cliffs began, upward still farther to the man-made structure at its apex – the Druid's Keep. The Keep was castlelike, age-old walls of blocked stone rising to peaked turrets and spiraled towers that cut the sky in proud defiance. It was unmistakably a fortress built to withstand assault by the strongest army, the ancient home and protectorate of the all but extinguished race of men called Druids. Within the heart of this stronghold of stone and iron had long rested the memorial of Man's triumph over the forces of the spirit world, the symbol of the courage and hope of the races in times long past, forgotten over the years as generations passed away and old legends died – the wondrous Sword of Shannara.

As the seven men stood there surveying the Druid's Keep, Flick's mind traveled back over the events that had taken place since the company had departed the Dragon's Teeth at sunset. They had traveled quickly over the open grasslands separating them from the forest surrounding Paranor, reaching the seclusion of its dark perimeter without incident in only a few short hours. At that time, Allanon briefed them on what to expect next. The forest, he said, was impenetrable unless one knew how to avoid the dangerous obstacles that the Warlock Lord had created to discourage any attempt to reach the Druid's Keep. Wolves prowled the entire woodland, huge, gray beasts that could catch anything on two or four feet and tear it to pieces within seconds. Beyond the wolves, surrounding the base of the cliffs beneath the Keep, was an impregnable barrier of thorns, coated with a poison for which there was no known cure. But the resourceful Druid was prepared. They moved quickly into the black forest, not bothering to choose any approach but the direct one, their path taking them straight for the fortress. Allanon warned them to stay close to him, but the warning was quite unnecessary. Only Menion seemed eager to forge ahead of the group, and the highlander rejoined them instantly at the first sound of the marauding wolves. The great, gray beasts attacked within minutes after the men entered the forest, their eyes blood-red in the darkness, their huge jaws snapping in blind hatred. But before they could reach the alarmed group, Allanon placed a strange whistle to his lips and blew softly. A sound so high pitched as to be indistinguishable to the men was emitted and the snarling wolves scattered brokenly, wheeling about and scurrying off with loud cries of dismay, their frightened whimpers still audible long after they were lost from sight.

The wolves appeared twice more during the remainder of the trek through the forest, although it was impossible to tell if it was the same pack or a different one. Flick was inclined to believe they were different packs after observing the effect of the strange whistle. Each time the wolves cringed in terror, leaving the travelers untouched. The company reached the thorny barrier without difficulty. But the bristling mass of poisonous spikes that confronted them seemed truly impenetrable, even by the redoubtable Allanon. Once again he reminded them that this was the homeland of the Druids, not the Warlock Lord. Leading them to the right, he skirted the edge of the barrier until he reached a point that seemed to satisfy him. Quickly pacing off a distance from a nearby oak that looked for all the world to Flick like any other oak, the Druid marked a spot on the ground before the thorny obstruction, nodding to the others that this was to be the spot of entry. Then to their amazement, the grim mystic simply walked up to the razor-sharp spikes and disappeared into the vegetation, only to reappear a moment later unharmed. In hushed tones he explained to them that at this point the barrier was fake and quite harmless, a secret passage to the fortress. There were others as well, all indistinguishable to any human eye unaware of what to look for. And so the company passed through the barrier, discovering that the spikes were indeed harmless, and stood at last before the walls of Paranor.

It seemed impossible somehow to Flick that they should be here at all. The journey had been an endless one while they were making it, the dangers encountered by them never conquered, only evaded and ultimately substituted, one for another. Yet here they were. All that remained was to scale the cliffs and seize the Sword, no simple task, but nevertheless no more difficult than the others they had faced and successfully completed. He gazed upward to the castle battlements, studying briefly the spaced torches that lit the ramparts, knowing that the enemy guarded those walls and the Sword within. He wondered who the enemy was, what it was. Not the Gnomes or the Trolls, but the real enemy – the creature that belonged in another world, but that had invaded this one in some inexplicable way to enslave the humans who inhabited it. He wondered vaguely if he would ever know the reason behind all that had happened to them, the reason why they stood here now, hunters for the legendary Sword of Shannara, of which none of them save the Druid mystic knew anything. He sensed that there was a lesson somewhere to be learned, but at the moment it eluded him. He only wanted to get the matter over with and get out of there alive.

His thoughts ended abruptly as Allanon motioned them forward along the steep walls of the cliff. Again, the Druid seemed to be searching for something. A few minutes later he halted before a smooth portion of the cliff face, touched something in the rock, and a concealed door swung open to reveal a hidden passageway. Allanon stepped inside for a moment and returned with unlit torches, giving one to each of the company and indicating that they were to follow him. They moved silently inside, halting momentarily in the small entryway as the stone door closed noiselessly behind them. Squinting in the near blackness, they saw a vague outline of stone steps leading upward into the rock, barely visible in the dim light of a lone torch flickering just ahead in the passage. They climbed carefully to that torch and each man lit his own to provide the necessary light for the ascent to the castle. Putting a single finger to his lips to indicate that he expected absolute silence, the dark figure of their leader turned and began to climb the damp stone steps, his black cloak billowing slightly as he walked, filling the entire passageway ahead with its shadow. The others followed without a word. The assault of the Druid's Keep had begun.

The staircase rose in a continual spiral, winding and twisting until at last no one knew how far they had come. The air in the passage became gradually warmer and more comfortable to breathe, and the dampness of the walls and steps diminished until it was entirely gone. Their heavy leather hunting boots scraped faintly against the stone, echoing through the deep silence of the caverns. Hundreds of steps and many minutes later, the company reached the end of the tunnel. A massive wooden door, bound with iron and fastened into the rock, blocked their passage. Allanon again proved that he knew the way well. A single touch on the binding and the door swung silently open to admit the men into a large chamber with numerous passages leading out of it, all of them well lit by burning torches. A quick look around revealed no one in sight, so Allanon brought the company around him once again.

'We are directly below the castle proper,' he explained in a barely audible whisper as the others crowded close. 'If we can reach the room where the Sword of Shannara rests without being seen, then we may be able to escape without a fight.'

'Something's wrong,' Balinor cautioned shortly. 'Where are the guards?'

Allanon shook his head to indicate he couldn't answer, but the others saw the concern in his eyes. Something was amiss.

'The passage we will take runs to the main heating ducts and a back stairway that leads to the central hall. Say nothing more until we are there, but keep your eyes open!'

Without waiting for any response, he turned and moved quickly toward one of the open tunnels, and the others followed hastily. The passage led upward, twisting tightly around after a short distance until it seemed they must be cutting back on themselves. Balinor had discarded his torch and drawn his broadsword after only a few steps, then the rest of the company was quick to follow his lead. The flickering light from the torches, fastened in iron racks to the bedrock of the cavern, cast their crouched shadows against the stone walls, their reflected images moving like furtive creatures seeking to escape the light. They crept warily through those ancient tunnels – the Druid, the two Princes, the Valeman, the Elven brothers and the Dwarf – all watching expectantly, caught up in the guarded excitement that comes with the end of a long hunt. Apart from one another, spread out along the walls of the passage, weapons held ready, eyes and ears straining for any hint of danger, they moved steadily forward, farther upward, deeper into the core of the Druid's Keep. Then the silence slowly faded, and there was a muffled sound like heavy breathing and the heat became more intense. Ahead, the passageway ended and a stone door with an iron handle came into view, its edges outlined sharply by a piercing light from the chamber just beyond. The mysterious sound increased in volume and became identifiable. It was the throbbing hum of machinery lodged in the rock beneath them, pumping with steady rhythm. Apprehensively, the members of the company approached the closed door on Allanon's silent command.

As the giant Druid opened the heavy stone barrier, the unsuspecting men were struck by a blast of hot air that surged violently through their lungs to lodge in the pits of their stomachs. Gasping for air, they momentarily hesitated, then moved reluctantly into the room. The door swung shut behind them. They knew where they were in an instant. The room was actually little more than a circular catwalk above a huge pit that dropped off into the rock for well over a hundred feet. At the bottom burned a fierce blaze, fed by some unknown source, its red-orange flames leaping into the air toward the top of the deep well. The pit cut away the greater portion of the chamber, leaving only the small walkway several feet wide with a short iron guard rail that rimmed its inner edge. From the ceiling and walls ran various heating ducts which carried the hot air to other parts of the structure. A concealed pumping system controlled the amount of heat generated by the open furnace. Because it was night, the pumping system had been shut down, and the temperature level along the catwalk was still tolerable, despite the intense heat of the pit fire below. When the bellows were in full operation, any human passing through the chamber would be fried in a matter of seconds.

Menion, Flick and the Elven brothers paused by the railing to get a closer look at the system. Hendel hung back, uncomfortable in this confining rock structure, comparing it unfavorably to the open woodlands with which he was familiar. Allanon moved to Balinor's side and conversed with him for a few moments, glancing uneasily at the several closed doors leading into the chamber and pointing to the open spiral staircase that led to the upper halls of the castle. Finally, the two seemed to settle on something, nodding in agreement, and signaled the others to catch up. Hendel was only too glad to comply. Menion and the Elven brothers moved away from the railing to join him. Only Flick lingered a second, strangely attracted by the fascinating blaze below. This slight delay produced an unexpected result. As he lifted his eyes with a parting glance to the other side of the chamber, he saw the dark figure of a Skull Bearer appear out of nowhere.

Flick froze instantly. The creature remained in a half-crouch directly across the pit from him, its body a black mass even in the light of the pit fires, the caped wings billowing out slightly behind it. Its legs were crooked, the feet ending in cruel-looking claws that seemed capable of rending the stone itself. Hunched low between the massive shoulders, the head and face bore a vague resemblance to scarred coal. The wicked eyes fastened on the speechless Valeman, their depths drawing him closer to the reddish glow that burned within, an open invitation to death. With slow, dragging steps, it began to make its way around the chamber, its breath rasping with every labored step as it drew closer and closer to the spellbound Flick. He wanted to cry out, run away, do anything but stay where he was, yet the strange eyes held him motionless. He knew he was finished.

But the others had noticed his immobile form; following his frightened gaze across the chamber, they had discovered the black Skull Bearer creeping noiselessly around the rim of the pit. In a flash, Allanon leaped in front of Flick, yanking him around to break the spell of the creature's terrible eyes. Dazed, Flick stumbled backward into the waiting arms of Menion, who had rushed to his assistance. The others stood just behind the Druid, their weapons held ready. The creature stopped several yards from Allanon, still in a half-crouch, hiding the hideous face from the fire's glow with one raised wing and clawed hand. Its breath sounded in slow, steady rasps as its cruel eyes rested on the tall figure that stood between it and the little Valeman.

'Druid, you are a fool to oppose me.' The voice hissed from somewhere deep within the creature's formless face. 'You are all doomed. You were doomed from the moment you chose to come after the Sword. The Master knew you would come, Druid! He *knew*.'

'Get away while you can, hateful one!' Allanon commanded in the most menacing tone any of the members of the company had ever heard him use. 'You frighten no one here. We will take the Sword, and you will not stand in our way. Step aside, lackey, and let your Master show himself!'

The words burned into the air, cutting through to the Skull Bearer like knives. The creature hissed its fury, the rasping breath coming in quick gasps as it took another step, crouching lower, its eyes frightful to look into as they blazed with new hatred.

'I will destroy you, Allanon. Then no one will be left to oppose the Master! You have been our pawn from the start, though you could not have guessed. Now we have you within our reach, along with your most valuable allies. And look what you have brought us, Druid – the last heir of Shannara!'

To the shock of everyone, the claw like hand pointed to an astonished Flick. The creature did not seem to realize that Flick was not the heir or that Shea had been lost to them on the Dragon's Teeth. For a moment no one spoke. The fire roared in the pit below, billowing up suddenly with a gust of boiling air that singed the unprotected faces of the mortals. The claws of the black spirit creature seemed to reach toward them.

'Now, fools,' the hate-filled voice rasped at them, 'you shall receive the kind of death your species deserves!'

CHAPTER

3

As the final words of the black creature hissed away in the flame-lit air, everything seemed to happen at once. With a dramatic sweep of one lean arm and a command so sharp it jarred them all into instant action, the giant Druid sent the tensed members of his little company charging toward the open staircase that led to the main hall of the Druid's Keep. As the six men broke in a mad dash for the winding stairway behind them, the Skull Bearer lunged for Allanon. The thudding impact of their collision could be heard even by the fleeing men, who were already starting up the staircase – save for one. Flick hesitated, torn by the desire to escape, but held spellbound by the titanic struggle between the two powerful beings locked in combat only inches from the rising flames of the great open furnace. He stood at the bottom of the staircase, hearing the disappearing footfalls of his companions as they raced for the upper hall. A moment later the footsteps were gone, leaving him the sole witness to the incredible struggle between Druid and Skull Bearer.

The black-garbed figures were immobile at the edge of the furnace, statues frozen in place with the great strain of their battle, dark faces only inches apart, the lean arms of the giant Druid holding firm the claw-tipped limbs of the deadly spirit creature. The Skull Bearer was attempting to

41

bring his razor-sharp hands close enough to the mystic's unprotected throat to rip the life out of him and end the battle quickly. The black wings heaved with the exertion, flapping in fury to add momentum to the assault, the unmistakable rasp of its breathing cutting the heated air with ragged desperation. Then suddenly the Northland creature's wiry leg shot out, tripping the Druid so that he fell backward onto the stone floor at the edge of the pit. Like a shot, the attacker was upon him, one clawed hand sweeping downward for the kill. But the victim was too quick, rolling deftly away from the deadly talons and free from the creature's grasp. Nevertheless, Flick saw the blow catch a portion of the shoulder and heard the distinct rending of cloth as first blood was drawn. Flick gave a gasp of dismay, but a moment later the Druid was on his feet, showing no sign of injury. Twin bolts of blue flame shot out of the extended fingers of his hands, striking the rising Skull Bearer with shattering force, throwing the infuriated creature back against the railing. But while the mystic bolts had visibly hurt the serpent during the battle in the Hall of Kings, they did little more than slow the Northland creature for a few brief seconds. Roaring in fury, it counterattacked. Blazing red bolts shot from its burning eyes. Allanon brought his cloak up in a sweeping movement, and the bolts appeared to deflect into the stone walls of the chamber. For a moment, the creature hesitated, and the two opponents circled each other warily in the manner of two beasts of the forest, locked in a life-and-death struggle which only one could survive.

For the first time, Flick noticed that the temperature was rising. With the approach of dawn, the furnace tenders had risen to care for the heating needs of the awakening castle. Unaware of the battle taking place in the walkway overhead, they had activated the dormant bellows machinery at the bottom of the pit, stoking the fire to build it up to an intensity which would enable heated air to warm all the chambers of the Druid's Keep. As a result, flames were now visible above the edge of the pit and the temperature of the chamber was rising steadily. Flick felt the sweat pouring down over his face, soaking through his warm hunting outfit. But still he would not leave. He sensed that if Allanon were defeated, they would all be doomed, and he was determined to know the outcome. The Sword of Shannara would mean nothing to them if the man who had brought them to this final battleground were destroyed. With rapt fascination clouding his stocky face, Flick Ohmsford watched what might be the fate of the races and the lands being decided by the two seemingly indestructible protagonists of mortal man and Spirit Lord.

Allanon had attacked again with the flashing blue bolts, striking at the circling Skull Bearer in brief, biting blows, trying to force it into a hasty move, trying to cause it to slip, to make a single fatal mistake. The spirit creature was no fool, but an evil spawned of a hundred hunts in which it alone had been the victor and the victims all lay forgotten beyond the world of mortal men. It dodged and twisted with frightening ease, always coming back to he same tense crouch, watching and waiting for its own moment to strike. Then, in a totally unexpected move, the black wings spread wide and it circled into the air in a sweep that carried it soaring around the flames of the furnace and down again with vicious speed onto the tall figure of Allanon. The clawed hands raked downward, and for a moment Flick thought all was surely lost. Miraculously, the floored Druid escaped the deadly hands, throwing the Skull Bearer completely over him with one mighty heave of his powerful arms. The hapless creature flew wildly through the air and crashed with an audible thud into the stone wall beyond. It struggled to its feet in an instant, but the force of the blow had shaken it, slowing it down just enough, and before it could escape, the giant Druid was upon it.

The two black figures thrashed about against the wall as if inextricably joined, their limbs locked onto each other like twisted branches. When they reared to full height, Flick could see that Allanon was behind the struggling Skull Bearer, his mighty arms locked viselike about the head of the creature, the straining muscles slowly crushing the life away. The victim's wings beat madly, its hooked arms clutching vainly for something to break the hold that was destroying it. The fire-red eyes burned with the fury of the furnace pit itself, shooting forth bolts of fire that tore into the stone walls, leaving gaping, blackened holes. The combatants lurched away from the wall and rocked wildly toward the blazing pit at the center of the heated chamber until they were against the low iron railing. For a moment it appeared to the wide-eyed Valeman that both would lose their balance and plunge into the flames below. But abruptly Allanon straightened with a mighty effort, dragging his captive back from the railing a few scant feet. It was this sudden movement that brought the entangled spirit creature about, its hate-filled eyes coming to rest directly on the partially hidden Valeman. Grasping at any opportunity to divert the clinging Druid for the instant that would permit it a chance to break free of those crushing arms, the Skull Bearer struck at the unprepared Flick. Twin bolts of flame shot out of the burning eyes, shattering the stone blocks of the staircase into deadly fragments which flew in all directions like little knives. Flick acted instinctively, diving out of the staircase onto the walkway, his hands and face cut by the stone, but his life saved by his quickness. As he leaped clear, the entire entryway shuddered abruptly and collapsed in a cascade of broken stone blocks that completely shut off the passage upward, the dust billowing out of the rubble in heavy clouds.

In that same instant, as Flick lay frightened and shaken but still conscious on the stone floor of the furnace chamber, with the flames from the roaring pit rising higher to meet the clouds of dust from the blocked passage, Allanon's grip relaxed just enough to permit the crafty spirit creature to break loose. Whirling about with a cry of hatred, it struck the distracted Druid a crushing blow on the head, knocking the tall wanderer to his knees. The Northlander moved in for the kill, but somehow the dazed mystic was on his feet again, the blue bolts from the lean hands flashing fiercely as they struck the unprotected head of the attacker. Powerful fists rained resounding blows on both sides of the creature's black head, turning the battered figure about once again as the great arms wound with crushing force about its chest, pinning the wings and claw-tipped hands back against the writhing body. Holding the creature thus, the steel-eyed Druid gritted his gleaming teeth in fury and squeezed. Flick, still lying on the floor as the two combatants loomed above him several yards away, heard a horrible crunching sound as something snapped inside the Skull Bearer. Then with a lurch the two figures were again next to the low iron railing, every straining feature clearly revealed in the flames, the thunder of the burning pit matched in its power and its fury by the wail of agony from the shattered victim as the black, hooked body shuddered once. From some deep well of strength and hatred buried within, the Skull Bearer summoned one last desperate surge of power, throwing itself over the iron railing, its clutching fingers embedded in the black-cloaked attacker as it fell, dragging its hated enemy with it, and both figures were lost in the glow of the hungry flames.

The fallen Flick climbed dazedly to his feet, shock slowly spreading over his battered face. He tottered unsteadily toward the edge of the furnace pit, but the heat was so intense that he was forced back. He tried once more without success, the sweat pouring down from his forehead into his eyes and mouth, mingling slowly with tears of helpless anger. The flames from the pit soared above the low iron railing, licking hungrily at the stone and crackling with new life as if to acknowledge the addition of the two black-garbed creatures to the fuel it greedily consumed. Through the mist that coated his burning eyes, the Valeman gazed fixedly toward the bottomless pit. There was nothing beyond the red glow of the flames and the unbearable heat. Hopelessly, he called out the Druid's name over and over in futile desperation, each call sending the echoes bouncing off the stone walls and dying in the heat of the fire. But the Valeman found himself alone with the roar of the flames, and he knew at last that the Druid was gone.

He panicked then. In a mad dash, he scrambled back from the fiery pit. He reached the rubble of the stairway before he remembered that it had been blocked, and he collapsed for a moment amid the broken rock. Shaking his head to clear his muddled brain, he felt the full intensity of the fire. He knew instinctively that if he did not escape the chamber in a matter of minutes, the heat would bake him alive. He bounded up and ran to the closest stone door, pushing and pulling on it in desperation. But the door did not move, and at last he stopped, his hands bloody from the effort. He looked down the wall, his eyes finding a second door. He stumbled on to this one, but it, too, was secured from the other side. He felt his hopes dim into nothingness, certain now that he was trapped. Woodenly, he forced himself to move on to the third. It was with the last of his fading strength, as he pushed and pulled frantically on the stubborn barricade, that he touched something hidden in the rock and triggered the mechanism that permitted it to open. With a cry of relief, the battered Valeman fell through the opening into the passageway beyond, kicking the stone door shut as he lay in the semidarkness, locking himself away from the heat and the death that remained behind.

For many long minutes he lay exhausted in the darkness of the corridor, his burning body soaking up the cool of the stone floor and the soothing air. He didn't try to think, didn't care to remember, but wished only to lose himself in the peace and quiet of the tunnel rock. At last he forced himself wearily to his knees, then to his feet in a final effort, leaning dazedly against the cold stone of the passage wall as he waited for his strength to return. He realized for the first time that his clothing was torn and burned almost beyond recognition, his hands and face signed and blackened from the heat. He looked around slowly, his stocky frame straightening itself as he pushed away from the wall. The dim light of the torch on the wall ahead indicated the direction in which the winding corridor ran, and he stumbled forward until he was able to grasp the burning piece of wood from its rack. He shuffled along slowly, the torch extended to light his way. Somewhere ahead he heard shouting, and instinctively his free hand went to the handle of his short hunting knife, drawing the weapon from its sheath. After several minutes, the noise seemed to move farther away and at last die out altogether, and still the Valeman had seen nothing. The corridor wound through the rock in curious fashion, taking Flick past several doors, all of which were closed and barred, but never leading upward and never branching off into other passageways. Ever so often the darkness ahead was broken by the dim light of a burning torch securely fastened to the stone, its yellow light casting his shadow against the far wall like a misshapen wraith fleeing into the darkness.

Then abruptly the passage widened and the light ahead grew stronger. Flick hesitated a moment, grasping his weapon tightly, his face streaked with lines of smoke and sweat, but grimly determined in the flickering glow. There was no sound as he inched his way forward. He knew that somewhere there had to be a stairway leading to the main hall of the Druid's Keep. So far, it had been a long and futile search, and he was becoming exhausted. He wished belatedly that he hadn't been so eager to remain behind, allowing himself to be cut off from the main party. Now he was trapped in these unfathomable corridors at the center of Paranor. Anything could have happened to the others by this time, he thought dismally, and he might never find them wandering through this maze. He edged his way a little farther around a bend in the rock, his muscles tensed, peering carefully into the light. To his surprise he found himself at the entrance to a round chamber with numerous other passages leading into it. A dozen or so torches burned cheerfully from the circular wall. He breathed a sigh of relief when he saw that the rotunda was deserted. Then he realized that he was no better off than he had been before. The other passages looked exactly like the one he had come through. There were no doors leading to other rooms, no stairways leading to the upper level, and no indication as to which way he should go. He looked around in bewilderment, desperately trying to identify one passage from another, his hope fading with each passing second and each repeated survey. At last he shook his head in confusion. Moving to one of the walls, he sat down wearily, closing his eyes as he forced himself to accept the bitter fact that he was hopelessly lost.

On Allanon's command, the remainder of the company had broken for the stairway. Durin and Dayel were closest to the stone passage and, being the fastest in the group, found themselves halfway up the steps before the others had even begun the short climb. Their lithe Elven limbs carried them up the flight of stairs in gliding, bounding leaps, barely touching the stone as they ran. Hendel, Menion, and Balinor came in a rush behind, their progress partially impeded by their heavy weapons and greater weight, and partially by each other as they tried to avoid stumbling over one another in the narrow, winding staircase. It was a wild, disorganized charge to the upper hall, each man scrambling to reach the object of the long quest and to escape the terrifying spirit creature. In their haste to accomplish both ends, the hapless Flick was not even missed.

Durin was first through the stairway entrance of the Druid's Keep, nearly stumbling into the great hall as he broke clear, the smaller form of his brother close behind. The hall was lavishly impressive, a huge, high-ceilinged corridor whose great walls were solid wood, polished until they shone with burnished magnificence in the mixed yellow light of burning torches and the reddish tinges of the dawn seeping through high, slanted windows. The panels were adorned with paintings, carved figures of stone and wood on mosaic display stands and long, handwoven tapestries that hung in folds to the polished marble floor that ran the length of the corridor. At various intervals, there were great statues of iron and fine stone, sculptures of another age preserved through the long centuries by the shelter of this timeless refuge. They seemed to be guarding the heavy, carved wooden doors that were beautifully ornamented with handles of copper-colored brass held fast by iron studs. A few of these stood open, and in the chambers that lay beyond could be seen the same carefully designed splendor, glowing radiantly as tall, open glass windows let in the sunshine in long streams of lingering color, fresh with the new day.

The Elven brothers had little time to admire the ageless beauty of Paranor. An instant after they were through the open staircase, they were set upon by Gnome guards, who seemed to come from everywhere at once, the gnarled, yellow bodies sliding from concealment behind doors, statues, the walls themselves. Durin met the rush with his long hunting knife and withstood the assault only a moment before they were on him. Dayel came to his brother's rescue, swinging his long bow as a weapon, knocking the attackers aside until the sturdy ash broke with an audible snap. For a moment it seemed they would be torn to pieces before their stronger comrades could come to their aid, until Durin broke free and snatched a long, wicked-looking pike from an iron warrior of another age and scattered the scrambling Gnomes with sweeping cuts, knocking them away from his struggling brother. But they were reinforced in an instant and quickly reassembled for a second charge. The Elven brothers had moved back to the wall, panting with the strain and covered with slashes and the blood of their attackers. The Gnomes gathered together in a yellow group, their deadly short swords held before them, intent on breaking past Durin's swinging pike and hacking both Elves to pieces. With a wild piercing cry, they charged in for the kill.

Unfortunately for the Gnomes, they had forgotten to watch the open stairway against the possible chance that the Elves were not alone. At the instant they rushed Durin and Dayel, the other three members of the company burst through the doorway and fell upon the unprepared attackers. The Gnomes had never in their lives encountered men such as these. In the center came the huge borderman from Callahorn, his gleaming sword cutting a path through the shorter swords with such ferocity that the Gnomes fell over each other trying to escape. On one side they ran headlong into the bludgeoning mace of the powerful Dwarf, while on the other they faced the quick blade of the swift, agile highlander. For a moment they stood and fought against the five madmen, then wavered slightly as the attack pressed ahead, and finally broke and ran, all thoughts of winning abandoned. Without a word, the five battered warriors charged down the magnificent hall, leaping over the wounded and dead, their hunting boots ringing on the polished marble. The few Gnomes who stood against them as they came soon went down before the rush, to lie in silent, unmoving heaps. After all that they had suffered and lost, the five who remained from the little company would not be denied any longer the victory they had sought so desperately.

Near the end of the ancient corridor, now littered with dead and wounded Gnomes, the tapestries and paintings torn and scattered from the sharp battle, a last desperate band of guards crowded together in tight formation before a set of tall, carved wooden doors that stood closed and barred. Their short hunting swords held before them like a wall of spikes, the determined Gnomes prepared to make a final stand. The attackers made a short rush at the deadly wall, trying to break through at the center behind the long swords of Balinor and Menion, but the battle-hardened guards repulsed the assault after several minutes of bitter fighting. The five withdrew in exhaustion, panting and sweating freely with the exertion, their bodies cut and battered. Durin dropped heavily to one knee, both an arm and a leg badly slashed by Gnome swords. Menion had been clipped along one side of his head by a pike edge, and the blood rose to the wound in a vivid red streak. The highlander seemed unaware of the injury. Again the five attacked and again, after long minutes of bitter hand-to-hand combat, they were repulsed. The number of Gnomes had diminished by almost half, but time was running out for the men of the company. There was no sign of Allanon, and the Gnomes would have reinforcements on the way to protect the Sword of Shannara, if indeed it did stand within the chamber they now so desperately sought to hold.

Then, in an amazing display of raw strength, the towering Balinor rushed to the other side of the hall and with one mighty heave overturned a huge stone pillar, at the top of which was affixed a metal urn. Pillar and urn struck the stone floor with a crash that jarred everyone to the bone, the echoes reverberating through the bloodied hall. Stone should have shattered, but the pillar remained whole. With the aid of Hendel, the giant borderman began to roll the rounded battering ram sideways toward the wedge of Gnomes and the closed doors to the chamber beyond, the monstrous roller gathering speed and power with each revolution as it thundered toward the hapless guards. For an instant the wiry yellow creatures hesitated, their short swords held ready as the crushing weight of the stone pillar bore down on them. Then they broke, bolting for safety, their spirit gone, the battle lost. Even so, several were not fast enough to escape the makeshift ram and were caught beneath its great bulk as it crashed amid a shower of stone and wood splinters into the barred doors. The doors shuddered and buckled with the blow, the wood cracking and the iron fastenings snapping like the crack of a whip, yet somehow they withstood the force of the ram. But an instant later they flew off their hinges with a resounding crash as the weight of the Prince of Callahorn struck them, and the five men rushed into the chamber beyond to claim the Sword of Shannara.

To their amazement, the room stood empty. There were tall windows and long, flowing curtains, masterful paintings that lined the walls, and even several small pieces of ornate furniture placed carefully about the large chamber. But nowhere was there any trace of the coveted Sword. In shocked disbelief, the five gazed slowly about the closed room. Durin dropped heavily to his knees, weak from loss of blood and close to passing out. Dayel came quickly to his aid, tearing up strips of cloth to bind the open wounds, then helping his brother to one of the chairs, where he collapsed in exhaustion. Menion looked from one wall to the next, searching for another exit to the room. Then Balinor, who had been pacing the floor of the chamber in slow scrutiny of its marble finish, gave a low exclamation. A portion of the floor at the very center of the room was scarred and discolored beneath a poor attempt to conceal the fact that something large and square had stood there for many years.

'The block of Tre-Stone!' exclaimed Menion quickly.

'But if it has been moved, it must have been recently,'

Balinor speculated, his breathing labored, his voice weary as he tried to think. 'So why did the Gnomes try to keep us out . . .?'

'Maybe they didn't know it had been moved,' suggested Menion desperately.

'Perhaps a decoy . . .?' ventured Hendel abruptly. 'But why waste time with a decoy unless . . .?'

'They wanted to keep us busy here, because the Sword was still in the castle and they hadn't gotten it out!' finished Balinor excitedly. 'They haven't had time to get it out, so they tried to decoy us! But where is the Sword now – who has it?'

For a moment all three were at a loss. Had the Warlock Lord known that the company was coming all along, just as the Skull Bearer in the furnace had seemed to indicate? If their attack had caught everyone by surprise, what could have happened to the Sword since Allanon had last seen it in this chamber?

'Wait!' exclaimed Durin weakly from across the room, rising slowly to his feet. 'When I came through the staircase, there was something happening on another set of stairs down the hall – men moving up those stairs.'

'The tower!' shouted Hendel, racing for the open doorway. 'They've got the Sword locked in the tower!'

Balinor and Menion hurried after the disappearing Dwarf, the weariness gone. The Sword of Shannara was still within reach. Durin and Dayel followed at a slower pace, the former still weak and leaning heavily on his younger brother for support, but their eyes bright with hope. A moment later, the chamber stood empty.

Flick climbed despondently to his feet after a few minutes' rest and decided that the only course of action left to him was to choose one of the passageways and follow it to the end, hoping that it would take him to a stairway leading upward to the fortress. He thought briefly of the others, somewhere in the corridors above, perhaps already in possession of the Sword. They could not know of Allanon's fall nor of his own fate, lost in these impossible tunnels. He hoped they would search for him, but realized at the same time that, if they did get the Sword, there would be no time to waste looking for him. They would have to make their escape before the Warlock Lord could send the Skull Bearers to retrieve the coveted blade. He wondered what had become of Shea, if he had been found alive, if he had been rescued. Somehow he knew that Shea would never leave Paranor while Flick was alive; but then there was no way for his brother to know that he had not perished in the furnace chamber. He had to admit that his own situation looked pretty hopeless.

At that instant there was a loud clamor from one of the tunnels, the sound of boots thudding on the stone floor, of men rushing directly toward the rotunda. In a flash, the Valeman crossed the room and hastened into concealment down a different tunnel, keeping flat against the rock in the protective shadows. He paused just within sight of the lighted rotunda and drew his short hunting knife. A few moments later a swarm of fleeing Gnome guards charged into the connecting room and disappeared down another of the passageways without pausing. The sounds of their flight were soon lost in the bends and turns of the rock. Flick had no idea what they were running from or perhaps running to, but wherever they had been was where he wanted to be. It was a good bet that they had come from the upper chambers of the Druids' Keep, and that was the place the Valeman had to reach. He moved cautiously back into the lighted chamber and crossed to the tunnel from which the Gnomes had come. Backtracking their path of flight, he entered the now-deserted corridor and disappeared into the darkness beyond. He held his knife before him, groping his way along the dimly lit walls toward the first torch rack. Freeing the burning wood from its clasp, he proceeded deeper into the passage, his eager eyes scanning the rough walls for signs of a door or an open stairway. He had only gone about a hundred yards when without warning a portion of the rock slid open almost at his elbow, and a single Gnome stepped into view.

It was disputable as to which of the two was more surprised at the appearance of the other. The Gnome guard was a straggler from the larger group fleeing the battle in the halls above, and the sight of another of the invaders here in the tunnels momentarily startled him. Although smaller than the Valeman, the Gnome was wiry and armed with a short sword. He attacked immediately. Flick dodged instinctively as the sweeping blade went wide of the mark. The Valeman leaped onto the Gnome before he could recover and wrestled him to the stone floor, trying vainly to take the sword away from his agile opponent, his own knife lost in the scuffle. Flick was not trained in hand-to-hand combat, but the Gnome was, and this gave the little yellow man a distinct advantage. He had killed before and would do so again without a second thought, while Flick sought only to disarm his attacker and escape. They rolled and fought across the floor for several long minutes before the Gnome again broke free and took a vicious cut at his adversary, barely missing the exposed head. Flick threw himself back, desperately looking for his knife. The little guard charged at him just as his groping fingers closed over the heavy wood of the torch he had dropped at the first assault. The short sword came down, glancing off Flick's shoulder and cutting into the exposed flesh of his arm painfully. At the same moment, the stunned Valeman brought the torch up with a powerful swing and felt it strike the Gnome's raised head with jarring impact. The guard sprawled forward with the force of the blow and did not move again. Flick slowly regained his footing and recovered his knife after a moment's search. His arm throbbed painfully and the blood had soaked into his hunting tunic, running down his arm and into his hand where he could clearly see it. Afraid that he was bleeding to death, he quickly tore up strips of cloth from the fallen Gnome's short cloak and bound them about the injured limb until the bleeding had stopped. Picking up the other's sword, he moved over to the still partially open rock slab to see where it led.

To his relief, he found a winding staircase beyond the doorway that spiraled upward. He slipped into the passage, closing the rock slab behind him with several pulls of his good arm. The stairs were dimly outlined by the familiar torchlight, and he proceeded to climb with slow, cautious steps. All was quiet in the passage as he moved steadily upward, the long torches in iron racks giving him enough light to pick out his footing on the rough stone. He reached a closed door at the top of the stairway and paused there to listen, his ear placed next to the cracks between the iron bindings. There was only silence beyond. Cautiously, he pushed the door open a bit and peered through into the ancient halls of Paranor. He had reached his goal. He opened the door a bit farther and stepped watchfully into the silent corridor.

Then the steel grip of a lean dark hand came down on his extended sword arm and yanked him into the open.

Hendel paused hesitantly at the bottom of the stairway that led to the tower of the Druids' Keep, peering upward into the gloom. The others stood quietly at his back, following his gaze intently. The stairway consisted of little more than a set of open stone steps, narrow and treacherous-looking, that wound upward in a spiral along the walls of the rounded turret. The entire tower was shrouded in gloomy darkness, unlighted by torches or openings in the dark stone. From their poor vantage point, the members of the company could see little beyond the first few turns in the staircase. The open stairwell dropped away from where they stood into a blackened pit. Menion crossed to the edge of the landing and peered downward, mindful of the absence of any guard rail either here or along the stairs. He dropped a small pebble into the black abyss and waited for it to hit bottom. No sound came back to him. He glanced again at the open stairs and the gloom above, then turned to the others.

'Looks like an open invitation to a trap,' he declared pointedly.

'Very likely,' Balinor agreed, stepping forward for a closer look. 'But we have to get up there.'

Menion nodded, then shrugged casually, moving toward the stairway. The others followed without a word, Hendel right at the highlander's heels, Balinor next and the Elven brothers bringing up the rear. They moved cautiously up the narrow stone steps, alert for any sign of a trap, their shoulders close to the wall, away from the dangerous open edge of the stairwell. They wound their way steadily through the musty gloom. Menion studied each step as he went, his keen eyes searching the seams of the stone-block wall for hidden devices. From time to time, he tossed stones onto the steps ahead of them, testing for traps that might be released by any sudden weight on the steps. But nothing happened. The abyss below was a silent black hole cut into the heavy gloom of the tower air, no sound penetrating its dark serenity save the soft scraping of hunting boots ascending the worn steps. At last, the faint light of burning torches cut through the darkness far above them, the small fires flickering briskly with the gusting of an unknown source of wind from the turret peak. A small landing came into view at the summit of the staircase, and beyond, the dim shape of a huge stone door, bound with iron and standing closed. The top of the Druids' Keep.

Then Menion sprang the first hidden trap. A series of

long, barbed spikes shot out of the stone wall, triggered by the pressure of Menion's foot on the stone stairway. Had Menion still been on the step, they would have cut into his unprotected legs, crippling him and forcing him over the edge of the open stairwell into the black abyss below. But Hendel had heard the click of the released spring an instant before the trap opened. With a quick pull he yanked the astonished highlander backward to the others, almost knocking them all off the narrow steps. They staggered wildly in the heavy gloom, inches from the sharpened steel spikes. Regaining their footing, the five remained flattened against the wall for several long minutes, breathing audibly in the still darkness. Then the taciturn Dwarf smashed the spikes before them with several well-placed blows of his great mace, opening the route once more. Now he led the way in alert silence, while the shaken Menion dropped back behind Balinor. Quickly Hendel found a second trap of the same type and triggered it, breaking the spikes and moving on.

They were almost to the landing now, and it appeared they would reach it without further difficulty when Dayel called out sharply. His keen Elven hearing had caught something that the others had missed, a small click that signaled the triggering of still another trap. For a moment everyone froze in position as alert eyes searched the walls and steps. But they found nothing, and at last Hendel ventured a single step farther on the stairs. Surprisingly, nothing happened, and the cautious Dwarf proceeded to the top of the stairway while the others remained in position. Once he had safely reached the landing, the others hastened after him until at last all five stood together at the top, looking anxiously down the winding staircase into the black pit. How they had managed to escape the third trap they could not imagine. Balinor was of the opinion that it had failed to function properly due to long years of neglect, but Hendel was not so easily persuaded. He could not shake the feeling that somehow they had overlooked the obvious.

The tower hung like a huge shadow over the open stairwell, its dark stone chill and wet to the touch, a mass of giant blocks that had been assembled ages ago and had stubbornly withstood the ravages of time with the endurance of the earth itself. The huge door at the landing appeared to be immovable, its surface scarred, the iron bindings as sturdy as the day they had been imbedded in the rock. Great iron spikes, hammered into the stone, held the hinges and lock in place, and it appeared to the five who stood before it that nothing less than an earthquake could force the monstrous slab of stone open even an inch. Balinor approached the formidable barrier cautiously and ran his hands along the seams and lock, trying to find some hidden device that might release it. Gingerly, he turned the iron handle and pushed forward. To the astonishment of all, the stone slab slid partially open with a shudder and a grinding of rusted iron. A moment later, the mystery of the tower was revealed as the door swung open all the way, striking the inner walls with a sharp crash.

In the exact center of the rounded chamber, set in the polished black surface of the giant Tre-Stone block, blade downward so that it rose before them like a gleaming cross of silver and gold, they beheld the legendary Sword of Shannara. Its long blade flashed brightly in the light of the sun streaming through the high, iron-barred windows of the tower, reflecting sharply off the mirror finish of the square stone. None of the five had ever seen the fabulous Sword, but they were instantly sure this was it. For a moment they remained framed in the doorway, gazing in astonishment, unable to believe that at last, after all their effort, the endless marches, the miserable days and nights of hiding, there before them stood the ancient talisman they had risked everything to find. The Sword of Shannara was theirs! They had outwitted the Warlock Lord. Slowly they filed into the stone chamber, smiles on their faces, the weariness gone, their wounds forgotten. They stood for long moments staring at it, silent, wondering, grateful. They could not bring themselves to step forward and take the treasure from the stone. It seemed too sacred for mortal hands. But Allanon was missing, and Shea was lost as well, and where . . .

'Where is Flick?' Dayel voiced the question suddenly. For the first time they realized that he was missing. They glanced about the chamber, looking blankly at one another for an explanation. Then Menion, who had turned apprehensively back to the gleaming Sword, watched the impossible happen. The great block of Tre-Stone and its precious display began to shimmer and dissolve before his astonished eyes. It took only seconds for the entire image to fade into smoke, then into a heavy haze, and at last into the air itself, until the five men stood alone in an empty room staring into space.

'A trap! The third trap!' roared Menion, recovering from the initial shock.

But behind him, he could already hear the huge rock slab swing shut on their inescapable prison, creaking and groaning sharply as the rusted hinges gave way under the monstrous weight of the stone. The highlander launched himself across the room, crashing into the door just as it closed on them, the sharp snap of its locks clicking firmly into place. He collapsed slowly to the worn stone floor, his heart beating violently in rage and frustration. The others had not moved, but stood in silent despair as they watched the slim figure at the door bury his face in his hands. The faint but unmistakable sound of muffled laughter echoed brokenly off the chill walls in long peals, mocking their foolishness and their bitter, inevitable defeat.

CHAPTER

4

The cheerless cold of the Northland sky hung in thin strips of gray fog against the dull edges that formed the peaks of the solitary mountain of pitted blackness that was the castle of the Warlock Lord. Above and below the surrounding plain of the Skull Kingdom, standing like rusted sawteeth, were the blunted tips of the Razor Mountains and the Knife Edge, an impenetrable barrier to mortal life. Between them stood the dying mountain of the Spirit Lord, forgotten by nature, spurned by the seasons as it wasted slowly away. The shroud of death that claimed its tall peaks, clinging with pitiless certainty to its shattered faces, spread its evil aura across the entire land with unmistakable hatred toward the few vestiges of life and beauty that had somehow managed to survive. A doomed era waited quietly in the Northland kingdom of the Warlock Lord. Now was the hour of death, the last signs of life slowly fading back into the ground as only the shell of nature's touch, once bright and magnificent, remained.

Within the skull of the lone mountain ran hundreds of timeless caverns, their enduring rock walls sunless in the never-changing grayness of the sky beyond. They wound about with the ruthless coiling of a cornered snake, twisting violently through the core of the rock. All was silence and death in the gray mist of the spirit kingdom, a permeating somber air that marked the total extinction of hope, the complete burial of gaiety and lightness. There was movement even here, however, but it was life unlike anything known to mortal man. Its source was the single, black chamber at the peak of the mountain, a monstrous room with its north face open to the dim light of the cheerless sky beyond and the endless stretch of forbidding mountains that formed the north gate to the kingdom. In this cavernous room, its walls wet with the cold that cut knifelike through the rock, scurried the inky minions of the Warlock Lord. Their small, black forms crawled about the floor of the silent chamber, their spineless frames bent and shattered with the terrible, wrenching power their Master wielded over them. Even walking would have been redemption in their existence. They were mindless wraiths, kept only to serve the one who held them enslaved. They muttered as they hustled about, small cries and weepings that sounded of unforgettable agony. In the center of the room rose a large pedestal that held a basin of water, its murky surface placid and deathly. From time to time, one of the little crawling creatures would hasten to its edge and peer cautiously into the cold water, eyes darting furtively about, waiting, watching expectantly. A moment later, with a small whimper, it would scurry away to blend back in the shadows of the cavern. 'Where is the Master, where is the Master?' the sounds would cry like whispers in the grayness as the little beings moved about uneasily. 'He will come, he will come, he will come,' the answer echoed back hatefully.

Then the air stirred violently as if wrenching free of the space that held it, and the mist seemed to come together in a huge black shadow that tightened slowly into material form at the edge of the basin. The mist gathered and swirled and became the Spirit Lord, a huge, cloaked figure of black that seemed to hang in the air. The sleeves rose, but there were no arms within, and the folds of the trailing robes covered nothing but the floor. 'The Master, the Master,' the terrified creatures' voices sounded in unison, and their bent shapes groveled obediently before him. The faceless cowl turned to them and looked down, and they could see within the blackness the tiny glints of flame that burned with satisfied hatred, flashing sparklike in a hazy green mist that hung all about the inner recesses of the shroud. Then the Warlock Lord turned from them, and they were forgotten as he gazed steadily into the waters of the strange basin, waiting for the commanded mental picture to appear. Seconds later the darkness was gone and in its place was the furnace room at Paranor where the company of Allanon again stood face to face with the dreaded Skull Bearer. The fiery eyes in the green mist stared first at the Valeman, then watched the battle between the two dark figures until both tumbled over the edge of the pit and were lost in the flames below. At that moment a sudden noise behind him caused the Spirit Lord to pause and turn slightly. Two of his Skull Bearers entered the room from one of the dark tunnels of the mountain to stand silently, awaiting his attention. He was not ready for them, and so returned to the waters of the basin. Again they cleared, forming a picture of the tower, where the astonished members of the company stood frozen in excited relief before the Sword of Shannara. He waited a few seconds, toying with them, enjoying his mastery of the situation as they moved closer to the Sword like mice to the baited trap of cheese. Seconds later, the trap was sprung as he dissolved his illusion before their startled eyes and watched the tower door fly shut, trapping them in the keep for eternity. Behind him, the two winged servants could sense the chilling laugh that rolled through his substance-less frame into the cavern air.

Without turning to face them, the Warlock Lord gestured abruptly toward the open wall facing north, and the Skull Bearers moved off without hesitation. They knew without asking what was expected of them. They would fly to Paranor and destroy the captured son of Shannara, the sole heir to the hated Sword. With the last member of the House of Shannara dead and the Sword itself within their grasp, they no longer need fear a mystical power greater than their own. Even now, the precious Sword was en route from the halls of Paranor to the Northland kingdom where it would be buried and forgotten in the endless caverns of the Skull Mountain. The Warlock Lord turned slightly to watch his two servants shuffle awkwardly across the dark chamber until they reached the open wall, where they rose heavily into the gray sky and wheeled southward. To be sure, the Elf king, Eventine, would attempt to intercept the Sword, to regain it for his own people. But the attempt would fail, and Eventine would be taken – the last great leader of the free lands, the last hope of the races. With Eventine his prisoner, the Sword in his possession, the last heir to the House of Shannara dead, and the most hated enemy of all, the Druid Allanon, destroyed in the furnace at Paranor, the battle was ended before it had begun. There would be no defeat in the Third War of the Races. He had won.

A wave of his cloak sleeve and the water again turned murky, the picture of the Druids' Keep and the trapped mortals gone. Then the air rushed violently about the black spirit and his form began to dissolve back into the mist of the chamber, fading gradually until there was nothing left but the basin and the empty room. Long moments passed in silence until at last the groveling minions of the Warlock Lord were certain the Master had again gone from them, and they came forth from the shadows, their small, black shapes creeping eagerly to the basin edge where they peered curiously, crying and whimpering their misery to the placid waters.

In the high tower of Paranor, in the remote and now inaccessible room of the Druids' Keep, four silent, tired members of the little company from Culhaven paced dejectedly about their prison. Only Durin sat quietly against one wall of the tower, his wound so painful that he could no longer move about. Balinor rocked slightly on his heels as he stood close to a high, barred window of the Keep, watching the faint rays of the sun filter down in long streamers of floating dust to light the otherwise gloomy chamber with small squares of sunlight that fell carelessly across the stone slabs of the floor. They had been there for over an hour now, hopelessly imprisoned behind the mammoth, ironbound door. The Sword was lost to them and with it their hopes of any victory. At first they had waited patiently in the belief that Allanon would soon reach them, smashing through the great stone barrier that barred the way to freedom. They had even called his name, hoping he could hear them and follow their voices to the tower. Menion had reminded them that Flick was still missing, possibly wandering about the halls of Paranor searching for them. But before very long their faith faltered and at last faded entirely, as each forced himself to admit inwardly, though none would speak the words, that there would be no rescue, that the courageous Druid and the little Valeman had fallen prey to the deadly Skull Bearer, that the Warlock Lord had won.

Menion was thinking once again of Shea, wondering what had befallen his friend. The company had done all it could, but it had not even been enough to save the life of one small human being, and now no one could guess what end he had come to, left alone in the wilds of the Eastland border plains to fend for himself. Shea was gone, probably dead. Allanon had believed they would find Shea when they found the Sword, but the Sword had been lost and there was no sign of the missing heir. Now Allanon was gone as well, killed in the furnace room of the Druids' Council, his ancestral home – or if not killed, then taken prisoner, chained and shackled in some dungeon just as they were locked in this tower. They would be left to rot, or worse, and it had all been for nothing. He smiled grimly as he considered their fate, wishing he could have had at least one opportunity to confront the real enemy, to take one swift cut at the all-powerful Warlock Lord.

Suddenly a short hush of warning from the ever-alert Dayel caused the others to freeze where they were, eyes fixed on the great door, listening guardedly to the sound of faint footfalls on the stone steps beyond. Menion dropped his hand to the sword of Leah resting in the leather sheath on the floor and noiselessly pulled it free. The giant borderman at his elbow already held his drawn broadsword. All moved in short, hurried steps to encircle the entrance. Even the wounded Durin staggered to his feet, limping painfully over to stand with his companions. The footsteps reached the landing and stopped. There was a moment of ominous silence.

Then the great stone door suddenly opened, swinging ponderously inward, its iron hinges groaning only slightly as they took the full weight of the rock slab. From out of the darkness beyond appeared the frightened features of Flick Ohmsford, his eyes darting wildly as he beheld his imprisoned friends armed and ready to strike. Swords and maces lowered slowly as if the astonished men holding them were mechanical toys. The little Valeman moved reluctantly into the dim light of the tower, partially shadowed by the tall black figure following.

It was Allanon.

They stared at him wordlessly. Streaked with sweat, his dark form coated with several layers of ash and soot, he moved silently into their midst, one great hand resting gently on Flick's small shoulder. He smiled at their reaction.

'I'm all right,' he assured them.

Flick was still shaking his head in disbelief at having been found by Allanon.

'I saw him fall . . .' he tried to explain to the others.

'Flick, I'm all right.' Allanon patted the little Valeman's shoulder.

Balinor came a step closer, as if to convince himself that this was indeed Allanon and not another apparition.

'We thought you were . . . lost,' he managed.

The familiar mocking grin appeared on the lean face.

'The blame for that lies in part at least with our young friend here. He saw me tumble into the furnace pit with the Skull Bearer and presumed me dead. What he did not realize is that the furnace is equipped with a series of iron rungs, which allow workmen to descend into the pit for the purpose of making repairs. Since Paranor has for centuries been the ancestral home of the Druids, I knew of the existence of the rungs. When I felt the evil one pull me over the railing, I reached for them and caught myself several feet below the rim. Flick, of course, could see none of this, and the roar of the fire drowned out my voice as I called out to him.'

He paused to brush some of the dirt from his robe.

'Flick was fortunate enough to escape the chamber, but then he lost his way in the tunnels. The battle with the Skull Bearer left me weakened, and even though I enjoy special protection from fire, it took me quite some time to pull myself out of the pit. I went looking for Flick, lost in that maze of underground corridors, found him at last and frightened him half to death when I pulled him into the light. Then we came after the rest of you. But now we must leave – quickly.'

'The Sword . . .?' Hendel asked sharply.

'Gone – removed sometime earlier. We can speak of that later. It is dangerous for us to remain here any longer. The Gnomes will send reinforcements to secure Paranor and the Warlock Lord will dispatch others of his winged bearers to be certain you cause him no further trouble. With the Sword of Shannara still in his possession and believing you trapped in the Druids' Keep, he will quickly turn his attention to his plans for an invasion of the four lands. If he can seize Callahorn and the border countries quickly enough, the rest of the Southland will fall without a struggle.'

'Then we're too late – we've lost!' exclaimed Menion bitterly.

Allanon shook his head emphatically.

'We have only been outmaneuvered, not defeated, Prince of Leah. The Warlock Lord rests easy in the belief that he has won, that we are destroyed and no longer a threat. Perhaps we can use that against him. We must not despair. Now come with me.'

He led them quickly through the open doorway. A moment later, the tower chamber stood empty.

CHAPTER

5

The little band of Gnomes marched Shea northward until sunset. The Valeman was exhausted when the march began and by the time the group finally halted for the night, he immediately collapsed and was asleep before the Gnomes had even finished binding his legs. The long trek took them from the banks of the unknown river northward into hill country west of the upper Anar Forest bordering on the Northland. Travel became considerably rougher, the terrain changing from the flat grasslands of the Rabb Plains into choppy, rolling hillocks. After a time, the band found itself doing more climbing than walking, with constant changes of direction made to avoid the bigger hills. It was beautiful country, grasslands patched with small forests of aged shade trees, their bending limbs graceful in the light spring winds. But its beauty was lost on the exhausted Valeman, who could only concentrate on putting one foot ahead of the other as his disinterested captors pushed him along without rest. By nightfall, the group was deep into the hill country, and had Shea been able to consult a map of the region, he would have discovered that they were camped directly east of Paranor. As it was, sleep came to him so fast that he could only remember dropping wearily to the grassy earth and then nothing more.

The industrious Gnomes finished tying him and then prepared a fire for their meager dinner. One Gnome was placed on sentry duty, mostly out of habit, since they felt there was little to fear this far into their own homeland, and a second was ordered to keep a close watch over the sleeping captive. The Gnome leader still did not realize who Shea was, nor did he realize the importance of the Elfstones, though he was intelligent enough to conclude that they must be worth something. His plan was to take the Valeman to Paranor where he could consult with his superiors concerning the fate of both the youth and the stones. Perhaps they would know the significance of these matters. The Gnome's only concern was doing the right thing in accordance with his orders to patrol this region, and beyond that duty, he did not care to know anything.

The fire was completed in short order, and the Gnomes ate a hastily prepared meal of bread and stripped meat. When the meal was finished, they gathered eagerly about the warm blaze and contemplated curiously the three small Elfstones which the leader had produced for inspection at his followers' urging. The wizened yellow faces bent closer to the fire and to the outstretched hand of the leader where the stones twinkled brightly in the glowing light. One eager follower tried to touch one, but a stinging blow from his superior sent him sprawling back into the shadows. The Gnome leader touched the stones curiously and rolled them about in his open palm as the others watched in fascination. Finally, the Gnomes tired of the sport, and the stones were put back in the small leather pouch and returned to the leader's tunic. A bottle of ale was broken out to ward off the chill in the night air as well as to aid the weary Gnomes in forgetting their immediate troubles. The bottle was passed around freely, and the little yellow soldiers laughed and joked far into the night, keeping the fire blazing for warmth. Even the lone sentry wandered in, knowing that his guard duty was unnecessary. At last the ale was gone, and the weary hunters turned in, pulling up their blankets in a tight circle about the fire. The sentry even had presence of mind enough to throw a blanket over the sleeping captive, concluding that it would do no good to bring him into Paranor suffering from a fever. Moments later, the campsite was silent, all asleep save the sentry who stood drowsily in the shadows just beyond the light of the small campfire that was dying slowly into coals.

Shea slept fitfully, his slumber disturbed by recurring nightmares of his harrowing flight with Flick and Menion to reach Culhaven, and from there, the ill-fated journey to reach Paranor. He relieved in his dreams the battle with the Mist Wraith, feeling its cold, slimy grip about his body, experiencing terror at the touch of the deadly swamp waters lapping about his legs. He felt desperation creeping all through him as the three again became separated in the Black Oaks, only this time he was alone in the great forest, and he knew there was no way out. He would wander until he died there. He could hear the cries of the hunting wolves closing in about him as he struggled to run, dodging madly through the endless maze of giant trees. A moment later the scene changed, and the company stood in the ruins of the city in the middle of the Wolfsktaag Mountains. They were looking curiously at the metal girders, unaware of the danger lurking silently in the jungle beyond. Only Shea knew what was about to happen, but when he tried to warn the others, he found he could not speak. Then he saw the giant creature creeping forth from its concealment to strike the unsuspecting men, and he could not move to warn them. They seemed unaware of what was about to happen, and the creature attacked, a mass of black hair and teeth. Then Shea was in the river, tossing and turning madly as he sought futilely to keep his head above the swift waters, to breathe the life-giving air. But he was being pulled down, and he knew he was suffocating. Desperately he sought to fight it, thrashing wildly as he was pulled farther and farther down.

Then suddenly he was awake and staring into the first faint tinges of light from the approaching dawn, his hands and feet cold and numb from the biting leather thongs that bound him. He looked anxiously about the clearing at the dying coals of the fire and the motionless Gnome bodies huddled in deep slumber. The hills were silent in the semi-darkness, so quiet that the Valeman could hear his own breathing, rasping heavily in the stillness. To one side of the campsite was the lone figure of the sentry, his small form a dim shadow on the far edges of the clearing, near some heavy brush. His figure was so vague in the mistiness of the dying night that for several seconds Shea was not really sure he was not a part of the brush. Shea glanced about the silent camp a second time, twisting himself up on one elbow and wiping the sleep from his eyes as he peered cautiously about. Briefly, he tried to work on the thongs that bound him, hoping vaguely that he might be able to work himself loose and make a dash for freedom before the sleeping Gnomes could catch him. But after long minutes of trying to free himself, he was forced to give up the idea. The bonds were too well tied to be worked loose, and he did not have the strength to break them. For a moment he stared helplessly at the ground in front of him, convinced that he had reached the end of the line, that once the Gnomes reached Paranor, he would be turned over to the Skull Bearers and disposed of quickly.

Then he heard something. It was only a faint rustle from somewhere in the darkness beyond the clearing, but it caused him to look up alertly, listening for something further. His Elven eyes traveled quickly over the campsite and the Gnomes, but nothing seemed out of place. It took him several moments to relocate the lone guard at the edge of the brush, but the man had not moved from his position. Then a huge black shadow detached itself from the brush, and the sentry was enveloped and suddenly gone. Shea blinked in disbelief, but there was no mistake. Where the figure of the sentry had stood a moment before, there was nothing. Long moments passed as Shea waited for something further to happen. It was sunrise now. The last traces of the night faded rapidly, and the edge of the golden morning sun appeared on the tips of the distant eastern hills.

There was a soft sound off to his left, and the Valeman twisted about sharply. From behind the cover of a small grove of trees emerged one of the strangest sights that the youth had ever seen. It was a man clad all in scarlet, the like of which no one in Shady Vale had ever encountered. At first the Valeman thought it might be Menion, recalling an outlandish red hunting outfit he had once seen the highlander wearing. But it became apparent almost immediately that this stranger was not Menion, nor in any way like him. The size, the stance, the manner of approach were all different. It was impossible to make out his features in the dim light. In one hand he carried a short hunting knife and in the other was a strange pointed object. The scarlet figure crept slowly over to his side and moved in back of him before he could get a good look at his face. The hunting knife went through the leather bonds silently and easily, freeing the captive Valeman. Then the other hand came around in front of his face, and Shea's eyes went wide in shock as he saw that the man's left hand was missing and in its place a deadly looking iron pike protruded.

'Not a word,' the leather-edged voice sounded in his ear. 'Don't look, don't think, just move out for the trees to the left and wait there. Now move!'

Shea did not stop to ask questions, but quickly did as he was told. Even without seeing the face of the rescuer, he could guess from the rough voice and the severed limb that it would be wise to do as he was told. He scurried silently from the camp, running in a low crouch until he had reached the cover of the trees. He stopped there and turned back to wait for the other, but to his astonishment the scarlet figure was prowling noiselessly through the midst of the sleeping Gnomes, apparently searching for something. The sun had risen into full view in the east now, and its light framed the stranger as he bent over the huddled form of the sleeping Gnome leader. One gloved hand reached cautiously into the Gnome's tunic, fumbled about for a moment, and came forth holding the small leather pouch with the precious Elfstones. As the hand with the pouch remained poised for an instant, the Gnome awakened, one hand coming up to seize the stranger's wrist as the other whipped a short sword around to finish the thief with one blow. But Shea's rescuer was too quick to be caught off guard. The long iron pike blocked the blow in a sharp clash of metal, and then came back in a long swipe across the Gnome's exposed throat. As the stranger rose to his feet and bounded away from the lifeless body, the entire camp came awake with the sound of the struggle. The Gnomes were on their feet in an instant, swords in hand, charging after the intruder before he could make a complete escape. The scarlet rescuer was forced to turn and fight, the short knife held in one hand as he faced a dozen attackers.

Shea was certain that this was the end for the man, and he prepared to leap from the cover of the trees to try to aid him. But the amazing stranger shrugged off the first onslaught of Gnome hunters as if they were mice, cutting through their disorganized assault and leaving two writhing on the earth with fatal wounds. Then he gave a sharp cry as the second wave of attackers moved in, and from out of the shadows on the other side of the camp charged a massive black figure bearing a huge club. Without slowing once, the black shape tore into the surprised Gnomes with indescribable fury, scattering them with great blows of the mace as if they were no more than fragile leaves. In less than a minute all the Gnomes lay motionless on the ground. Shea watched in astonishment at the edge of the trees as the huge figure approached Shea's rescuer, somewhat in the manner of a faithful dog seeking its master's approval. The stranger spoke softly to the giant for several moments, and then sauntered over to Shea while his companion remained to look after the Gnomes.

'I think that's about all of it,' the voice rolled out as the scarlet figure came up to the Valeman, hefting the leather pouch in his good hand.

Shea took a moment to study the man's face, still uncertain as to who his benefactor might be. The way the man swaggered, there was no question in Shea's mind but that he was an arrogant fellow whose unshakable confidence in himself was probably matched only by his undeniable efficiency as a fighter. The tanned, worn face was clean-shaven except for a small mustache cut evenly above the upper lip. He had one of those faces that defied age; he looked neither old nor young, but somewhere in between. Yet his manner was youthful, and only the leathery skin and deep eyes revealed that he would never see forty years again. The dark hair seemed flecked slightly with bits of gray, though in the misty dawn light it was difficult to be certain. The face was broad and his features prominent, particularly the wide, friendly mouth. It was a handsome, beguiling type of face, but one that Shea instinctively felt was a carefully worn mask that hid the true nature of the man. The stranger stood easily before the uncertain Valeman, smiling and waiting for some indication of his attitude toward his rescuers, apparently unsure of what it might be.

'I want to thank you,' Shea quickly sputtered. 'It would have been all over for me if you hadn't . . .'

'Quite all right, quite all right. Rescuing people is not exactly our business, but those devils would cut you up for sport. I'm from the Southland myself, you know. Haven't been back in quite awhile, but it's my home nevertheless. You're from there, I can tell. One of the hill communities, maybe? Of course, you have Elven blood in you, too . . .'

He trailed off abruptly, and for an instant Shea was certain that the man not only knew who he was, but what he was, and that he had stepped from the frying pan into the fire. A quick look back at the huge creature by the fallen Gnomes was necessary to reassure the youth that this was not a Skull Bearer.

'Who are you, friend, and where are you from?' the stranger demanded suddenly.

Shea gave him his name and explained that he was from Shady Vale. He told him that he had been exploring on a river to the south when his boat overturned, and he had been washed downstream and left unconscious on a bank where the band of Gnomes had found him. The fabricated tale was close enough to the truth so that the man might believe him, and Shea was not yet ready to trust strangers with the whole truth until he knew more than he knew about these two. He concluded his story by stating that the Gnomes had found him and decided to take him prisoner. The man looked at him for a long moment, an amused smile crossing his lips as he played idly with the leather pouch.

'Well, I doubt that you have told me the whole truth.' He laughed shortly. 'But I can't blame you. If I were in your place, I wouldn't tell me everything either. There will be time enough for the truth later. My name is Panamon Creel.'

He extended his one broad hand which Shea accepted and shook heartily. The stranger had a grip like iron and the Valeman winced involuntarily at the strong handshake. The man smiled faintly and released his grip, pointing to the dark giant behind them.

'My companion, Keltset. We've been together for almost two years now and I never had a better friend, although I could have wished for a more talkative one, perhaps. Keltset is a mute.'

'What is he?' asked Shea curiously, watching the great figure lumber slowly about the little clearing.

'You certainly are a stranger to this part of the world.' The other laughed in amusement. 'Keltset is a Rock Troll. His home was in the Charnal Mountains until his people made an outcast of him. We're both outcasts in this thankless world, but life deals a different hand to each, I suppose. We have no choice in the matter.'

'A Rock Troll,' Shea repeated wonderingly. 'I've never seen a Rock Troll before. I thought they were all savage creatures, almost like animals. How could you . . .?'

'Watch your tongue. friend,' the stranger warned sharply. 'Keltset doesn't like that kind of talk, and he is just sensitive enough to step on you for using it. Your problem is that you look at him and see a monster, a misshapen creature unlike you or me, and you wonder if he's dangerous. Then I tell you that he's a Rock Troll, and you're twice as certain he's more animal than man. Part of your limited education and lack of practical experience, I warrant. You should have traveled with me during the last few years – ha, you would have learned that even a friendly smile shows the teeth behind!'

Shea looked closely at the giant Rock Troll as Keltset bent idly over the fallen Gnomes, glancing about for anything he might have missed in his extensive search of their garments and packs. Keltset was basically man-shaped, dressed in knee-length pants and a tunic belted with a green cord. About the neck and wrists he wore protective metal collars. His really different feature was the strange, almost barklike skin that covered the entire body, coloring it something on the order of meat well done, but not yet charred. The dark face was small featured, blunt and nondescript, with a heavy brow and deep-set eyes. The extremities were the same as a man's except for the hands. There was no little finger on either hand – only a thumb and three stout, powerful fingers nearly as large as the Valeman's small wrists.

'He doesn't look very tame to me,' Shea declared quietly.

'There you are! The perfect example of a hasty opinion totally without foundation. Just because Keltset doesn't look civilized and doesn't appear an intelligent creature on the face of things, you label him an animal. Shea, my boy, you may believe me when I say that Keltset is a sensitive man with the same feelings as you or I. Being a Troll in the Northland is every bit as normal as being an Elf in the Westland and so on! You and I are the strangers in this part of the world.'

Shea looked carefully at the broad, reassuring face, the easy smile that seemed to come so naturally, and he instinctively distrusted the man. These two were more than travelers passing through this country who had seen his plight and had come to his aid out of love for their fellowman. They had stalked that Gnome encampment with skill and cunning, and when discovered, destroyed the entire Gnome patrol with ruthless efficiency. As dangerous as the Rock Troll appeared, Shea was certain that Panamon Creel was twice as deadly.

'You are most certainly better informed on the matter than I,' admitted Shea, choosing his words carefully. 'Being from the Southland, and having traveled little outside of its borders, I am unfamiliar with all life in this region of the world. I owe you both my life, and my thanks go to Keltset as well.'

The dashing stranger smiled happily at the expression of gratitude, obviously pleased at the unexpected compliment.

'No thanks are necessary; I told you that,' he replied. 'Come over here and sit with me for a moment while we wait for Keltset to finish his task. We must talk more about what brought you to this part of the country. It's very dangerous in these parts, you know, especially traveling alone.'

He led the way over to the nearest tree where he sat down wearily, resting his back against the slender trunk. He still held the pouch with the Elfstones in his one good hand, and Shea did not feel that he should bring that subject up just yet. Hopefully, the stranger would ask if they belonged to him, and he could recover them and be on his way to Paranor. The others in the company would be looking for him by now, either along the eastern edge of the Dragon's Teeth or farther up near Paranor.

'Why is Keltset searching those Gnomes?' the youth asked after a moment's silence.

'Well, there might be some indication of where they are from, where they were going. They might have some food, which we could use right now. Who knows, they might even have something valuable . . .?'

He trailed off sharply and looked questioningly at Shea, one hand balancing the leather pouch with the Elfstones before the Valeman's eyes, holding it like bait before the hunted animal. Shea swallowed hard and hesitated, realizing suddenly the man had sensed all along that the stones belonged to him. He had to do something quickly, or he would give himself away.

'They belong to me. The pouch and the stones are mine.'

'Are they now?' Panamon Creel grinned wolfishly at the youth. 'I don't see your name on the pouch. How did you come by them?'

'They were given to me by my father,' Shea lied quickly. 'I've had them for years. I carry them everywhere – a sort of good-luck piece. When the Gnomes captured me, they searched me and took the pouch and the stones away. But they are mine.'

The scarlet-clad rescuer smiled faintly and opened the pouch, pouring the stones into his open palm, holding the pouch with the wicked-looking pike. He hefted them and held them up to the light, admiring their brilliant blue glow. Then he turned back to Shea, raising his eyebrows quizzically.

'What you say may be true, but it may be that you stole

them. They look rather valuable to be carrying around as a good-luck charm. I think I should keep them until I am satisfied that you are the true owner.'

'But I have to go – I have to meet my friends,' Shea sputtered desperately. 'I can't stay with you until you're certain I own the stones!'

Panamon Creel rose slowly to his feet and smiled down, tucking the pouch and its contents into his tunic.

'That should pose no problem. Just tell me where I can reach you, and I'll bring the stones to you there after I've checked out your story. I'll be down in the Southland in several months or so.'

Shea was absolutely beside himself with anger, and he leaped to his feet in a rage.

'Why, you're nothing but a thief, a common highwayman!' he stormed, bracing the other defiantly.

Panamon Creel erupted suddenly into a fit of uncontrollable laughter, holding his sides in mirth. He finally regained control of himself, shaking his head in disbelief as the tears rolled down his broad face. Shea looked on in astonishment, unable to see what was so humorous about the accusation. Even the huge Rock Troll had stopped momentarily and turned to look at them, his placid face dark and expressionless.

'Shea, I have to admire a man who speaks his mind,' exclaimed the stranger, still chuckling in delight. 'No one could accuse you of being unperceptive!'

The irate Valeman started to make a hasty retort and then caught himself quickly as the facts of the situation recalled themselves sharply in his puzzled mind. What were these two strange companions doing in this part of the Northland? Why had they bothered to rescue him in the first place? How had they even known he was a prisoner of the small band of Gnomes? He realized the truth in an instant; it had been so obvious that he had overlooked it.

'Panamon Creel, the kind rescuer!' he mocked bitterly.

'No wonder you found my remark so amusing. You and your friend are exactly what I called you. You are thieves, robbers, highwaymen! It was the stones you were after all along! How low can you be . . . ?'

'Watch your tongue, youngster!' The scarlet stranger leaped in front of him, brandishing the iron pike. The broad face was distorted in sudden hate, the constant smile suddenly villainous beneath the small mustache as anger flashed sharply in the dark eyes. 'What you may think of us had best be kept to yourself. I've come a long way in this world, and no one has ever given me anything! Since this is so, I let no man take anything away!'

Shea backed away guardedly, terrified that he had foolishly overstepped his bounds with the unpredictable pair. Undoubtedly, his own rescue had been almost an afterthought on their part, their primary concern having been the theft of the Elfstones from the Gnome raiders. Panamon Creel was no one to fool around with, and a reckless tongue at this stage of the game could cost the Valeman his life. The tall thief stared balefully at his frightened captive a moment longer and then stepped back slowly, the angered features relaxing and a faint hint of his former good-naturedness returning in a quick smile.

'Why should we deny it, Keltset and I?' He swaggered backward and around a few paces, wheeling abruptly on Shea again. 'We are wayfarers of fortune, he and I. Men who live by their wits and by their cunning – yet we are no different than other men, save in our methods. And perhaps our disdain for hypocrisy! All men are thieves in one way or another; we are simply the old-fashioned type, the honest type who are not ashamed of what they are.'

'How did you happen on this camp?' Shea asked hesitantly, fearful of aggravating the temperamental man further.

'We came across their fire last night, just after sunset,' the other replied easily, all traces of hostility gone. 'I came down to the edge of the clearing for a closer look and saw my little yellow friends playing with those three blue gems. I saw you as well, all trussed up for delivery. So I decided to bring Keltset down and kill two birds with one stone – ah, ha, you see, I wasn't lying when I told you that I did not like to see a fellow Southlander in the hands of those devils!'

Shea nodded, happy to be free, but unsure whether he was better off now than when he had been a prisoner of the Gnomes.

'Quit worrying, friend.' Panamon Creel recognized the unspoken fear. 'We don't mean you any harm. We only want the stones – they'll bring a good price, and we can use the money. You're free to go back to where you came from anytime.'

He turned away abruptly and walked over to the waiting Keltset, who was standing obediently next to a small pile of arms, clothing, and assorted articles of value that he had collected from the fallen Gnomes. The huge frame of the Troll dwarfed the normally large figure of his companion; the dark, barklike skin made him appear somewhat like a gnarled tree casting its shadow over the scarlet-clad human. The two conversed briefly, Panamon speaking in low tones to his giant friend while the other replied with sign language and nods of his broad head. They turned to the pile of goods, which the man shuffled through quickly, casting most of the effects aside as useless junk. Shea watched momentarily, uncertain what he should do next. He had lost the stones, and without them he was virtually defenseless in this savage land. He had lost his companions in the Dragon's Teeth, the only ones who would stand with him, the only ones who could really help him recover the stones. He had come so far that it was unthinkable to turn back now, even if he thought he could do so safely. The others in the company depended on him, and he would never desert Flick and Menion whatever the dangers involved.

Panamon Creel cast a short glance over his shoulder to see if the Valeman had made any move to leave, and a faint trace of surprise registered on his handsome face when he saw the youth still standing where he had left him.

'What are you waiting for?'

Shea shook his head slowly, indicating that he wasn't quite sure. The tall thief watched him a moment longer, and then waved him over with a short smile.

'Come on and have a bite to eat, Shea,' he invited. 'The least we can do is feed you before you start back for the Southland.'

Fifteen minutes later the three were seated around a small campfire, watching strips of dried beef warm enticingly in the smoking heat. The mute Keltset sat silently next to the little Valeman, the deep eyes fixed on the smoking meat, the huge hands clasped childlike as he squatted before the small fire. Shea had an uncontrollable urge to reach out and touch the strange creature, to feel the rough, barklike skin. The features of the Troll were indescribably bland even from this close distance. The Troll never moved while the meat was cooking, but sat absolutely still like some immobile rock that time and the ages had passed by without changing. Panamon Creel glanced over once and noticed Shea casting a watchful eye on the huge creature. He smiled broadly, one hand coming across to clap the startled Valeman on the shoulder.

'He won't bite – long as he gets fed! I keep telling you the same thing, but you don't listen. That's youth for you – wild and fancy free and no time for the old folks. Keltset is just like you and me, only bigger and quieter, which is what I like in a partner in this line of work. He does his job better than any man I've ever worked with, and I've worked with quite a few, I can tell you.'

'He does what you tell him, I suppose?' Shea asked shortly.

'Sure he does, sure he does,' came the quick answer; then the scarlet figure bent closer to the other's pale face,

83

the iron pike coming up sharply in emphasis. 'But don't get me wrong, boy, because I don't mean to say he's any kind of animal. He can think for himself when it's needed. But I was his friend when no one else would even look his way – no one! He's the strongest living thing I've ever seen. He could crush me without half thinking about it. But do you know what? I beat him, and now he follows me!'

He paused to judge the other's reaction, eyes wide with delight at the Valeman's startled look of disbelief. He laughed merrily and slapped his knee with exaggerated humor at the reaction he had drawn.

'I beat him with friendship, not strength! I respected him as a man, treated him as an equal, and for that cheap price, I won his loyalty. Hah, surprised you!'

Still chuckling at his thin attempt at humor, the thief lifted the strips of beef from the fire and held out the stick on which they rested to the silent Troll, who removed several and began munching hungrily. Shea helped himself slowly when offered and suddenly realized that he was starving. He couldn't even remember when he had eaten last, and gnawed ravenously at the tasty beef. Panamon Creel shook his head in amusement and offered the Valeman a second piece before taking one himself. The three ate in silence for several minutes before Shea ventured a further inquiry concerning his companions.

'What made you decide to become . . . robbers?' he asked guardedly.

Panamon Creel shot a quick look at him, arching his eyebrows in surprise.

'What do you care what the reasons were? Plan on writing our life story?' He paused and caught himself suddenly, smiling quickly at his own irritability. 'There's no secret to it, Shea. I've never been much at making an honest living, never very good at common work. I was a wild kid, loved adventure, loved the outdoors – hated work. Then I lost my hand in an accident, and it became even harder to find work that would make me a comfortable living, get me what I wanted. I was deep in the Southland then, living in Talhan. I got in a little trouble and then a lot more. The next thing I knew I was roaming the four lands robbing for a living. The funny thing was I found myself so good at it that I couldn't quit. And I enjoyed it – all of it! So here I am, maybe not rich, but happy in the prime of my youth – or at least, my manhood.'

'Don't you ever think about going back?' Shea persisted, unable to believe the man was being honest with himself. 'Don't you ever think about a home and . . .?'

'Please, let's not be maudlin, lad!' The other roared in laughter. 'Keep this up and you'll have me in tears, begging for forgiveness on my tired old knees!'

He broke into such an uncontrollable fit of raucous guffaws that even the silent Troll glanced over in quiet contemplation for a moment before returning to his meal. Shea felt a fierce flush of indignation spreading over his face and turned slowly back to his food, chewing the beef with grinding bites of anger and embarrassment. After several moments the laughter died into small chuckles, the thief shaking his head in amusement as he tried to swallow a little food. Then without further prompting, he continued his narration in a quieter tone of voice.

'Keltset has a different story than mine, I want to make that clear. I had no reason to take up this kind of life, but he had every reason. He was a mute since birth, and the Trolls don't like deformed people. Kind of a joke on them, I guess. So they made life pretty rough for him, kicked him around and beat him when they were mad at anything that they couldn't take their anger out on directly. He was the butt of every joke, but he never fought back because those people were all he had. Then he became big, so big and strong that the others were frightened of him. One night some of the young ones tried to hurt him, really hurt him so he might go away, even die. But it didn't work out quite as they expected. They pushed him too far, and he fought back and killed three of them. As a result he was driven from the village, and an outcast Troll has no home once outside his own tribe or whatever they are. So he wandered around on his own until I found him.'

He smiled faintly and looked over at the massive, placid face bent intently over the last several strips of beef, eating hungrily.

'He knows what we're doing, though, and I guess he knows that it's not honest work. But he's like a child who's been so badly mistreated that he has no respect for other people because they never did him any good. Besides, we stay in this part of the country where there's only Gnomes and Dwarfs – a Troll's natural enemies. We steer away from the deep Northland and seldom get south very far. We do all right.'

He returned to his piece of beef, munching absently as he stared into the dying embers of the fire, poking them with the toe of his leather boot, the sparks rising in small showers and fading into dust. Shea finished his own food without further comment, wondering what he could possibly do to regain the Elfstones, wishing that he knew where the other members of the company were now. Moments later the meal was ended, and the scarlet-clad thief rose abruptly, scattering the embers of the fire with a swift kick of his boot. The massive Rock Troll rose with him and stood quietly waiting for his friend to make the next move, his great bulk towering over Shea. The Valeman stood at last and watched Panamon Creel gather up several small trinkets and a few weapons to place in a sack which he handed to Keltset to carry. Then he turned to his small captive and nodded shortly.

'It's been interesting knowing you, Shea, and I wish you good luck. When I think of the little gems in this pouch, I shall think of you. Too bad it couldn't work out so that you could save them, but at least you saved your life – or rather, I saved it. Think of the stones as a gift for services rendered. It may make losing them easier. Now you'd better be moving along if you plan to reach the safety of the Southland in the next several days. The city of Varfleet lies just to the south and west, and you'll find help there. Just stick to the open country.'

He turned to leave, motioning Keltset to follow and had taken several long strides before he glanced back over his shoulder. The Valeman had not moved, but was looking after the departing men as if in a trance. Panamon Creel shook his head in disgust and walked a bit farther, then stopped in annoyance and wheeled about, knowing the other was still standing immobile where he had left him.

'What's the matter with you?' he demanded angrily. 'Now don't tell me that you have any foolish ideas about trailing us and trying to get the gems back? That would spoil a very nice relationship because I'd have to cut your ears off – maybe worse! Now get going, get out of here!'

'You don't understand what those stones mean!' Shea shouted desperately.

'I think I do,' came the quick reply. 'They mean that for a while Keltset and I will be more than merely poverty-stricken thieves. It means we won't have to steal or beg for a handout for quite some time. It means money, Shea.'

Desperately, Shea dashed after the two robbers, unable to think of anything but recovering the precious Elfstones. Panamon Creel watched him approach in astonishment, certain that the Valeman was crazed to the point of daring to attack them to regain possession of the three blue gems. Never had he encountered such a persistent fellow in all his days. He had spared the lad's life and graciously given him his freedom, but still it didn't seem to be enough to satisfy him. Shea came to a panting halt several yards away from the two tall figures, and the thought flashed through his mind that he had reached the end of his rope. Their patience was exhausted and now they would dispose of him without further consideration.

'I didn't tell you the truth before,' he gasped finally. 'I couldn't . . . I don't know it all myself. But the stones are very important – not only to me, but to everyone in all the lands. Even to you, Panamon.'

The scarlet robber looked at him with a mixture of surprise and distrust, the smile gone, but the dark eyes still free of anger. He said nothing, but stood motionless waiting for the exasperated Valeman to speak further.

'You've got to believe me!' Shea exclaimed vehemently. 'There's more to this than you realize.'

'You certainly seem to believe so,' admitted the other flatly. He looked over at the huge Keltset, who stood at his elbow, and shrugged his incredulity at Shea's strange behavior. The Rock Troll made a quick move toward Shea, and the Valeman shrank back in terror; but Panamon Creel stopped his massive companion with a raised hand.

'Look, just grant me one favor,' Shea pleaded desperately, grasping at any chance to gain a little time to think. 'Take me north with you to Paranor.'

'You must be mad!' cried the thief, aghast at the suggestion. 'What possible reason could you have for going to that black fortress? It's extremely unfriendly country. You wouldn't last five minutes! Go home, boy. Go home to the southland and leave me in peace.'

'I've got to get to Paranor,' the other insisted quickly. 'That was where I was going when the Gnomes captured me. I have friends there – friends who will be searching for me. I have to join them at Paranor!'

'Paranor is an evil place, a spawning ground for Northland creatures even I would be afraid to run into!' Panamon said heatedly. 'Besides, if you do have friends there, you probably plan to lead Keltset and me into some sort of trap so you can get your hands on the stones. That's your plan, isn't it? Forget it right now. Take my advice and turn south while you still can!'

'You're afraid, aren't you?' Shea sputtered angrily. 'You're afraid of Paranor and afraid of my friends. You haven't the courage . . .'

He trailed off sharply as the deep fires of anger kindled explosively in the scarlet thief, the broad face flushing heatedly at the accusation. For a moment Panamon Creel stood motionless, his entire frame quivering with rage as he glared at the small Valeman. Shea stood his ground, gambling everything on this final plea.

'If you won't take me with you – just to Paranor – then I'll go alone and take my chances,' he promised. He watched their reaction for a moment and then continued: 'All I'm asking is to be taken just to the borders of Paranor. I won't ask you to go beyond; I won't lead you into a trap.'

Panamon Creel shook his head once again in disbelief, the anger gone from his eyes and a faint smile playing over his tightened lips as he turned from the Valeman to look at the giant Rock Troll. He shrugged shortly and nodded.

'Why should we be worried?' he mused mockingly. 'It's your neck on the block. Come on along, Shea.'

CHAPTER

6

The three strange companions journeyed northward through the rough hill country until midday, when they paused for a quick meal and a few welcome minutes of rest. The terrain of the country had remained changeless during the morning's march, a consistently rugged series of elevations and depressions that made traveling extremely difficult. Even the powerful Keltset was forced to climb and scramble with the two men, unable to find sure footing or level ground that would permit him to walk upright. The land was not only humped and misshapen, but also rather barren and unfriendly in appearance. The hills were grass-covered and dotted with brush and small trees, but they conveyed a lonely and wild emptiness to the travelers that caused them to feel uneasy and moody. The grass was a tall, whiplike weed so strong that it slapped at the men's pants legs with stinging swipes. When crushed down by their heavy boots, it lay matted only seconds before springing back into place. Upon looking back in the direction from which they had come, Shea could not tell from the appearance of the land that anyone had passed that way. The scattered trees were gnarled and bent, filled with small leaves, but giving the overall impression that they were nature's stepchildren, stunted at birth and left to survive in this lonely country as best they could. There was no sign at all of any animal or bird life, and since dawn, the three men had neither seen nor heard another living creature.

Conversation was not lacking, however. In fact, there were several times when Shea wished that Panamon Creel would tire of his own voice for a few minutes. The tall thief carried on a steady conversation with his companions, with himself, and on occasion with no one in particular, for the entire morning. He talked about everything imaginable, including a good many things about which he seemed to know nothing. The one topic of conversation he scrupulously avoided was Shea. He acted as if the Valeman were merely a comrade in arms, a fellow thief with whom he could freely speak about his own wild experiences without fear of reprimand. But he meticulously avoided mentioning Shea's background, the Elfstones, or the purpose of this journey. Apparently he had concluded that the best way to handle the matter was to get the bothersome Valeman to Paranor as quickly as possible, reunite him with his friends, and without further delay continue on. Shea had no idea where the two had intended to travel before encountering him. Perhaps even they had been uncertain of their destination. He listened attentively while the thief rambled on, interjecting comments of his own when he thought it appropriate or the other seemed interested in his opinion. But for the most part, he concentrated on the journey and tried to decide the best way to go about recovering the stones. The situation was somewhat untenable no matter how he went about it; both the thieves and he knew that he was going to try to get the stones away from them. The only question remaining was the method he would try. Shea was convinced that the clever Panamon Creel would merely toy with him, give him enough rope to find out how he planned to get the stones, and then gaily haul in the noose about the Valeman's neck.

Occasionally while they walked and conversed, Shea

glanced at the silent Rock Troll, wondering what sort of person lay beneath the expressionless exterior. Panamon had said the Troll was a misfit, a creature spurned by his own people, a companion to the flashy thief because the man had proved to be his friend. This could be true, as trite as the tale seemed on first appraisal, but there was something about the Troll's bearing that caused the Valeman to question that he was an exile driven out by his own people. The Troll carried himself with undeniable dignity, head erect, the massive frame ramrod straight. He never spoke, apparently because he really was mute. Yet there was an intelligence in the deep-set eyes that led Shea to believe Keltset was far more complex than his companion had indicated. Just as with Allanon, Shea felt that Panamon Creel had not told him the whole truth. But unlike the Druid, the clever thief was probably a liar, and the youth felt that he should not believe anything he had been told. He was certain that he did not know the whole story behind Keltset, whether because Panamon had lied or because the man simply didn't know it. He was equally sure that the scarlet-clad adventurer, who had in one instant saved his life and in the next calmly stolen the precious Elfstones, was more than an ordinary road agent.

They finished the midday meal quickly. As Keltset packed up their cooking implements, Panamon explained to Shea that they were not far from the Jannisson Pass at the northern borders of the hill country. Once through this pass, they would cross the Plains of Streleheim to the west to reach Paranor. There they would part ways, the thief declared pointedly, and Shea could meet with his friends or go to the Druids' Keep as he saw fit. The Valeman nodded his understanding, catching the hint of eagerness in the other's voice, knowing that they expected him to make his move to recover the stones soon. He said nothing, however, and gave no indication that he suspected they were baiting him, but picked up what little gear he still had, to continue the journey. The three men wound their way slowly through the foothills toward the low mountains that had appeared ahead. Shea was certain the distant mountains on his left were an extension of the formidable Dragon's Teeth, but this new set of mountains appeared to be a completely different range, and it was between the two chains that the Jannisson Pass must lie. They were very near the Northland now, and for the Valeman there was no turning back.

Panamon Creel had launched into another in the seemingly never-ending series of tales about his adventures. Strangely, he seldom mentioned Keltset, another indication to Shea that the thief knew less about the Rock Troll than he professed. It was beginning to appear to Shea that the giant Troll was as much a mystery to his companion as he was to the Valeman. If they had lived together as thieves for two years, as Panamon had claimed, then some of the tales certainly ought to include Keltset. Moreover, while at first it had seemed to Shea that the Troll was a doglike follower of the crimson thief, it was beginning to appear on closer observation that he traveled with the man for entirely different reasons. It was not a conclusion Shea arrived at so much by listening to Panamon as from observing the mute conduct of the Troll. Shea was mystified by his proud bearing and detached attitude. Keltset had been swift and deadly in his extermination of the Gnome hunting party, but in retrospect it seemed almost as if he had done it because it had to be done – not to please his companion or to gain possession of the stones. Shea found it difficult to surmise who Keltset might be, but he was certain that he was not a downtrodden, shunned misfit who had been driven from his people as a hated outcast.

It was a particularly warm day, and Shea was beginning to perspire freely. The terrain had failed to level off at all, and traversing the stubborn, winding hills was laborious and slow. Panamon Creel talked on all the while, laughing and joking with Shea as if they were old friends, companions on the road to high adventure. He told him about the four lands; he had traveled them all, seen their people, studied their ways of life. Shea thought he seemed a bit vague about the Westland, and seriously doubted that the thief had learned much about the Elven people, but decided it would be unwise to pursue the matter. He listened dutifully to the tales of the women Panamon had met in his travels, including a standard narration about a beautiful king's daughter whom he had saved and fallen in love with, only to lose her when her father stepped between them and spirited her away to distant lands. The Valeman sighed with exaggerated pity, inwardly chuckling at the tale, as the anguished thief ended by confiding that to this day he continued his search for her. Shea remarked that he hoped Panamon would find her and she might persuade him to give up this way of life. The man looked at him sharply, studying the serious face, and for a few moments he was silent as he mulled the prospect over.

They reached the Jannisson Pass about two hours later. The pass was formed by a break at the meeting of the two mountain chains, a wide, easily accessible passage leading to the broad plainland beyond. The great mountain range coming up from the south was an extension of the towering Dragon's Teeth, but the northern range was unfamiliar to Shea. He knew that the Charnal Mountains, the home of the huge Rock Trolls, lay somewhere to the north of them, and this second range could be a southerly extension. Those desolate and relatively unexplored peaks had for centuries remained a vast wilderness inhabited solely by the ferocious and warlike Troll colonies. While the Rock Trolls were the largest of that breed, there were several other types of Trolls living in that sector of the Northland. If Keltset were any example of the Rock Trolls, then Shea imagined they must be a more intelligent people than Southlanders believed. It seemed somehow strange that his own countrymen should be so misinformed about another race inhabiting the same world. Even the textbooks he had studied when he was younger had described the Troll nations as ignorant and uncivilized.

Panamon called a sudden halt at the entrance to the wide pass and walked ahead several yards, peering cautiously up into the high slopes to either side, obviously wary of what might be waiting there. After several minutes' perusal, he ordered the stolid Keltset to investigate the pass to be certain it was safe for them to proceed. Quickly the giant Troll lumbered forward and was soon lost between the hills and rocks. Panamon suggested Shea sit down to wait, smiling that unforgivably smug smile that indicated the thief thought he was incredibly clever to take this added precaution to avoid any traps that friends of Shea might have arranged for him. While he felt safe enough keeping Shea with him, being reasonably certain that Shea posed no threat by himself, he was concerned that the Valeman might have friends powerful enough to cause trouble if they found the opportunity. While waiting for his companion to return, the garrulous adventurer decided to launch into still another wild tale of his hairraising life as a road agent. Shea found this one, like the others, incredible and obviously exaggerated. Panamon seemed to enjoy telling these stories far more than anyone could possibly enjoy listening, as if each were the very first and not the five hundredth. Shea endured the tale in stoic silence, trying to look interested as he thought about what lay ahead. They had to be quite close to the borders of Paranor now, and once they reached that point, he would be left on his own. He would have to find his friends quickly if he expected to stay alive in this region of the country. The Warlock Lord and his hunters would be searching tirelessly for any trace of him, and if they reached him before he gained the protection of Allanon and the company, his death was certain. Still, it was possible that by this time they had taken possession of the Druid's Keep and seized the precious Sword of Shannara. Perhaps the victory was already won.

Keltset appeared suddenly in the pass and signaled for them to come forward. They hastened to his side and together the three proceeded. There was little cover in the Jannisson Pass that would hide an ambush party, and it was apparent that there would be no trouble at this point. There were a few stray clumps of boulders and a few narrow hillocks, but none of these was big enough to hide more than one or two men. The pass was quite long, and it took the three travelers almost an hour to reach the other end. But it was a pleasant walk and the time passed quickly. When they reached the northern entrance, they could see plains stretching northward and beyond these still another mountain range which appeared to run toward the west. The travelers marched out of the pass onto the smooth floor of the plains which were set in a pocket, surrounded on three sides in horseshoe fashion by mountains and forests and opening out to the west. The plains were sparsely covered with a thin, pale green grass which grew in shaggy tufts over the dry earthen land. There were small bushes, all only knee-high on Shea, and these were bent and gaunt in appearance. Apparently, even in the spring, these plains were never very green, and little life existed in the lonely expanse of country beyond Paranor.

Shea knew they were nearing their destination when Panamon turned the little group westward, keeping their line of march several hundred yards north of the forest and mountain bordering to their left, careful to protect against any surprise assaults. When the Valeman asked the scarlet-clad leader where they were in relation to Paranor, the thief only smiled slyly and assured him they were getting closer all the time. Further questioning was pointless, and the youth resigned himself to being kept in the dark as to where they were until the other decided he was ready to let his uninvited guest go on alone. Instead, Shea turned his attention to the plains ahead, their barren vastness awesome and fascinating to the Southlander. It was an entirely new world for him, and while he was understandably afraid for his life, he was determined that he would miss nothing. This was the fabulous odyssey Flick and he had always dreamed they would someday make, and while its end might find them both dead and forgotten, the quest a failure and the Sword lost, still he would see it all in the time remaining to him.

By midafternoon, the three were sweating and tempers were growing short in the steady heat of the open plainlands. Keltset walked slightly apart from the other two, his pace steady and unwavering, his rough face expressionless, his eyes dark and unfriendly in the hot, white sunlight. Panamon had stopped talking and was interested only in completing the day's march and being rid of Shea, whom he had begun to regard as an unnecessary burden. Shea was tired and sore, his limited stamina greatly sapped by the two long days of constant travel. The three were walking right into the face of the burning sun, unprotected and unshaded on the open plains, their eyes squinting sharply in the piercing light. It became increasingly harder to distinguish the land ahead as the sun moved closer toward the western horizon, and after a while Shea gave up trying, relying on Panamon's skill to get them to Paranor. The travelers were drawing closer to the end of the mountain range northward on their right, and it appeared that where the mountain peaks ceased the plains opened into an endless expanse. It was so vast that Shea could see the lateral line of the horizon where the sky dropped to the parched earth. When he asked at last if these were the Streleheim Plains, Panamon gave no immediate answer, but after a few moments' consideration nodded shortly.

Nothing further was said about their present location or Panamon Creel's unspoken plans for Shea. They passed out of the horseshoe valley onto the eastern borders of the Streleheim Plains, a wide, flat expanse extending north and west. The land immediately before them, running parallel to the cliff face and forest land on their left, was surprisingly hilly. It was not a change in terrain that could be distinguished by one still in the valley, but became distinct only when one was nearly on top of it. There were even groves of small trees and dense stretches of brush farther on, and . . . something else, something foreign to the land. All three travelers spotted it at the same moment, and Panamon signaled a sharp halt, peering suspiciously into the distance. Shea squinted into the strong light of the afternoon sun, shading his eyes with one hand. He saw a series of strange poles set in the earth, and scattered about for several hundred yards in every direction were heaps of colored cloth and bits of shining metal or glass. He could just barely make out the movement of a number of small, black objects amid the cloth and debris. Finally Panamon called out loudly to whomever might be up ahead of them. To their shock, there was a flurried rushing of raven-black wings, accompanied by a frightful shrieking of disrupted scavengers as the black objects turned suddenly into great vultures rising slowly and reluctantly as they scattered into the brilliant sunlight. Panamon and Shea stood rooted in mute astonishment as the giant Keltset moved several yards closer and peered carefully ahead. A moment later, he wheeled about and motioned sharply to his watchful comrade. The scarlet thief nodded soberly.

'There's been a battle of some sort,' he announced curtly. 'Those are dead men up there!'

The three moved forward toward the grisly scene of battle. Shea hung back slightly, suddenly afraid that the still, tattered forms might be his friends. The strange poles became distinct after the men had gone only several yards; they were lances and standards of battle. The bright bits of light were the blades of swords and knives, some discarded by fleeing men, others still clenched by the dead hands of their fallen owners. The cloth heaps became men, their still, blood-soaked forms sprawled in death, baking slowly in the white heat of the sun. Shea choked as the smell of death struck his nostrils for the first time and his ears caught the sound of flies buzzing busily about the human carcasses. Panamon looked back and smiled grimly. He knew that the Valeman had never before seen death at close range, and it would be a lesson he would not forget.

Shea fought the sickening feeling creeping through his stomach and forced himself to move with the other two onto the battleground. Several hundred bodies lay on the little stretch of rolling land, sprawled carelessly in death. There was no movement anywhere; they were all dead. From the random scattering of the bodies and the lack of any single concentration of men, Panamon quickly concluded in his own mind that it had been a long, bitter struggle to the death – no quarter asked and none given. he recognized the Gnome standards immediately, and the gnarled yellow bodies were easily distinguishable. But it was not until he had looked closely at several huddled forms that he realized that the opposing force had been composed of Elven warriors.

Finally Panamon halted in the middle of the slain men, uncertain what he should do next. Shea could only stare in horror at the carnage, his shocked gaze moving robot-like from one dead face to the next, from Gnome to Elf, from the raw, open wounds to the bloodied ground. At that moment, he knew what death really meant and he was afraid. There was no adventure in it, no sense of purpose or choice, nothing but a sickening disgust and shock. All those men had died for some senseless reason, died perhaps without ever knowing exactly what they had fought to accomplish. Nothing was worth such terrible slaughter – nothing.

A sudden movement by Keltset snapped his attention

back to his companions, and he saw the Troll pick up a fallen standard, its pennant torn and bloodied, the pole broken in half. The insignia on the pennant was a crown seated over a spreading tree surrounded by a wreath of boughs. Keltset seemed very excited and gestured vigorously to Panamon. The other frowned sharply and hurriedly made a quick study of the faces of the nearby bodies, working his way outward from his companions in a widening circle. Keltset looked around anxiously, suddenly stopping as his deep-set eyes came to rest on Shea, apparently fascinated by something he saw in the little Valeman's face. A moment later Panamon was back at his side, an unusually worried expression clouding his broad features.

'We've got real trouble here, friend Shea,' he announced solemnly, resting his hands determinedly on his hips and planting his feet. 'That standard is the banner of the royal Elven house of Elessedil – the personal staff of Eventine. I can't find his body among the dead, but that doesn't make me feel any easier. If anything has happened to the Elven king, it could start a war of unbelievable proportions. The whole country will go up in smoke!'

'Eventine!' exclaimed Shea fearfully. 'He was guarding the northern borders of Paranor in case . . .'

He caught himself abruptly, afraid that he had given himself away, but Panamon Creel was still talking and apparently hadn't heard.

'It doesn't make any sense – Gnomes and Elves fighting out here in the middle of nowhere. What would bring Eventine this far away from his own land? They must have been fighting for something. I can't under . . .' He paused with the thought left hanging, unspoken in the silence. Suddenly he stared at Shea.

'What did you just say? What was that about Eventine?'

'Nothing,' the Valeman stammered fearfully. 'I didn't say . . .'

The tall thief snatched the hapless Valeman by his tunic

100

front, dragging him close and raising him bodily off the ground, until their faces were only inches away.

'Don't try to be clever, little man!' The flushed, angered face seemed gigantic and the fierce eyes were narrowed with suspicion. 'You know something about all of this – now talk. All along I've suspected you knew a lot more than you were telling about those stones and the reason those Gnomes bothered to take you prisoner. Now your time for fooling around is over. Out with it!'

But Shea would never know what his response would have been. As he hung in midair, struggling violently in the powerful thief's ironhanded grip, a huge black shadow suddenly fell over them and then passed on in a great rustling of wings as a monstrous shape descended from the late afternoon skies. Its giant, black bulk swooped slowly, gracefully to the battlefield only yards away from them, and in horror Shea felt the familiar chilling fear surge through him at the sight of its deathlike form. Panamon Creel, still angered, but now bewildered by the sudden appearance of this creature, lowered Shea to the earth abruptly and turned to face the strange newcomer. Shea stood on shaking legs, his blood turned to ice, his senses raw and distorted with terror, the last vestiges of his courage gone. The creature was one of the dreaded Skull Bearers of the Warlock Lord! There was no time left to run; they had found him at last.

The cruel red eyes of the creature passed quickly over the giant Troll, who had remained motionless to one side, stopped for a moment on the scarlet thief, then passed on to the little Valeman, burning into him, probing his scattered thoughts. Panamon Creel, while still bewildered at the sight of this winged monster, was nevertheless not in the least panicked. He turned fully about to face the evil being, the broad, devilish grin spreading slowly over his flushed countenance as he raised one arm and pointed in warning.

'Whatever manner of creature you might be, keep your distance,' he warned sharply. 'My concern is with this man alone, and not . . .'

The burning eyes fastened hatefully on him, and suddenly he was unable to continue. He stared at the black creature in shock and surprise.

'Where is the Sword, mortal?' the voice rasped menacingly. 'I can sense its presence. Give it to me!'

Panamon Creel stared uncomprehendingly at the dark speaker for a long moment, then shot a sharp look at the frightened face of Shea. For the first time, he realized that for some unknown reason this terrible creature was the Valeman's enemy. It was a dangerous moment.

'It is useless to deny you have it!' The grating voice pierced the distressed mind of the thief. 'I know it is here among you, and I must have it. It is useless to fight me. The battle is over for you. The last heir to the Sword has long since been taken and destroyed. You must give me the Sword!'

For once, Panamon Creel was speechless. He had no idea what the huge black creature was talking about, but he realized that there was no point in trying to tell him that. The winged monster was determined to finish them all anyway, and the time for any explanations was past. The tall thief raised his left hand and stroked the tips of his small mustache with the deadly pike. He smiled bravely, looking aside fleetingly at the motionless form of his giant companion. They both knew instinctively that this would be a battle to the death.

'Do not be foolish, mortals!' The command rang out in a sharp hiss. 'I care nothing for you – only the Sword. I can destroy you easily – even in daylight.'

Suddenly Shea saw a glimmer of hope. Allanon had once said that the power of the Skull Bearers faded with the light of day. Perhaps they were not invincible while the sun shone. Perhaps the two battle-hardened thieves would have a chance. But how could they expect to destroy something that was not mortal, but only the spirit of a dead soul, a wraith of deathless existence embodied in physical form? For a few moments no one moved, and then abruptly the creature took a step forward. Immediately Panamon Creel's good right hand unsheathed the broadsword at his side in a lightninglike motion and the thief crouched for the attack. The great form of Keltset moved forward a few paces at the same instant, changing from a motionless statue into an iron-muscled fighting machine, the heavy mace in one hand, the thick legs braced for the assault. The Skull Bearer hesitated and his burning eyes fastened momentarily on the face of the approaching Rock Troll, studying the huge being closely for the first time. Then the crimson eyes went wide in astonishment.

'Keltset!'

Only an instant remained to ponder how the Bearer could have known the mute giant – a split second of astonished disbelief in the creature's eyes, mirroring similar incomprehension in the eyes of Panamon Creel, and then the huge Troll attacked with blinding speed. The mace hurtled through the air, powered by Keltset's massive right arm, striking the black Skull creature directly in the chest with a sickening crunch. Panamon was already leaping forward, pike and sword blade sweeping downward toward the Bearer's chest and neck. But the deadly Northland creature was not to be so easily finished. Recovering from the blow dealt by the mace, it parried Panamon's weapons with one clawed hand, knocking the man sprawling. In the next instant the burning eyes began to smolder, and bolts of searing red light shot out at the dazed thief. He lunged quickly to one side, and the bolts caught him only a glancing blow, singeing his scarlet tunic and knocking him down again. Before the attacker could find his target for a second assault, the huge form of Keltset was upon him, bearing him heavily to the earth. Even the comparatively large size of the winged monster was dwarfed in comparison to the massive Rock Troll as the two rolled and battled over the bloodied ground. Panamon was still on his knees, shaking his dazed head, trying to regain his senses. Realizing that he had to do something, Shea rushed to the fallen thief and grabbed one arm in desperation.

'The stones!' he begged wildly. 'Give me the stones, and I can help!'

The battered face turned up to him for a moment, and then the familiar look of anger crept into his eyes, and he shoved the Valeman rudely away.

'Shut up and keep out of this,' he roared, climbing unsteadily to his feet. 'No tricks now, friend. Just stay put!'

Retrieving his fallen sword, he rushed to the aid of his giant companion, trying vainly to strike a solid blow at the caped Skull Bearer. For long minutes the three struggled fiercely back and forth across the rolling battleground, thrashing madly over the still bodies of the fallen Gnomes and Elves. Panamon was not nearly as strong as the other two, but he was quick and extremely durable, bouncing away from the blows struck at him, dancing nimbly aside when the Northlander sent the reddish bolts flashing his way. The incredible strength of Keltset was proving to be a match for even the spirit powers of the Skull creature, and the evil being was becoming desperate. The rough Troll skin was singed and burned in a dozen places from the fire that struck it, but the giant merely shrugged the powerful jolts aside and fought on. Shea desperately wanted to help, but he was dwarfed by their power and size, and his weapons were ridiculously inadequate. If only he could get the stones . . .

At last the two mortals began to tire in the face of the repeated, inexhaustible assaults from the spirit creature. Their blows were not having any lasting effect and they began slowly to realize that human strength alone could not destroy the attacker. They were losing the battle. Suddenly the valiant

Keltset stumbled and fell to one knee. Instantly the Skull creature lashed out with one clawed limb, slashing the unprotected Troll from neck to waist, knocking him backward to the earth. Panamon cried out in fury and struck wildly at the spirit creature, but his blows were parried, and in his haste he dropped his guard and left himself momentarily vulnerable. The emissary of the Warlock Lord struck viciously, one arm knocking aside the thief's piked hand as the narrowed eyes sent their fiery blasts directly into the man's chest. The deadly bolts seared the hapless Panamon Creel about the face and arms, and burned right through the chest covering with such force that he was knocked unconscious. The Skull Bearer would have finished him then had not Shea, disregarding his own fears at the other's grave peril, thrown a piece of a lance at the attacker's unprotected head, striking it full in the evil face. The clawed hands came up too late to ward off the painful blow, and they gripped the blackened visage in fury, trying angrily to recover. Panamon was still lying motionless on the ground, but the durable Keltset was back on his feet, seizing the Skull creature in an agonizing headlock, desperately trying to crush the life out of it.

There were only seconds left to act before the deadly monster was free again. Shea rushed to Panamon Creel's side, shouting at him to get up. The battered figure responded with inhuman courage, but fell back a moment later, blinded and exhausted. Shea pleaded with him, shaking him into consciousness, begging him to give him the stones. Only the stones could help now, the Valeman cried desperately! They were the only chance for survival! He glanced back at the two dark combatants, and to his horror he saw that Keltset was slowly losing his hold on the spirit creature. In seconds the evil being would be free, and they would all be finished. Then abruptly the little leather pouch was thrust into his hand by the bloodied fist of Panamon, and he had the precious stones once more.

Leaping clear of the fallen thief, the little Valeman tore

open the drawstrings to the leather pouch and emptied the three blue stones into his open hand. At that moment the Skull Bearer broke free from Keltset's powerful grip and turned to finish the battle. Shea yelled wildly, holding the stones stretched forth toward the attacker, praying for their strange power to aid him now. The blinding blue glow spread outward just as the creature turned. Too late the Skull Bearer saw the heir to Shannara bring the power of the Elfstones to life. Too late he focused his burning eyes on the Valeman, the red bolts of searing fire flashing menacingly. The great blue light blocked and shattered the attack, slicing through in a powerful, blazing surge of energy to reach the crouched black figure beyond. The light struck the immobile Skull creature with a sharp crackle, holding him fast and draining the dark spirit from the mortal shell as the creature writhed in agony and screamed its loathing of the power destroying it. Keltset came to his feet in a bound, picked up a fallen lance, reared back his giant frame, the arms extended high, and with a lunge shoved the spear completely through the creature's caped back. The Northlander shuddered horribly, twisting almost completely about with one final shriek, and then slid slowly to the earth, the black body crumbling into dust as it sank. In another second it was gone, and only a small pile of black ashes remained. Shea stood motionless, the stones extended, their piercing blue light still concentrated on the dust. Then the dust stirred in still another shudder and from its midst rose a whipish black cloud that shot upward like a thin stream of smoke and disappeared into the air. The blue light abruptly ceased and the battle was ended, the three mortals positioned like statues in the silence and emptiness of the bloodied ground.

For long seconds no one moved, still stunned by the sudden finality of the violent combat. Shea and Keltset stood staring at the small pile of black ashes as if waiting for it to come back to life. Panamon Creel lay wearily on the earth to one side, propped up on one elbow, his singed eyes trying vainly to grasp what had just transpired. Finally Keltset stepped forward gingerly and prodded the ashes of the Skull Bearer with one foot, stirring them about to see if anything had been missed. Shea watched quietly, mechanically replacing the three Elfstones in the leather pouch and dropping it back into the front of his tunic. Remembering Panamon, he turned quickly to check on the injured thief, but the durable Southlander was already struggling to a sitting position, his deep brown eyes fixed wonderingly on the Valeman. Keltset hastened over and gently raised his companion to his feet. The man was burned and cut, his face and bared chest blackened and raw in places, but nothing seemed to be broken. He stared at Keltset as well for a moment, then shrugged off the other's strong arm and tottered over to a waiting Shea.

'I was right about you after all,' he growled, breathing heavily and shaking his broad head. 'You did know a lot more than you were telling – especially about those stones. Why didn't you tell me the truth from the start?'

'You wouldn't listen,' Shea alibied shortly. 'Besides, you didn't tell me the truth about yourself – or Keltset either.' He paused to glance sharply at the massive Troll. 'I don't think you know very much about him.'

The battered face stared at the Valeman incredulously, then the broad smile slowly spread over his handsome features. It was as if the scarlet thief suddenly saw new humor in the whole situation, but Shea thought he caught a hint of grudging respect in the dark eyes for his candid evaluation.

'You may be right. I'm beginning to think I don't know anything about him.' The smile turned into a hearty laugh, and the thief looked sharply at the rough, expressionless face of the great Rock Troll. Then he looked back to Shea.

'You saved our lives, Shea, and that's a debt we can never repay. But I'll start by saying that the stones are yours to keep. I'll never argue that point again. More than that, you have my promise that should the need ever arise, my sword and my skill, such as it is, shall be in your service at a word.'

He paused wearily to catch his breath, still shaken badly from the blows he had received. Shea stepped hurriedly forward to offer his aid, but the tall thief held him away, shaking his head negatively.

'I assume that we shall be great friends, Shea,' he murmured seriously. 'Still, we cannot be friends when we hide things from each other. I think you owe me some sort of explanation about those stones, about that creature that nearly put an end to my illustrious career, and about this confounded sword I've never seen. In return, I shall enlighten you on a few, ah, misunderstandings concerning Keltset and myself. Do you agree?'

Shea frowned at him suspiciously, trying to read behind the battered visage into the man himself. Finally he nodded affirmatively and even managed a short smile.

'Good for you, Shea,' Panamon commended heartily, clapping the Valeman on his slender shoulder. A second later, the tall thief had collapsed, weakened by loss of blood and dizzy from trying to move about too quickly. The other two rushed to his side, and despite protestations that he was quite all right, forced him to remain in a supine position while the giant Keltset cleaned his face with a wetted cloth like any mother would a small, injured child. Shea was amazed at the Troll's quick change from a nearly indestructible fighting machine to a gentle, concerned nurse. There was something very extraordinary about him, and Shea was certain that in some strange way Keltset was connected with the Warlock Lord and the quest for the Sword of Shannara. It had been no accident that the Skull Bearer had known the Rock Troll. The two had encountered each other before – and had not parted as friends.

Panamon was not unconscious, but it was clear that he

was not yet in any condition to travel very far on his own legs. He tried vainly to rise several times, but the watchful Keltset gently pushed him back. The irascible thief swore vehemently and demanded to be let to his feet, all to no avail. Finally, he realized that he was getting nowhere and asked that he be taken out of the sun to rest for a while. Shea looked around the barren plainland and quickly concluded they would find no shelter there. The only shade within reasonable walking distance was to the south – the forests surrounding the Druids' Keep within the borders of Paranor. Panamon had previously indicated that he would not go anywhere near Paranor, but the decision was no longer entirely his to make. Shea pointed to the forests to the south, less than a mile's walk, and Keltset nodded his agreement. The injured man saw what Shea was suggesting and cried out furiously that he would not be carried into those forests even if it meant he would die where he lay. Shea tried to reason with him, assuring him that they would face no danger from his companions if by chance they managed to find them, but the thief seemed more disturbed by the strange rumors he had heard concerning Paranor. She had to laugh at this, recalling Panamon's boasts of all the past hair-raising perils he had survived. While the two men conversed, Keltset had risen slowly to his feet and was scanning the land about them, apparently in idle speculation. The two were still talking when he bent down to them and gave a sharp signal to Panamon. The thief started, the color drained from his face as he nodded shortly. Shea started to rise in apprehension, but the thief's strong hand held him down.

'Keltset has just spotted something moving in the brush to the south of us. He can't tell from here what it is; it's just on the fringes of this battlefield, about halfway between us and the forest.'

Shea immediately turned ashen.

'Get your stones ready in case we need them,' the other

ordered quietly, an unmistakable indication that he thought it might be a second Skull Bearer lurking in the cover of the brush, waiting for sundown and a chance to catch them off guard.

'What are we going to do?' Shea asked fearfully, clutching the little pouch.

'Get him before he gets us – what other choice do we have?' Panamon declared irritably, motioning to Keltset to pick him up.

The obedient giant bent down and carefully lifted Panamon in the cradle of his two massive arms. Shea retrieved the wounded thief's fallen broad-sword and followed the slowly departing form of Keltset, who proceeded southward with relaxed, easy strides. Panamon talked steadily as they walked, calling on Shea to hurry, chiding Keltset on being too rough in his duty as bearer of the wounded. Shea could not bring himself to be quite so relaxed, and was content with bringing up the rear, glancing uneasily from side to side as they moved southward, searching vainly for some sign of movement that might indicate where the danger lay. In his right hand he clutched tightly the leather pouch with the invaluable Elfstones, their only weapon against the power of the Warlock Lord. They were about a hundred yards from the scene of their battle with the Skull Bearer when Panamon called a sudden halt, complaining bitterly of an injured shoulder. Gently, Keltset lowered his burden to the ground and stood up.

'My shoulder is never going to stand such wanton disregard of its tissues and bones,' growled Panamon Creel irritably, and looked meaningfully at Shea.

Instantly the Valeman knew that this was the place, and his hands shook as he loosened the strings on the pouch and withdrew the Elfstones. A moment later Keltset stood leisurely beside the still-muttering thief, the great mace held loosely in one hand. Shea glanced around hastily, his eyes coming to rest directly on the huge clump of brush immediately to the left of the other two. His heart jumped to his throat as one section of the brush moved ever so slightly.

Then Keltset made his move. With a sharp lunge he whirled about, leaped into the center of the brush, and was lost from view.

CHAPTER

7

What followed was complete pandemonium. A terrible high-pitched shriek sounded from the bushes and the entire mass of shrubbery shook violently. Panamon struggled wildly to his knees, calling to Shea to throw him the great broadsword which the fear-struck Valeman still clutched tightly in his left hand. Shea stood frozen in place, his other hand clasping the power-ful Elfstones in readiness, waiting in terror for the assault that surely would come from the unknown creature in the brush. Panamon finally fell back in hopeless exhaustion, unable to get Shea's attention and incapable of walking over to where he stood. There were a few more cries from the heavy bushes, some vague thrashing within, and then silence. A moment later the durable Keltset emerged, the heavy mace still held in one lowered hand. In the other was the squirming, twisting body of a Gnome, his neck held fast in the iron grip of the Troll. The gnarled yellow body appeared childlike next to the huge frame of its captor, the arms and legs moving all at once in different directions like snakes caught by their tails. The Gnome was one of the familiar hunters, clothed in a leather tunic, hunt-ing boots, and sword belt. The sword was missing, and Shea correctly surmised that the struggle in the bushes involved the disarming of the little fellow. Keltset came over to Panamon, who had managed to raise himself back up to a sitting position, and dutifully held forth the struggling captive for inspection.

'Let me go, let me go, curse you!' the thrashing Gnome cried venomously. 'You have no right! I have done nothing – I'm not even armed, I tell you. Let me go!'

Panamon Creel looked at the little creature humorously, shaking his head in relief. Finally, as the Gnome continued to plead, the thief burst out laughing.

'What a terrible foe, Keltset! Why, he might have destroyed us all had you not captured him. That must have been a fearful struggle! Ha, ha, I can't believe it. And we were afraid of another of those winged black monsters!'

Shea was not quite so inclined to be amused by the incident, recalling clearly the close calls the company had already had with the little yellow creatures while traveling through the Anar. They were dangerous and crafty – a foe whom he did not regard as harmless. Panamon looked over and, upon spying the serious countenance, ceased his chiding of the captive and turned his attention to Shea.

'Do not be angry, Shea. It's more habit than stupidity when I laugh at these things. I laugh at them to stay a sane man. But enough of all this. What do we do with our little friend, eh?'

The Gnome stared fearfully at the no longer laughing man, the large eyes wide as the insistent voice died away to a low whine.

'Please, let me go,' he begged subserviently. 'I will go away and say nothing to anyone about you. I will do whatever you say, good friends. Just let me go.'

Kelset still held the hapless Gnome by the scruff of his neck about a foot off the ground in front of Shea and Panamon, and the little fellow was beginning to choke violently from the tight clasp. Seeing the prisoner's plight, Panamon at last motioned for the Rock Troll to lower his victim to the ground and release his grip. Pausing for a moment's serious contemplation of the Gnome's eager plea, the thief looked over at Shea and winked quickly, turning back to the captive sharply and snapping the pike at the end of his left arm up to the yellow throat.

'I can see no reason for permitting you to live, let alone go free, Gnome,' he announced menacingly. 'I think it would be best for all concerned if I just cut your throat right here and now. Then none of us would have to worry about you further.'

Shea did not believe the thief was serious, but his voice sounded as if he were in deadly earnest. The terrified Gnome gulped and held forth his hands in a final desperate cry for mercy. He whined and cried so that Shea finally became almost embarrassed for him. Panamon made no move, but only sat there staring into the unfortunate fellow's horror-stricken face.

'No, no, I beg you, don't kill me,' the frantic Gnome pleaded, his wide green eyes shifting from one face to the next. 'Please, please let me live – I can be of use to you – I can help! I can tell you about the Sword of Shannara! I can even get it for you.'

Shea started involuntarily at the unexpected mention of the Sword, and he placed a restraining hand on Panamon's wide shoulder.

'So you can tell us about the Sword, can you?' The icy voice of the thief sounded only slightly interested, and he ignored Shea completely. 'What can you tell us?'

The wiry yellow frame relaxed slightly, and the eyes returned to normal size, shifting about eagerly, seizing on any chance to stay alive. Yet Shea saw something else there, something he could not quite define. It was almost a fervid cunning, revealed as the Gnome momentarily relaxed his carefully masked feelings. A second later it was gone, replaced by a look of total subjugation and helplessness.

'I can lead you to the Sword if you wish,' he whispered harshly as if he were afraid someone would hear. 'I can take you to where it is – if you let me live!'

Panamon moved the sharp iron tip of his piked hand back from the throat of the cringing Gnome, leaving just a small trace of blood on the yellow neck. Keltset had not moved and gave no indication that he had any interest in what was happening. Shea wanted to warn Panamon how important that Gnome might be if there was even the slightest chance of finding the Sword of Shannara, but he realized the thief preferred to keep the captive Gnome guessing. The Valeman could not be sure how much Panamon Creel knew about the legend; so far, he had shown little concern with the races generally and had not indicated he knew anything about the history of the Sword of Shannara. The grim features of the thief relaxed briefly and a faint smile crossed his lips as he eyed the still quivering captive.

'Is this Sword valuable, Gnome?' he queried easily, almost slyly. 'Can I sell it for gold?'

'It is priceless to the right people,' the other promised, nodding eagerly. 'There are those who would pay anything, give anything to get possession of it. In the Northland . . .'

He ceased talking abruptly, afraid that he had already said too much. Panamon smiled wolfishly and nodded to Shea.

'This Gnome says it could be worth money to us,' he mocked quietly, 'and the Gnome wouldn't lie, would you, Gnome?' The yellow head shook vehemently. 'Well, then, perhaps we should let you live long enough to prove you have something of value to barter for your worthless hide. I wouldn't want to throw away a chance to make money simply to satisfy my inborn desire to cut the throat of a Gnome when I get one within my grasp. What do you think, Gnome?'

'You understand perfectly, you know my value,' whined

the little fellow, fawning at the knees of the smiling thief. 'I can help; I can make you rich. You can count on me.'

Panamon was smiling broadly now, his big frame relaxed and his good hand on the Gnome's small shoulder as if they were old friends. He patted the stooped shoulder a few times, as if to put the captive at ease, and nodded reassuringly, looking from the Gnome to Keltset to Shea and back again for several long seconds.

'Tell us what you're doing way out here by yourself, Gnome,' Panamon urged a moment later. 'By the way, what are you called?'

'I am Orl Fane, a warrior of the Pelle tribe of the upper Anar,' he answered eagerly. 'I . . . I was on a courier mission from Paranor when I came upon this battlefield. They were all dead, all of them, and there was nothing I could do. Then I heard you and I hid. I was afraid you were . . . Elves.'

He paused and looked fearfully at Shea, noting the youth's Elven features with dismay. Shea made no move, but waited to see what Panamon would do. Panamon just looked understandingly at the Gnome and smiled in friendly fashion.

'Orl Fane – of the Pelle tribe,' the tall thief repeated slowly. 'A great tribe of hunters, brave men.' He shook his head as if deeply regretting something and turned again to the mystified Gnome. 'Orl Fane, if we are going to be of any service to one another, we must have mutual trust. Lies can only hinder the purpose binding our new partnership. There was a Pelle standard on the battlefield – the standard of your tribe in the Gnome nation. You must have been with them when they fought.'

The Gnome stood speechless, a mixture of fear and doubt creeping slowly back into his shifting green eyes. Panamon continued to smile easily at him.

'Just look at yourself Orl Fane – covered with specks of blood and a bad cut on your forehead at the hairline. Why

hide the truth from us? You had to be here, isn't that right?'
The persuasive voice coaxed a quick nod out of the other,
and Panamon laughed almost merrily. 'Of course you were
here, Orl Fane. And when you were set upon by the Elf
people, you fought until you were wounded, perhaps
knocked unconscious, eh, and you lay here until just before
we came along. That's the truth of the matter, isn't it?'

'Yes, that's the truth,' the Gnome agreed eagerly now.

'No, that's not the truth!'

There was a moment of stunned silence. Panamon was
still smiling, and Orl Fane was caught between emotions,
a trace of doubt still in his eyes, a half-smile forming on
his lips. Shea looked at both curiously, unable to follow
exactly what was happening.

'Listen to me, you lying little rodent.' The smile was
gone from Panamon's face, the features hardened as he
spoke, the voice cold and menacing once more. 'You have
lied from the beginning! A member of the Pelle would wear
their insignia – you wear none. You weren't wounded in
battle; that little scratch on your forehead is nothing! You
are a scavenger – a deserter, aren't you? Aren't you?'

The thief had seized the terrified Gnome by the front
of his hunting tunic and was shaking him so hard that Shea
could hear his teeth rattle with the force. The wiry captive
was struggling to catch his breath, gasping in disbelief at
this sudden turn of events.

'Yes, yes!' The admission was throttled out of him at
last, and Panamon released him with a quick thrust backward into the grip of the watchful Keltset.

'A deserter from your own people.' Panamon spat the
words out in distaste. 'The lowest form of life that walks
or crawls is a deserter. You've been scavenging this battlefield for valuables from the dead. Where are they, Orl Fane?
Shea, check in those bushes where he was hiding.'

As Shea moved toward the brush, the struggling Gnome
let out the most frightful shriek of dismay imaginable,

causing the youth to believe Keltset had twisted his neck off. But Panamon just smiled and nodded for the Valeman to proceed, certain now that the Gnome had indeed hidden something in the bushes. Shea pushed his way past the thick branches into the center of the clump, searching carefully for any sign of a cache. The ground and the limbs in the center were badly torn up from the struggle between Keltset and the Gnome, and there was nothing immediately visible. He hunted about unsuccessfully for several minutes. He was just about to give up, when his eye caught a glimpse of something half buried at the far end of the bushes beneath leaves, branches, and dirt. Using his short hunting knife and his hands, he quickly uncovered a long sack containing metal objects that rattled against one another as he worked. He called out to Panamon that he had discovered something, which immediately set off another series of whining cries from the distraught captive. When the sack was uncovered, he pulled it out of the brush into the fading afternoon sunlight and dropped it before the others. Orl Fane was in a frenzy by this time, and Keltset was forced to use both hands just to hold him.

'Whatever's in here is certainly important to our little friend.' Panamon grinned at Shea and reached for the sack.

Shea moved to his side and peered over the broad shoulders as Panamon untied the leather thong binding the top and reached eagerly into the dark interior. Changing his mind suddenly, the scarlet thief removed his hand and, grabbing the other end of the sack, turned it upside down and poured the contents onto the open earth. The others stared at the cache, looking from item to item curiously.

'Junk,' growled Panamon Creel after a moment's consideration. 'Just junk. The Gnome is too stupid even to bother with valuable things.'

Shea looked at the contents of the sack without answering. Nothing but assorted daggers, knives, and swords in the collection, some still in their leather sheaths. A few pieces of cheap jewelry sparkled in the sunlight, and there were one or two Gnome coins, practically worthless to anyone but a Gnome. It certainly appeared to be useless junk, but the whining Orl Fane had evidently considered it worth something to him. Shea shook his head in pity for the little Gnome. He had lost everything when he turned deserter, and all he had to show for it were these few worthless pieces of metal and cheap jewelry. Now it seemed certain that he would lose his life as well for having dared to lie to the volatile Panamon Creel.

'Hardly worth dying for, Gnome,' Panamon growled, nodding shortly to Keltset, who raised the heavy mace to finish the hapless fellow.

'No, no, wait, wait a minute, please,' the Gnome cried, his voice edged with a harsh note of desperation. It was the end for him; this was his final plea. 'I didn't lie about the Sword – I swear I didn't! I can get it for you. Don't you realize what the Sword of Shannara is worth to the Dark Lord?'

Without thinking, Shea put out a hand to grasp Keltset's massive arm. The giant Troll seemed to understand. Slowly he lowered the mace and looked curiously at Shea. Panamon Creel opened his mouth angrily and then hesitated. He wanted to learn the truth behind Shea's presence in the Northland, and the secret of this Sword evidently had much to do with it. He stared momentarily at the Valeman, then turned back to Keltset and shrugged disinterestedly.

'We can always kill you later, Orl Fane, if this is another deception. Put a rope around his worthless neck and bring him along, Keltset. Shea, if you would give me a hand up and an arm to lean on, I think I can make it to the woods. Keltset will keep a close watch over our clever little deserter.'

Shea helped the injured Panamon to his feet and tried to support him as he took a few careful test steps. Keltset tied Orl Fane and placed a length of rope about his neck so that he could be led. The Gnome allowed himself to be bound without complaining, though he was visibly distraught about something. Shea imagined that the fellow was still lying when he said he knew where the Sword could be found and was desperately trying to figure out how he would get free from his captors before they discovered his treachery and killed him. While Shea would not himself kill the Gnome, nor even agree to have it done, nevertheless he felt little compassion for the deceitful creature. Orl Fane was a coward, a deserter, a scavenger – a man without a people or a country. Shea was certain now that the whining, groveling attitude the Gnome had displayed earlier was a carefully studied shield for the crafty, desperate creature that lay hidden beneath. Orl Fane would cut their throats without the slightest compunction if he thought there would be no danger to himself. Shea almost wished that Keltset had ended their worries a few minutes earlier by finishing the fellow. Shea would have felt easier in his own mind.

Panamon signaled that he was ready to proceed toward the woodland, but before they had taken two steps, the whining pleas of Orl Fane had stopped them. The unhappy Gnome refused to go farther if he were not allowed to keep his sack and its treasures. He set up such a stubborn howl of protest that Panamon was again on the verge of bashing in the hateful yellow head.

'What does it matter, Panamon?' Shea finally asked in exasperation. 'Let him have his trinkets if it will make him happy. We can get rid of them later after he quiets down.'

Panamon shook his handsome face in dismay, finally nodding his reluctant acquiescence. He was fed up with Orl Fane already.

'Very well, I'll give in just this once,' the thief agreed. Orl Fane immediately quieted down. 'However, if he opens his mouth like that once more, I'll cut out his tongue.

Keltset, you keep him away from that sack. I don't want him getting hold of one of those weapons long enough to cut himself free and do us in! Worthless blades probably wouldn't do a neat job of it anyway, and I'd die of blood poisoning.'

Shea had to laugh in spite of himself. They were poor-looking weapons, though he rather fancied the slim broadsword with the extended arm and burning torch cut into the hilt. Even that one was rather gaudy, the cheap gold paint chipped and flecked about the hilt. Like several of the others, it rested in a worn leather sheath so it was difficult to tell what condition the blade might be in. At any rate, it could prove dangerous in the hands of the wily Orl Fane. Keltset hoisted the sack and its contents over one shoulder, and the party continued on its way toward the woodland.

It was a comparatively short hike, but by the time they reached the perimeter of the forest Shea was exhausted from supporting the weight of the injured Panamon. The little group stopped on the thief's command; as an after-thought, he sent Keltset back to cover their trail and to create a number of false trails that would confuse anyone following. Shea did not object, for although he hoped that Allanon and the others were searching for him, there was a dangerous possibility that patrolling Gnome hunters or, worse still, another Skull Bearer might come across their tracks instead.

After tying the captive Orl Fane to a tree, the Rock Troll backtracked onto the battlefield to erase any sign of their passage in this direction. Panamon collapsed wearily against a broad maple, and the tired Valeman took up a position opposite him, lying peacefully back on a small, grassy knoll, staring absently into the treetops and breathing deeply the forest air. The sun was fading rapidly now with the close of the afternoon and the faint beginnings of evening crept into the western sky in streaks of purple and deep blue. Less than an hour of sunlight remained, and the night would help to hide them from their enemies. Shea fervently wished now for the aid of the company, for the strong, wise leadership and fantastic mystical prowess of Allanon, for the courage of the others – Balinor, Hendel, Durin, Dayel, and the fiery Menion Leah. Most of all he wished Flick were with him – Flick, with his unwavering, unquestioning loyalty and trust. Panamon Creel was a good man to have on his side, but there were no real ties between them. The thief had lived too long by his wits and cunning to understand basic honesty and truth. And what about Keltset – an enigma, even to Panamon?

'Panamon, you said back there you would explain about Keltset,' Shea remarked quietly. 'About how the Skull Bearer knew him.'

For a moment there was no answer, and Shea raised up to see if the man had heard him. Panamon was staring quietly at him.

'Skull Bearer? You seem to know a great deal more about this whole matter than I. You tell me about my giant companion, Shea.'

'That wasn't the truth you told me when you saved me from those Gnomes, was it?' Shea asked him. 'He wasn't a freak driven from his village by his own people. He didn't kill them for attacking him, did he?'

Panamon laughed merrily, the pike coming up to scratch the small mustache.

'Maybe it was the truth. Maybe those things did happen to him. I don't know. It always seemed to me that something of the sort must have happened to him to make him take up with someone like myself. He's no thief; I don't know what he is. But he is my friend – he is that. I didn't lie to you when I said that.'

'Where did he come from?' Shea asked after a moment's silence.

'I found him north of here about two months ago. He

wandered down out of the Charnal Mountains, battered, beaten, just barely alive. I don't know what happened to him; he never volunteered the information, and I didn't ask. He was entitled to keep his past hidden, just as I. I took care of him for several weeks. I knew a little sign language, and he understood it, so we could communicate. I guessed his name from his word signs. We learned a little about each other – only a little. When he was well, I asked him to come along and he agreed. We've had some good times, you know. Too bad he's not really a thief.'

Shea shook his head and chuckled softly at that last remark. Panamon Creel would probably never change. He didn't understand any other way of life and didn't want to. The only people who made any sense to him were those who told the world to hang by its thumbs and took by force what they needed for themselves. Yet friendship remained a prized commodity, even for a thief, and it was something that would not be tossed aside lightly. Even Shea was beginning to feel a strange sort of friendship for the flamboyant Panamon Creel, a friendship that was improbable because their characters and their values were complete opposites. But each had an understanding of what the other felt, though not why he felt it, and there was the experience of the battle shared against a common enemy. Perhaps that was all that anyone ever needed as a basis for friendship.

'How could the Skull creature have known him?' Shea persisted.

Panamon shrugged casually, indicating he neither knew nor cared. The watchful Valeman felt the latter was not the case, and Panamon would very much like to find out the truth behind Keltset's appearance two months earlier. His hidden past had something to do with the spirit creature's unexplained recognition of the giant Troll. There had been a trace of fear in those cruel eyes, and Shea found it difficult to imagine how anything mortal could have frightened the powerful Skull Bearer. Panamon had seen it, too, and certainly he must be asking himself the same question.

By the time Keltset rejoined them, it was sundown and the faint rays of the late afternoon sun only barely lit the dark forest. The Troll had carefully erased all signs of their passing from the battlefield, leaving a number of confusing false trails for anyone who attempted to follow. Panamon was feeling well enough to maneuver on his own strength, but requested that Keltset help support him until they reached a suitable campsite because it was becoming dark too quickly for travel. Shea was given the task of leading the docile Orl Fane by the rope leash, a chore he did not relish, but which he accepted without complaint. Again, Panamon tried to leave the worn sack and its contents behind, but Orl Fane was not to be deprived of his treasures so easily. He immediately set up such a howl of anguish that the thief ordered him bound about the mouth until the only sound the hapless Gnome could make was a muffled groan. But when they tried to move into the forest, the desperate captive threw himself on the ground and refused to rise, even when kicked painfully by a thoroughly irate Panamon. Keltset could have carried the Gnome and supported Panamon, too, but that was more trouble than it was worth. Muttering dire threats at the whining Gnome, the thief at last had Keltset pick up the sack, and the four began their journey into the darkening woods.

When it became too dark to tell with any certainty where they were going, Panamon called a halt in a small clearing between giant oaks whose interlocking boughs formed a weblike roof for shelter. Orl Fane was tied to one of the tall oaks while the other three set about building a fire and preparing a meal. When the food was ready, Orl Fane was unfettered long enough to allow him to eat. While Panamon did not know exactly where they were, he felt safe enough to permit a fire, relatively certain that no one would be trailing them at night. He might have felt a little less secure had he known of the dangers of the impenetrable forests that surrounded the dark cliffs of Paranor. As it happened, the four men were in an adjoining forest east of the dangerous woodlands ringing Paranor. The section of woods in which they were camped was seldom traveled by the minions of the Warlock Lord, and there was little possibility that anyone would happen along to discover them. They ate in silence, a hungry and tired group after the long day's travel. Even the whines of the bothersome Orl Fane were temporarily stilled as the little Gnome ate ravenously, his crafty yellow face bent close to the warmth of the small fire as the dark green eyes shifted warily from one face to the next. Shea paid no attention, concentrating instead on what he should tell Panamon Creel about himself, the company, and most important of all, the Sword of Shannara. He had not made up his mind when dinner was completed. The captive was again bound to the nearest oak and permitted to breathe without the gag after his solemn promise that he would not begin whining and crying again. Then placing himself comfortably close to the dying fire, Panamon turned his attention to the expectant Valeman.

'The time is here, Shea, for you to tell me what you know about all this Sword business,' he began briskly. 'No lies, no half-truths, and leave nothing out. I promised my help, but we must have mutual trust – and not the kind I spoke of to this pitiful deserter. I have been fair and open with you. Do likewise for me.'

So Shea told him everything. He didn't mean to when he started. He wasn't really sure how much he should tell but one thing led to another and before he knew it the whole tale was out in the open. He told about the coming of Allanon, and the subsequent appearance of the Skull Bearer which forced the brothers to flee from Shady Vale. He related the events surrounding the journey to Leah and the meeting with Menion, followed by the terrible flight through the Black Oaks to Culhaven, where they joined the rest of the company. He skimmed over the details of the journey to the Dragon's Teeth, a great part of which was still hazy in his own mind. He concluded by explaining how he had fallen from the Crease into the river and been washed out onto the Rabb Plain where he was captured by the Gnome hunting party. Panamon listened without interruption, his eyes wide in astonishment at the tale. Keltset sat next to him in impenetrable silence, the rough-hewn but intelligent face gazing intently at the little Valeman during the entire narration. Orl Fane shifted about uneasily, groaning and muttering unintelligibly as he listened with the other two, his eyes darting wildly about the campsite as if expecting the Warlock Lord himself at any minute.

'That is the most fantastic tale I have ever heard,' Panamon announced at last. 'It's so incredible that even I find it hard to believe. But I do believe you, Shea. I believe you because I've fought that black-winged monster on the plainlands and because I've seen the strange power you have over those Elfstones, as you call them. But this business about the Sword and your being the lost heir of Shannara – I don't know. Do you believe it yourself?'

'I didn't at first,' Shea admitted slowly, 'but now I don't know what to think. So much has happened that I can't decide who or what to believe anymore. In any case, I've got to rejoin Allanon and the others. They may even have the Sword by this time. They may have the answer to this whole riddle of my heritage and the power of the Sword.'

Orl Fane suddenly doubled up laughing, his voice high-pitched and frenzied.

'No, no, they don't have the Sword,' he shrieked like a fool caught up in his own madness. 'No, no, only I can show you the Sword! I can lead you to it. Only I. You can search and you can search and you can search, ha, ha, ha – go ahead. But I know where it is! I know who has it! Only I!'

'I think he's losing his mind,' Panamon Creel muttered humorlessly, and ordered Keltset to regag the bothersome Gnome. 'We'll find out exactly what he knows in the morning. If he knows anything about the Sword of Shannara, which I seriously doubt, he'll tell us or wish he had!'

'Do you think he might know who has it?' Shea asked soberly. 'That Sword could mean so much, not only to us, but to all the peoples of the four lands. We've got to try to find out what he really knows.'

'You bring tears to my eyes with that plea for the people,' Panamon mocked disdainfully. 'They can go hang for all I care. They've never done anything for me – except travel alone, unarmed, with fat purses, and that's been all too infrequently.' He looked up at Shea's disappointed face and shrugged nonchalantly. 'Still, I am curious about the Sword, so I might be willing to help you. After all, I owe you a great favor, and I'm not one to forget a favor.'

Keltset finished gagging the babbling Gnome once again and rejoined them next to the small fire. Orl Fane had lapsed into a series of small, shrill laughs coupled with incoherent mumblings that even the cloth gag did not completely muffle. Shea glanced uneasily at the little captive, watching the gnarled yellow body twist about as if possessed by some devil, the dark eyes wide and rolling wildly. Panamon gallantly ignored the moans for a brief time, but at last, losing all patience, leaped to his feet and drew his dagger to cut the Gnome's tongue out. Orl Fane immediately quieted down and for a while they forgot about him.

'Why do you suppose,' Panamon began after a moment, 'that Northland creature believed we were hiding the Sword of Shannara? It was strange he wouldn't even argue the point. He said he could sense that we had it. How do you explain that?'

Shea thought for a moment and finally shrugged uncertainly.

'It must have been the Elfstones.'

'You may be right,' Panamon agreed slowly, thoughtfully, his good hand rubbing his chin. 'I frankly don't understand any of this. Keltset, what do you think about it.'

The giant Rock Troll regarded them solemnly for a moment and then made several brief signs with his hands. Panamon watched intently, then turned to Shea with a disgusted look.

'He thinks the Sword is very important and that the Warlock Lord is a very great danger to us all.' The thief laughed humorously. 'He's a great help, I must say!'

'The Sword *is* very important!' Shea repeated, his voice trailing off in the darkness, and they sat quietly, lost in thought.

It was late evening now, the night around them black beyond the faint light of the fire's reddish embers. The woods were a wall of concealment, shutting them into the little clearing, surrounding them with the sharp sounds of the insect world and the occasional cry of some faraway creature. The sky above showed through the boughs of the great trees in patches of dark blue broken by one or two distant stars. Panamon talked on quietly for a few minutes more as the coals died into ashes. Then he rose, kicking the ashes and grinding them into the earth, bidding good night to his companions with a finality that discouraged further attempts at conversation. Keltset was wrapped in a blanket and sleeping before Shea had even selected a suitable patch of forest earth. The Valeman felt incredibly weary from the strain of the long day's march and the battle with the Skull Bearer. Dropping his blanket, he lay down on his back, kicked off the hunting boots and stared aimlessly at the blackness above him through which he could just barely discern the limbs of the trees and the shadows of the sky.

Shea thought about all that had happened to him, once again retracing mentally his long, endless journey from Shady Vale. So much of it was still a mystery. He had come so far, endured so much, and still he didn't know what it was all about. The secret of the Sword of Shannara, the Warlock Lord, his own heritage – it was no clearer now than before. The company was out there somewhere looking for him, led by the secretive, mystic Allanon, who seemed to be the only man with the answers to all the unanswered questions. Why had he not told Shea everything from the beginning? Why had he insisted on giving the company only a piece of the story at a time, always reserving that small bit, always holding back the key to their complete understanding of the unknown power locked in the elusive Sword of Shannara?

He rolled over on his side, peering through the darkness to the sleeping form of Panamon Creel just a few feet away. Beyond and to the other side of the clearing he could hear the heavy breathing of Keltset blending in with the sounds of the forest night. Orl Fane sat with his back straight against the tree to which he was bound, his eyes shining like a cat's in the dark, unmoving as they stared fixedly at Shea. The Valeman stared back for a moment, unnerved by the Gnome's gaze, but finally he forced himself to turn the other way and closed his eyes, dropping off to sleep in a matter of seconds. The last thing he remembered was clutching the small bulk of the Elfstones close to his chest within the tunic, wondering if their power would continue to protect him in the days ahead.

Shea was awakened abruptly to the gray light of an early forest morning by a long string of venomous oaths of dismay and frustration from a wrathful Panamon Creel. The thief was stamping about the campsite in absolute fury, shouting and cursing all at the same time. Shea could not decide what had happened right away, and it was several minutes before he had wiped the sleep from his eyes and propped himself up on one elbow, squinting wearily in the gloom. He felt as if he had slept no more than a few minutes, his muscles sore and strained, his mind hazy. Panamon continued to storm about the small clearing as Keltset knelt silently next to one of the great oaks. Then Shea realized that Orl Fane was missing. He leaped to his feet and rushed over, suddenly afraid. In a moment his worst fears were realized; the ropes that had bound the crafty Gnome lay in pieces about the base of the huge trunk. The Gnome had escaped, and Shea had lost his one chance to find the missing Sword.

'How did he get away?' Shea demanded angrily. 'I thought you tied him up, away from anything that might cut his bonds!'

Panamon Creel looked at him as if he were an idiot, disgust registered all over the flushed countenance.

'Do I look like a complete fool? Of course I tied him up away from any weapons. I even tied him to the confounded tree and had him gagged as an added precaution. Where were you? The little devil didn't cut these ropes and that gag. He chewed his way through them!'

Now it was Shea's turn to be amazed.

'I'm dead serious, I assure you,' Panamon continued angrily. 'The ropes were chewed through by teeth. Our little rodent friend was more resourceful than I imagined.'

'Or perhaps more desperate,' the Valeman added thoughtfully. 'I wonder why he didn't try to kill us. He had reason enough to hate us.'

'Very uncharitable of you to suggest such a thing,' the other declared in mock disbelief. 'I'll tell you why, though, since you asked. He was terrified that he might be caught in the act. That Gnome was a deserter – a coward of the lowest order. He didn't have the courage to do anything but run! What is it, Keltset?'

The huge Rock Troll had lumbered silently over to his comrade and made several quick gestures, pointing to the north. Panamon shook his head in disgust.

'The spineless mouse has been gone since early this morning – hours ago. Worse still, the fool fled north-ward, and it would not be healthy for us to chase him in that country. His own people will probably find him and dispose of him for us. They won't shelter a deserter. Bah, let him go! We're better off without him, Shea. He was probably lying about the Sword of Shannara anyway.'

Shea nodded doubtfully, unconvinced that the Gnome had been lying about everything he had told them. As unbalanced as the little fellow had seemed, he had nevertheless appeared certain that he knew where the Sword could be found and who had possession of it. The whole idea that he knew such a secret was unnerving to the Valeman. Suppose he had gone after the Sword? Suppose he knew where it was?

'Forget the whole matter Shea,' Panamon interjected in resignation. 'That Gnome was scared to death of us; his only thought was to escape. The story of the Sword was merely a trick to keep us from killing him until he found the opportunity to escape. Look at this! He left in such a hurry, he even forgot his precious sack.'

For the first time Shea noticed the sack lying partially open at the other side of the clearing. It was strange indeed that Orl Fane should abandon his treasures after going to so much trouble to persuade his captors to bring them along. That useless sack had been so important to him, and yet there it lay forgotten, its contents still visible as small bulks beneath the cloth. Shea walked over to it curiously, staring at it with visible suspicion. He emptied the contents onto the forest earth, the swords and the daggers and the jewelry clattering together as they tumbled out in a heap. Shea stared at them, aware that the giant form of Keltset was at his side, the dark, expressionless face bent next to his. They stood together, studying the Gnome's abandoned hoard as if somehow it held a mysterious secret. Their companion watched for a few seconds, then muttered in disgust and strolled over to join them, glancing down at the weapons and jewelry.

'Let's be on our way,' he advised lightly. 'We've got to find your friends, Shea, and perhaps with their help we can locate this elusive Sword. What are you staring at? You've already seen that worthless junk once. It hasn't changed.'

Then Shea saw it.

'It's not the same,' he announced slowly. 'It's gone. He's taken it.'

'What's gone?' snapped Panamon irritably, kicking at the pile of junk. 'What are you talking about?'

'That old sword in the leather scabbard. The one with the arm and the torch.'

Panamon looked quickly at the swords in the little heap, frowning curiously. Keltset straightened abruptly and looked at Shea with those deeply intelligent eyes fixed on the little Valeman. He realized the truth as well.

'So he took one sword,' Panamon growled without stopping to think. 'That doesn't mean he . . .' He caught himself, his jaw dropping open in dismay, his eyes rolling back in disbelief. 'Oh, no! That can't be – it can't. You mean he has . . . ?'

He couldn't finish the thought, but choked on his words. Shea shook his head in quiet despair.

'The Sword of Shannara!'

CHAPTER

8

The same morning that found Shea and his new companions facing the awful truth about the fleeing Orl Fane and the Sword of Shannara also found Allanon and the remaining members of the company embroiled in difficulties of their own. They had escaped from the Druids' Keep under the aged mystic's sure guidance, winding downward through the maze of tunnels in the core of the mountain to the forest land below. They had encountered no initial resistance to their escape, finding only a few scattered Gnomes scurrying about the passages, remnants of the broken palace guard that had fled earlier. It was early evening by the time the little band was clear of the forbidding heights and moving northward through the forests. Allanon was certain that the Gnomes had removed the Sword of Shannara from the Keep sometime before the encounter with the Skull Bearer in the furnace room, but it was impossible to tell exactly when the removal had been accomplished. Eventine was patrolling the northern perimeter of Paranor and any attempt to move the Sword would be met with resistance from his soldiers. Perhaps the Elven king had already gained possession of the Sword. Perhaps he had even intercepted the missing Shea. Allanon was extremely worried about the little Valeman, whom he had expected to find at the Druids' Keep. There had been no mistake when he had made his mental search for the youth back at the foot of the Dragon's Teeth. Shea was in the company of others, and they were moving northward toward Paranor. Something had diverted them. Still, Shea was a resourceful fellow, and he had the power of the Elf-stones to protect him from the Warlock Lord. The Druid could only hope that somehow they would find each other without further complications, and that when they did, Shea would be safe and unharmed.

Allanon had other worries, however, which demanded his immediate attention. Gnome reinforcements began to arrive in large numbers, and it did not take them long to conclude that Allanon and his little band of invaders had fled the castle and were somewhere in the dangerous Impregnable Forest surrounding Paranor. In truth, the Gnomes had no idea for whom they were searching; they only knew that the castle had been invaded, and the intruders had to be cap-tured or destroyed. The emissaries of the Warlock Lord had not arrived, and the Skull King himself did not yet realize his prey had escaped him once again. He rested content-edly in the dark recesses of his domain, assured that the troublesome Allanon had been destroyed in the furnaces of Paranor, that the heir of Shannara and the others with him were prisoners, and that the Sword of Shannara was safely on its way to the Northland, intercepted by this time by a Skull Bearer whom he had dispatched a day earlier to be certain the precious Sword was not retaken. So the newly arrived Gnomes began to comb the forests surrounding Paranor in an effort to find the unknown intruders, believ-ing that they would flee south and sending the majority of their hunters in that direction.

Allanon and his small band were moving steadily north-ward, but progress was slowed from time to time with the appearance of large Gnome search parties patrolling the woodlands. The little company would never have escaped undetected had they proceeded south, but the enemy numbers were reduced enough to the north that they managed to elude the hunting parties by hiding until they had passed and then pressing onward. It was light by the time they finally reached the fringes of the forest and could look northward over the awesome Plains of Streleheim, their pursuers momentarily behind them.

Allanon turned to them, his dark countenance worn and grim, but the eyes still bright with determination. His companions waited as he studied them one by one as if he were seeing each for the first time. Finally he spoke, the words slow and reluctant.

'We have reached the end of the road, my friends. The journey to Paranor is at an end, and it is time for the company to disband and each of us to go his own way. We have lost our chance to gain possession of the Sword – at least for the moment. Shea is still missing, and we cannot tell how long it may take to find him. But the greatest threat facing us is an invasion from the north. We must protect ourselves and the peoples of the lands south, east, and west of us from that. We have seen no sign of the Elven armies of Eventine, though they were supposed to be patrolling this region. It appears they have been withdrawn, and this would only be done if the Warlock Lord had begun to move his armies southward.'

'Then the invasion has begun?' Balinor asked shortly.

Allanon nodded solemnly, and the others exchanged startled looks.

'Without the Sword we cannot defeat the Warlock Lord, so we must attempt to stop his armies. To do this, we must unite the free nations quickly. We may already be too late. Brona will use his armies to seize all of the central Southland. To do this he need only destroy the Border Legion of Callahorn. Balinor, the Legion must hold the cities of Callahorn to give the nations enough time to unite their armies and strike back at the invader. Durin and Dayel can accompany you to Tyrsis and from there travel westward to their own land. Eventine must bring his Elven armies across the Plains of Streleheim to reinforce Tyrsis. If we lose there, the Warlock Lord will have succeeded in driving a wedge between the armies, and there will be little chance of uniting them. Worse still, the entire Southland will lie open and unprotected. Men will never be able to form their armies in time. The Border Legion of Callahorn is the only chance they have.'

Balinor nodded in agreement and turned to Hendel.

'What support can the Dwarfs give us?'

'The city of Varfleet is the key to the eastern sector of Callahorn.' Hendel pondered the situation carefully. 'My people must protect against any assault through the Anar, but we can spare enough men to help defend Varfleet as well. But you must hold the cities of Kern and Tyrsis yourself.'

'The Elven armies will help you on the west,' Durin promised quickly.

'Wait a minute!' exclaimed Menion incredulously. 'What about Shea? You've kind of forgotten about him, haven't you?'

'Still allowing your words to precede your thinking, I see,' Allanon said darkly. Menion turned scarlet with anger, but waited to see what the mystic had to say.

'I'm not abandoning the search for my brother,' Flick announced quietly.

'Nor am I suggesting you should, Flick.' Allanon smiled at the other's concern. 'You and Menion and I shall continue to search for our young friend and for the missing Sword. I suspect that where we find one, we shall find the other. Remember the words spoken to me by the Shade of Bremen. Shea shall be the first to lay hands on the Sword of Shannara. Perhaps he has already done so.'

'Then let's get on with the search,' suggested Menion irritably, avoiding the eyes of the Druid.

'We shall leave now,' Allanon announced, adding

pointedly, 'but you must see that you keep a closer guard over your tongue. A Prince of Leah should speak with wisdom and foresight, with patience and understanding – not with foolish anger.'

Menion nodded grudgingly. The seven said their farewells with mixed emotions and parted. Balinor, Hendel, and the Elven brothers turned westward past the forest in which Shea and his companions had spent the night, hoping to circle the Impregnable Forest and pass down through the hill country north of the Dragon's Teeth and thereby reach Kern and Tyrsis within two days. Allanon and his two youthful companions moved eastward, searching for some sign of Shea. Allanon was convinced that the Valeman must have eventually come northward toward Paranor and perhaps was a prisoner in one of the Gnome camps in that region. Rescuing him would not be easy, but the Druid's greatest fear was that the Warlock Lord would learn of his capture and find out who he was, then have him immediately executed. If that happened, the Sword of Shannara would be worthless to them anyway, and they would have no choice but to rely on the strength of the divided armies of the three besieged lands. It was not a promising thought, and Allanon quickly turned his attention to the land ahead. Menion walked slightly in front as they traveled, his keen eyes picking out the trails and studying the footprints of all who had passed. His concern was the weather. If it rained, they would never find the trail. Even if the weather stayed favorable for them, the sudden wind storms that blew across the Streleheim would have the same effect as a rainfall, erasing all traces of anyone's passage. Flick dutifully bringing up the rear, walked in abject silence, hoping against hope that they would find some sign of Shea, but fearful that he had seen the last of his brother.

By noonday, the barren plains were shimmering with the blistering heat of the white-hot sun, and the three travelers walked as close to the forest edge as possible to take advantage of small patches of shade from the great trees. Allanon alone seemed unperturbed by the fearful heat, his dark face calm and relaxed in the scorching sunlight, free from even the slightest trace of perspiration. Flick felt ready to collapse at any moment, and even the durable Menion Leah was beginning to feel ill. His sharp eyes were dry and blurred, and his senses were starting to play tricks on him. He was seeing things that weren't there, hearing and smelling images formed by his muddled brain in the seething flatlands ahead.

At last the two Southlanders could go no farther, and their tall leader called a brief halt, leading them into the cooling shade of the forest. In silence they ate a small, tasteless meal of bread and dried meats. Flick wanted to ask the Druid more about Shea's chances of surviving alone in that desolate land, but he couldn't bring himself to voice the questions. The answers were all too apparent. He felt strangely alone now that the others were gone. He had never felt close to Allanon, always plagued by nagging doubts about the Druid's strange powers. The mystic remained a giant shadowy figure, as mysterious and deadly as the Skull Bearers that pursued them so relentlessly. He remained a personification of the deathless spirit of Bremen that had risen from the nether world in the Valley of Shale. He was power and wisdom of such magnitude that he didn't seem a part of Flick's mortal world; he was more a part of the Warlock Lord's domain, that black, frightful corner of the mortal mind where fear is master and reason cannot penetrate. Flick could not forget the terrible battle between the great mystic and the treacherous Skull creature which had resulted in a fiery climax in the flames of the furnace beneath the Druids' Keep. Yet Allanon had saved himself; he had survived what no other man could have survived. It was more than merely uncanny – it was terrifying. Balinor alone had seemed able to deal with the giant leader, but now he was gone, and Flick felt very alone and vulnerable.

Menion Leah felt even less certain of himself. He was not really afraid of the powerful Druid, but he was aware that the giant did not think much of him and had brought him along primarily because Shea had wanted him. Shea had believed in the Prince of Leah when even Flick had doubted the adventurer's motives. But Shea was gone now. Menion felt he had only to anger the Druid once more and the unpredictable mystic would dispose of him for good. So he ate quietly and said nothing, believing that for the moment discretion was the better part of valor.

When the silent meal was concluded, the Druid motioned them to their feet. Again they marched eastward along the fringes of the forest, their faces bathed in the withering heat of the sun, their tired eyes scanning the barren plains for the missing Shea. This time they walked for only fifteen minutes before they found signs of something out of the ordinary. Menion spotted the tracks almost immediately. A large number of Gnomes had passed that way several days earlier, booted and undoubtedly armed. They followed the tracks northward for about half a mile. Upon topping a small rise of ground, they found the remains of the Gnomes and Elves who had died in battle. The decaying bodies lay where they had fallen, still untouched and unburied, less than a hundred yards from the rise. The three walked slowly down into the graveyard of bleached bones and rotting flesh, the terrible stench rising to their nostrils in sickening waves. Flick could go no farther, and stopped where he was to watch the other two walk into the midst of the dead bodies.

Allanon wandered in silent contemplation through the fallen men, studying discarded weapons and standards, glancing only briefly at the dead. Menion discovered a fresh set of tracks almost immediately and began moving mechanically about the battlefield, his eyes fixed on the dusty earth. Flick could not tell exactly what was going on from his distant vantage point, but it appeared that the highlander retraced his own steps several times, casting about for traces of new trails, the thin hands shading his reddened eyes. Finally, he turned southward toward the forest and began strolling slowly back toward Flick, his head lowered thoughtfully. He stopped at a large clump of bushes and dropped to one knee, apparently observing something of interest. Momentarily forgetting his distaste for the battlefield and its corpses, the curious Valeman hastened forward. He had just reached the kneeling man's side when Allanon, standing in the center of the battlefield, let out a shout of astonishment. The two men paused and watched silently while the tall black figure peered downward for a moment as if to be certain, then turned and moved toward them in long strides. The mystic's dark face was flushed with excitement when he reached them, and they were relieved to see the familiar mocking smile slowly spread into a wide grin.

'Amazing! It's amazing indeed. Our young friend is more resourceful than I had imagined. Up there, I found a small pile of ashes – all that remains of one of the Skull Bearers. Nothing mortal destroyed that creature; it was the power of the Elfstones!'

'Then Shea has been here ahead of us!' exclaimed Flick hopefully.

'No other has the power to use the stones.' Allanon nodded assuringly. 'There are signs of a terrific battle, tracks that show Shea was not alone. But I cannot tell whether those who were with him were friends or enemies. Nor can I tell if the creature of the north was destroyed during or after the battle between Gnome and Elf. What have you found, highlander?'

'A lot of false trails left by a very intelligent Troll,' Menion responded wryly. 'It's impossible for me to tell much from all the footprints, but I am sure that a large

140

RockTroll was among the prior occupants of this field. He left his tracks all over it but none of them lead anywhere. There are indications that some sort of scuffle took place within these bushes, though. See the bent branches and newly fallen leaves? But more important, there are footprints of a small man. They could be Shea's.'

'Do you think he was captured by the Troll?' Flick queried fearfully.

Menion smiled at his concern and shrugged.

'If he could handle one of those Skull creatures, then I doubt he would have much trouble with an ordinary Troll.'

'The Elfstones are no protection against mortal creatures,' Allanon pointed out chillingly. 'Is there any clear indication which way this Troll went?'

Menion shook his head negatively.

'To be certain, we would have had to find the tracks right away. These tracks are at least a day old. The Troll knew what he was doing when he left. We could search forever and never be sure which way he went.'

Flick felt his heart sink at this news. If Shea had been taken by this mysterious creature, then it appeared they had reached another dead end.

'I found something else,' Allanon announced after a moment. 'I found a broken standard from the house of Elessedil – Eventine's personal banner. He may have been present at the battle. He may have been taken prisoner or even killed. It seems possible that the slain Gnomes were attempting to escape from Paranor with the Sword and were intercepted by the Elf King and his warriors. If so, then Eventine, Shea and the Sword may all be in the hands of the enemy.'

'I'm sure of one thing,' Menion declared quickly. 'Those Troll footprints and this battle in the bushes took place yesterday, while the battle between the Gnomes and Elves is several days old.'

'Yes . . . yes, you're right, of course,' the Druid agreed

thoughtfully. 'There has been a sequence of events taking place that we can't piece together from the little we know. I'm afraid we won't find all the answers here.'

'What do we do now?' Flick asked anxiously.

'There are tracks leading westward across the Streleheim,' Allanon mused thoughtfully, gazing in that direction as he spoke. 'The tracks are blurred, but they may have been made by survivors of this battle . . .'

He looked questioningly at the silent Menion Leah for his opinion.

'Our mysterious Troll did not go that way,' Menion stated worriedly. 'He would not bother with a lot of false trails if he were going to leave a clear one when he left! I don't like it.'

'Do we have any choice?' Allanon persisted. 'The only clear set of tracks leaving this battleground leads westward. We'll have to follow them and hope for the best.'

Flick thought that such optimism was unwarranted in view of the hard facts of the situation and found the comments out of character for the grim Druid. Still, it seemed they had little choice in the matter. Perhaps whoever had made those tracks could tell them something about Shea. The little Valeman turned to Menion and nodded his willingness to follow the Druid's advice, nothing the look of consternation clouding the highlander's lean features. Clearly Menion was not happy with the decision, convinced that there was another trail to be found that would tell them more about the Troll and the slain Skull creature. Allanon beckoned to them, and retracing their steps they began the long march back across the Streleheim Plains to the lands west of Paranor. Flick cast one final look at the field of slain men, their carcasses rotting slowly in the boiling heat of the sun, shunned by man and nature in senseless death. He shook his broad head. Perhaps this was the way it would end for them all.

The three travelers walked steadily westward for the

remainder of the day. They spoke little, lost in private thoughts, their eyes following almost carelessly the blurred trail before them as they watched the brilliant sun turn red in the horizon and die into evening. When it was too dark to continue, Allanon directed them into the bordering forests where they made camp for the night. The trio had reached a point near the northwestern sector of the dreaded Impregnable Forest and they were once again in danger of discovery by Gnome hunting parties or prowling wolf packs. The resolute Druid explained that, while they were in some danger of discovery, he believed the search for them would have been abandoned by this time in favor of more urgent matters. As a necessary precaution, they would light no fire and would keep constant watch through the night for the wolves. Flick silently prayed that the wolf packs would not venture this close to the plainland, but would keep to the dark interior of the woods, closer to the Druids' Keep. They ate a brief, tasteless meal and quickly turned in for the night. Menion offered to stand the first watch. Flick was asleep in moments, but it seemed he had slept for only an instant when the highlander awoke him for his turn as guard. About midnight, Allanon approached without a sound and ordered Flick to go back to sleep. The Valeman had been guarding for only about an hour, but he did as he was told without arguing.

When Flick and Menion awoke again, it was dawn. In the faint red and yellow slivers of sunlight which crept slowly into the shadowed forest, they saw the giant Druid resting peacefully against a tall elm as he stared at them. The tall, dark figure seemed almost a part of the forest, sitting there motionlessly, the deep eyes black in the caverns beneath the great brow. They knew that Allanon must have stood guard over them all night without sleep. It seemed impossible that he could be rested, yet he rose without stretching, the grim face relaxed and alert. They ate a quick breakfast and marched out of the forest onto the Streleheim once more. A moment later they halted in shocked disbelief. All about them, the skies were clear and faintly blue in the new light of day, the sun rising in blinding brilliance above the mountain ranges far to the east. But to the north stood a gigantic, towering wall of darkness against the skyline, as if all the ominous thunderclouds of the earth had been massed together and piled one on top of the next to form a black wall of gloom. The wall rose into the air until it was lost in the curving atmosphere of the earth's horizon, and it stretched across all of the rugged Northland, huge, dark, and terrible – its center the kingdom of the Warlock Lord. It seemed to foreshadow the relentless, inevitable approach of an endless night.

'What do you make of that?' Menion could barely get the question out.

For a moment Allanon said nothing, his own dark face mirroring the blackness of the northern wall as he stared in silence. The muscles of his lean jaw seemed to tighten beneath the small black beard and the eyes narrowed as if deep in concentration. Menion waited quietly, and at last the Druid seemed to realize he had spoken, turning to him in recognition.

'It is the beginning of the end. Brona has signaled the start of his conquest. That terrible darkness will follow his armies as they sweep southward, then east and west, until the whole earth is blanketed. When the sun is gone in all the lands, freedom is dead, too.'

'Are we beaten?' Flick asked after a moment.' Are we really beaten? Is it hopeless for us, Allanon?'

His worried voice struck a responsive chord within the giant Druid, who turned quietly to him, gazing reassuringly into the wide, frightened eyes.

'Not yet, my young friend. Not yet.'

Allanon led them westward for several hours from that point, staying close to the fringes of the forest, warning

Menion and Flick to keep their eyes open for any sign of the enemy. The Skull Bearers would be flying in the day as well as by night, now that the Warlock Lord had begun his conquest, no longer afraid of the sunlight, no longer trying to conceal their presence. The Master was finished with hiding in the Northland; now, he would begin to move into the other lands, sending his faithful spirits ahead of him like great birds of prey. He would give them the power they needed to withstand the sun – the power he had harnessed in the great dark wall that shadowed his kingdom and would soon begin to shadow all of the lands beyond. The days of light were drawing to a close.

About midmorning, the three travelers turned southward on the Streleheim Plains, keeping close to the western fringes of the forests surrounding Paranor. The tracks they had been following merged at this point with others coming down from the north to continue southward toward Callahorn. The trail they left was broad and open; there had been no attempt to hide either their number or their direction. From the width of the trail and the impressions left by the footprints, Menion concluded that at least several thousand men had passed this way a few days earlier. The footprints were Gnome and Troll – obviously part of the Northland hordes of the Warlock Lord. Allanon was certain now that a giant army was massing on the plains above Callahorn to begin a sweep through the Southland that would divide the free lands and their armies. The trail had become so obscured by the intermingling of constant additional parties into the main body that it was no longer possible to tell whether a small group might have detached itself. Shea or the Sword could have been taken a different way at some point, and his friends would fail to catch it, continuing to follow the main army.

They walked southward all day with only occasional periods of rest, intent on catching the huge column of men ahead before nightfall. The trail of the invading army was so apparent that Menion merely glanced out of habit from time to time at the trampled earth. The barren Plains of Streleheim were replaced by green grasslands. To Flick, it almost seemed that they were going home again, and the familiar hills of Shady Vale might be just over the rise of the plains. The weather was warm and humid, and the terrain was considerably more friendly. They were still some distance from Callahorn, but it was clear that they were passing out of the bleakness of the Northland into the warmth and greenness of their home. The day passed quickly, and conversation between the travelers resumed. At Flick's urging, Allanon told them more about the Council of the Druids. He recounted in detail the history of Man since the Great Wars, explaining how their race had progressed to its present state of existence. Menion said little, content to listen to the Druid and keep a close watch over the surrounding countryside.

When they had begun the day's march, the sun had been bright and warm, and the sky clear. By midafternoon, the weather had changed abruptly and the brightness of the sun was replaced by low-hanging, gray rain clouds and an even more humid atmosphere that clung uncomfortably to the exposed skin. The air felt sticky and wet, and there was little doubt that a storm was approaching. They were near the southernmost boundaries of the Impregnable Forest by this time, and the jagged peaks of the Dragon's Teeth were visible in the dark horizon to the south. Still there was no sign of the massive army traveling ahead of them, and Menion was beginning to wonder how far south it might have already penetrated. They were not far now from the borders of Callahorn, which lay immediately below the Dragon's Teeth. If the Northland armies had already taken Callahorn, then the end had indeed come. The gray light of the afternoon dropped off sharply and the sky closed over in sullen darkness.

It was dusk when they first heard the ominous booming

rising out of the night, echoing off the giant peaks ahead of them. Menion recognized it at once – he had heard that sound before in the forests of the Anar. It was the sound of hundreds of Gnome drums, their steady rhythm throbbing through the stillness of the humid air, filling the night with a sinister tension. The earth shook with the force of the beat, and all life had gone mute in awe and fear. Menion could tell by the intensity of the drums that there were far more than they had encountered at the Pass of Jade. If the army of the Northland could be measured by the sound of those drums, then there must be thousands. As the three moved quickly ahead, the frightening sound enveloped them entirely, booming all about them in shuddering echoes. The gray clouds of late afternoon still masked the night sky, leaving the searching men shrouded in inky darkness. Menion and Flick could no longer find the way alone, and the silent Druid led them with uncanny precision into the rough lowlands below Paranor. No one spoke, each man frozen into watchful apprehension by the deathly booming of those Gnome drums. They knew that the enemy camp was just ahead.

Then the terrain changed abruptly from the low hills and scattered brush to steep slopes dotted with boulders and treacherous rock ledges. The surefooted Allanon moved steadily ahead, his tall form unmistakable even in the near blackness, and the two Southlanders followed dutifully. Menion estimated that they must have reached the smaller mountains and foothills just above the Dragon's Teeth and that Allanon had chosen to come this way to avoid any chance encounters with members of the Northland army. It was still impossible to tell where the enemy army was encamped, but from the sound of the drums, it seemed as if they were right on top of it. The three dark shapes wound their way cautiously through the night for what must have been almost an hour, at times feeling their way blindly through the boulders and brush.

Their clothes were scraped and torn, their exposed limbs scratched and bruised, but the silent Druid did not slacken the pace or pause to rest. At the end of that long hour's time, he halted abruptly and turned to them, placing a warning finger over pursed lips. Then slowly, cautiously, he led them forward into a huge mass of boulders. For several minutes, the three climbed noiselessly upward. Suddenly there were lights in the distance – dim, flickering yellow lights that came from burning fires. They crawled on hands and knees to the rim of the boulders. Upon reaching a tilted shelf of rock that sloped upward to the edge of the boulder cluster, they raised their heads slowly to the rim and peered breathlessly over.

What they saw was awesome and terrifying. As far as the eye could see, stretching miles in all directions, the fires of the Northland army burned in the night. They were like thousands of blazing yellow dots in the blackness of the plains, and moving busily about in their bright light were the dim shapes of wiry, gnarled Gnomes and bulky, thick-limbed Trolls. There were thousands of them, all armed, all waiting to descend on the kingdom of Callahorn. It was inconceivable to Menion and Flick that even the legendary Border Legion could hope to stand against such a mighty force. It was as if the entire Gnome and Troll population had been gathered on the plains below. Allanon had avoided any chance encounters with scouts or guards by approaching along the edges of the Dragon's Teeth on the western borders, and now the three were perched in a crow's nest of boulders several hundred feet up from the army encamped below. From this height, the shocked Southlanders could see the entirety of the massive force assembled to invade their poorly defended homeland. The drums of the Gnomes boomed out in steady crescendo as the men stared down, their eyes traveling from one end of the sprawled camp to the other in disbelief. For the first time, they understood fully what they were up against. Before, it had been only Allanon's words describing the invasion; now they could see the enemy and judge for themselves. Now they could feel the desperate need for the mysterious Sword of Shannara – a need for the one power that could destroy the evil being who had caused this army to materialize and march against them. But now was already too late.

For several long minutes, no one said anything as they stared down at the enemy encampment. Then Menion touched Allanon on the shoulder and started to speak, but the Druid clamped his hand quickly over the surprised highlander's mouth and pointed toward the base of the slope on which they lay concealed. Menion and Flick peered cautiously downward and to their surprise they made out the vague shapes of Gnome guards patrolling near the base of their hiding place. Neither had believed the enemy would bother to place guards this far from the actual camp, but apparently they were taking no chances. Allanon motioned for the two to move back from the edge of the boulders and they quickly complied, following his lead as he inched his way down into the tall rocks. Once they had reached the bottom of the boulder cluster, safely away from the rim of the ledge, the Druid huddled together with them in earnest council.

'We have to be very quiet,' he warned in a tense whisper. 'The sound of our voices would have echoed off the cliff face onto the plains from up there. Those Gnome guards would have heard us!'

Menion and Flick nodded in understanding.

'The situation is more serious than I thought,' Allanon continued, his voice a hushed rasp in the gloom. 'It appears the entire Northland army has bunched at this one point to strike at Callahorn. Brona intends to crush any resistance from the Southland immediately, dividing the better prepared armies of the East and West so he can deal with them separately. The evil one already holds everything north of Callahorn. Balinor and the others must be warned!'

He paused a moment, then turned expectantly to Menion Leah.

'I can't leave now,' Menion exclaimed heatedly. 'I've got to help you find Shea!'

'We haven't the time to argue the priorities of the situation,' Allanon declared almost menacingly, one finger coming up like a dagger at the highlander's face. 'If Balinor is not warned about the situation, Callahorn will fall and the rest of the Southland will follow, including Leah. The time has come for you to start thinking about your own people. Shea is only one man, and right now there is nothing you can do for him. But there is something you can do for the thousands of Southlanders who face enslavement at the hands of the Warlock Lord if Callahorn should fall!'

Allanon's voice was so cold that Flick could feel the chills run up his spine. He could sense Menion tensing expectantly, fearfully, at his side, but the Prince of Leah kept silent in the face of this stinging reprimand. Druid and Prince faced one another in the darkness for several interminable minutes, their eyes locked in open anger. Then Menion looked away abruptly and nodded shortly. Flick breathed an audible sigh of relief.

'I'll go to Callahorn and warn Balinor,' Menion muttered, his voice still muffled with fury, 'but I'll be back to find you.'

'Do as you wish when you have found the others,' replied Allanon coldly. 'However, any attempt to return through enemy lines would be foolhardy at best. Flick and I shall try to find out what has happened to Shea and the Sword. We will not desert him, highlander, I promise you.'

Menion looked back at him sharply, almost in disbelief, but the Druid's eyes were clear and undisguised. He was not lying.

'Keep close to these smaller mountains until you get past the enemy picket lines,' the giant wanderer advised quietly. 'When you reach the Mermidon River above Kern, cross there and enter the city before dawn. I expect the Northland army will march on Kern first. There is little chance that the city can be successfully defended against a force of that size. The people should be evacuated and moved into Tyrsis before the invaders can cut off their retreat. Tyrsis is built on a plateau against the back of a mountain. Properly defended, it can withstand any assault for at least several days. That should be time enough for Durin and Dayel to reach their homeland and return with the Elven army. Hendel should be able to offer some help from the Eastland. Perhaps Callahorn can be held long enough to mobilize and combine the armies of the three lands to strike back at the Warlock Lord. It is the only chance we have without the Sword of Shannara!'

Menion nodded in understanding and turned to Flick, extending his hand in a gesture of farewell. Flick smiled faintly and clasped the hand warmly.

'Good luck to you, Menion Leah.'

Allanon came forward and placed a strong hand on the highlander's lean shoulder.

'Remember, Prince of Leah, we depend on you. The people of Callahorn must be made aware of the danger they face. If they falter or hesitate, they are lost, and with them all of the Southland. Do not fail.'

Menion turned abruptly and moved like a shadow into the rocks beyond. The giant Druid and the little Valeman stood silently as the lean figure flitted agilely between the rocks and then disappeared from sight. They stood for a few minutes without speaking after he was gone, and then Allanon turned to Flick.

'To us is left the task of finding out what has happened to Shea and the Sword.' He spoke again in a lowered voice, sitting heavily down on a small rock. Flick moved closer to him. 'I'm worried about Eventine as well. That broken standard we found back at the battlefield was his personal banner. He may have been taken prisoner, and if he has, the Elven army may hesitate to act until he has been rescued. They love him too dearly to take a chance with his life, even to save the Southland.'

'You mean the Elven people don't care what happens to the people of the Southland?' Flick exclaimed incredulously. 'Don't they know what will happen to them should the Southland fall to the Warlock Lord?'

'It's not quite as simple as it seems,' Allanon stated, sighing deeply. 'Those who follow Eventine understand the danger, but there are others who believe that the Elven people should stay out of the affairs of the other lands unless they are directly attacked or threatened. With Eventine absent, the choice will not be so clear, and discussion of what is right and proper may delay any move by the Elven army until it is too late for them to help.'

Flick nodded slowly, thinking of another time at Culhaven when a bitter Hendel had reported much the same thing about the people of the Southland cities. It seemed incredible that people could be so undecided and confused in the face of such obvious danger. Yet Shea and he had been like that when they had first learned about Shea's birthright and the threat of the Skull Bearers. It was not until they had seen one crawling, searching for them . . .

'I've got to know what's happening in that camp.' Allanon's voice cut into Flick's thoughts with a sharp rasp of determination. He paused in thought a moment, staring at the little Valeman.

'My young friend, Flick . . .' He smiled faintly in the darkness. 'How would you like to be a Gnome for a little while?'

CHAPTER

9

With Shea still missing somewhere north of the Dragon's Teeth and Allanon, Flick, and Menion in search of some definite sign of his whereabouts, the remaining four members of the now divided company of friends drew within sight of the great towers of the fortress city of Tyrsis. It had taken them almost two days of constant travel, their hazardous journey through the lines of the Northland army further impeded by the formidable mountain barrier cutting off the Southland kingdom of Callahorn from the land of Paranor. The first day was long, but without incident, as the four wound southward through the forests adjoining the Gnome-patrolled Impregnable Forest to reach the lowlands beyond, which formed the doorstep to the awesome Dragon's Teeth. The mountain passes were all carefully guarded by Gnome hunters, and it seemed it would prove to be impossible to get past them without a fight. But a simple ruse lured most of the guards away from the entrance to the high, winding Kennon Pass, allowing the four an opportunity to get into the mountains. The difficult task of getting out again at the southern end was accomplished only after several Gnomes were silently dispatched at a midpoint check camp and twenty more were frightened into believing the entire Border Legion of

Callahorn had seized the pass and was descending on the luckless sentries with every intention of killing them all. Hendel was laughing so hard when they finally reached the safety of the forests south of the Kennon Pass that all four were forced to pause momentarily until he could recover his composure. Durin and Dayel looked doubtfully at one another, recalling the taciturn Dwarf's grim attitude during the journey to Paranor. They had never seen him laugh at anything, and somehow it seemed out of character. They shook their lean faces in disbelief and glanced questioningly at Balinor. But the giant borderman only shrugged. He was an old friend to Hendel and the Dwarf's changeable character was well known to him. It was good to hear his laughter again.

Now in the twilight of the early evening, with the sun's fading light a hazy purple and red in the vast horizon of the western plains, the four stood within sight of their destination. Their bodies were worn and sore, their normally keen minds numbed by lack of sleep and constant travel, but their spirits rose with unspoken excitement at the sight of the majestic city of Tyrsis. They paused for an instant at the edge of the forests that ran south from the Dragon's Teeth through Callahorn. To the east was the city of Varfleet, which guarded the only sizable passage through the Mountains of Runne, a small range that lay above the fabled Rainbow Lake. The sluggish Mermidon River wound its way through the forest at their backs above Tyrsis. Westward lay the smaller island city of Kern, and the source of the river was farther west in the vast emptiness of the Streleheim Plains. The river was broad at all points, forming a natural barrier against any would-be enemy and offering reliable protection for the inhabitants on the island. While the river ran full, which it did almost the year around, the waters were deep and swift, and no enemy had ever taken the island city.

Yet while both Kern, surrounded by the waters of the

Mermidon, and Varfleet, nestled in the Mountains of Runne, seemed formidable and well defended, it was the ancient city of Tyrsis that harbored the Border Legion – the precision fighting machine that had for countless generations successfully guarded the borders of the Southland against invasion. It was the Border Legion that had always taken the brunt of any assault against the race of Man, offering the first line of defense against an enemy invader. Tyrsis had given birth to the Border Legion of Callahorn, and as a fortress it was without equal. The old city of Tyrsis had been destroyed in the First War of the Races, but had been rebuilt and then expanded over the years until now it was one of the largest cities in all the Southland and by far the strongest city standing in the northern regions. It had been designed as a fortress capable of withstanding any enemy attack – a bastion of towering walls and jagged ramparts set on a natural plateau against the face of an unscalable cliff. Each generation of its citizens had contributed in the construction of the city, each making it more formidable. Over seven hundred years ago, the great Outer Wall had been built on the edge of the plateau, extending the boundaries of Tyrsis as far as nature would permit on the bluff face. In the fertile plains below the fortress were the farms and croplands that fed the city, the dark earth nurtured and sustained by the life-giving waters of the great Mermidon which ran east and south. The people had their homes scattered throughout the surrounding countryside, relying on the city's walled protection only in the event of invasion. For hundreds of years following the First War of the Races, the cities of Callahorn had successfully repelled assaults by unfriendly neighbors. None of the three had ever been seized by an enemy. The famed Border Legion had never been defeated in battle. But Callahorn had never faced an army the size of that sent by the Warlock Lord. The real test of strength and courage lay ahead.

Balinor looked upon the distant towers of his city with

mixed feelings. His father had been a great King and a good man, but he was growing old. For years he had commanded the Border Legion in its unceasing battle against persistent Gnome raiders from the Eastland. Several times he had been forced to wage long and costly campaigns against the great Northland Trolls, when scattered tribes had moved into his land, intent on seizing its cities and subjugating its people. Balinor was the elder son and the logical heir to the throne. He had studied hard under his father's careful guidance, and he was well liked by the people – people whose friendship could be won only through respect and understanding. He had worked beside them, fought beside them, and learned from them, so that now he could feel what they felt and look through their eyes. He loved the land enough to fight to hold it, as he was doing now, as he had been doing for a number of years. He commanded a regiment of the Border Legion, and they wore his personal insignia – a crouched leopard. They were the key unit of the entire fighting force. For Balinor, holding their respect and devotion was more important than anything. He had been gone from them for months now – gone, by his own choosing, to a self-imposed exile of travel with the mysterious Allanon and the company from Culhaven. His father had asked him not to go, pleaded with him to reconsider his decision. But he had already decided; he was not to be swayed, even by his father. His brow furrowed and a strange feeling of gloom settled into his mind as he looked down on his homeland. Unconsciously, he raised one gloved hand to his face, the cold chain mail tracing the line of the scar that ran down the exposed right cheek to his chin.

'Thinking about your brother again?' Hendel asked, although it was not so much a question as a statement of fact.

Balinor looked over at him, momentarily startled, then nodded slowly.

'You've got to stop thinking about that whole business, you know,' the Dwarf stated flatly. 'He could be a real threat to you if you persist in thinking of him as a brother and not as a person.'

'It is not so easy to forget that his blood and mine make us more than sons born to the same father,' the borderman declared gloomily. 'I cannot ignore nor forget such strong ties.'

Durin and Dayel looked at each other, unable to comprehend what the two were talking about. They knew that Balinor had a brother, but they had never seen him and had heard no mention of him since they had begun the long journey from Culhaven.

Balinor noticed the baffled looks on the faces of the two Elven brothers and shot a quick smile in their direction.

'It's not as bad as it might seem,' he assured them calmly.

Hendel shook his head hopelessly and lapsed into silence for the next few minutes.

'My younger brother Palance and I are the only sons of Ruhl Buckhannah, the King of Callahorn,' Balinor volunteered, his eyes wandering back toward the distant city as if looking for another time. 'We were very close while growing up – as close as you two. As we got older, we developed different ideas about life . . . different personalities, as all individuals must, brothers or not. I was the elder; I was next in line to the throne. Palance always realized this, of course, but it divided us as we grew older, mainly because his ideas of ruling the land were not always the same as mine. . . . It's difficult to explain, you understand.'

'It's not so difficult,' Hendel snorted meaningfully.

'All right, then, it's not so difficult,' Balinor conceded wearily, to which Hendel responded with a knowing nod. 'Palance believes Callahorn should cease to serve as a first line of defense in case of attack on the Southland people. He wants to disband the Border Legion and isolate

Callahorn from the rest of the Southland. We cannot agree at all on this point . . .'

He trailed off in bitter silence for a moment.

'Tell them the rest, Balinor.' Hendel again spoke icily.

'My distrustful friend believes my brother is no longer his own master – that he says these things without meaning them. He keeps counsel with a mystic known as Stenmin, a man Allanon feels is without honor and will guide Palance to his own destruction. Stenmin has told my father and the people that my brother should rule and not I. He has turned him against me. When I left, even Palance seemed to believe that I was not fit to rule Callahorn.'

'And that scar . . .?' Durin asked quietly.

'An argument we had just before I left with Allanon,' Balinor replied, shaking his head as he thought back on the matter. 'I can't even remember how it started, but all at once Palance was in a rage – there was real hatred in his eyes. I turned to leave, and he grabbed a whip from the wall, striking out at me, cutting into my face with the tip. That was the reason I decided to get away from Tyrsis for a time, to give Palance a chance to regain his senses. If I had stayed after that incident, we might have . . .'

Again he trailed off ominously, and Hendel shot the Elven brothers a glance that left no doubt in their minds what would have happened if the brothers had had another altercation. Durin frowned in disbelief, wondering what sort of person would take sides against a man like Balinor. The tall borderman had repeatedly proved his courage and strength of character during their dangerous journey to Paranor, and even Allanon had relied heavily on him. Yet his brother had deliberately and vindictively turned against him. The Elf felt a deep sadness for this brave warrior, returned to a homeland where peace even in his own family was denied him.

'You must believe me when I tell you that my brother was not always like that – nor do I believe he is now a bad man,' Balinor continued, more as if he were explaining it to himself than to the others. 'This mystic Stenmin has some kind of hold over Palance that provokes him into these rages, turning him against me and what he knows to be right.'

'There is more to him than that,' Hendel interrupted sharply. 'Palance is an idealistic fanatic – he seeks the throne and turns against you under pretext of upholding the interests of the people. He is choking on his own self-righteousness.'

'Perhaps you are right, Hendel,' Balinor conceded quietly. 'But he is still my brother, and I love him.'

'That's what makes him so dangerous,' the Dwarf declared, standing before the tall borderman, meeting his gaze squarely. 'He no longer loves you.'

Balinor did not reply, but stared into the plainlands to the west and toward the city of Tyrsis. The others remained silent for a few minutes, leaving the brooding Prince to his own thoughts. Finally he turned back to them, his face relaxed and calm, looking as if the whole matter had never come up.

'Time to be moving on. We want to reach the walls of the city before nightfall.'

'I'm going no farther with you, Balinor,' Hendel interjected quickly. 'I must return to my own land and help prepare the Dwarf armies against an invasion of the Anar.'

'Well, you can rest in Tyrsis for tonight and leave tomorrow,' Dayel replied quickly, knowing how tired they all were and anxious for the Dwarf's safety.

Hendel smiled patiently, then shook his head.

'No, I must travel at night in these lands. If I stay the night in Tyrsis, I lose a whole day's travel, and time is very precious to us all. The entire Southland stands or falls on how quickly we can assemble our armies into a combined fighting unit to strike back at the Warlock Lord. If Shea and the Sword of Shannara are lost to us, then our armies are all we have left. I will travel to Varfleet and rest there. Take care my friends. Luck to you in the days ahead.'

'And to you, brave Hendel.' Balinor extended a great hand. Hendel clasped it warmly, then those of the Elven brothers, and disappeared into the forests with a parting wave.

Balinor and the Elven brothers waited until they could no longer see him moving through the trees and then began their walk across the plains toward Tyrsis. The sun had dropped behind the horizon, and the sky had turned from dusky red to a deep gray and blue that signaled the momentary approach of night. They were about halfway when the sky turned completely black, revealing the first of the night's stars shining in a clear, cloudless sky. As they neared the fabled city, its vast bulk sprawling and dark against the night horizon, the Prince of Callahorn described in detail to the Elven brothers the history behind the building of Tyrsis.

A series of natural defenses protected the man-made fortress. The city had been built on a high plateau which ran back against a line of small, but treacherous cliffs. The cliffs bounded the plateau entirely on the south and partially on the west and east. While they were not nearly so high or formidable in appearance as the Dragon's Teeth or the Charnal Mountains of the far Northland, they were incredibly steep. That portion of the cliffs that faced north onto the plateau rose almost straight up, and no one had ever successfully scaled it. Thus, the city was well protected from the rear, and it had never been necessary to construct any defenses to the south. The plateau on which the city was built was a little over three miles across at its widest point, dropping off sharply onto the plainlands which ran unbroken and open all the way north and west to the Mermidon River and east to the forests of Callahorn. The swift Mermidon actually formed the first line of defense against invasion, and few armies had ever gotten beyond that point

160

to reach the plateau and the city walls. The enemy who did manage to cross the Mermidon onto the plainlands immediately found itself confronted by the steep wall of the plateau, which could be defended from above. The main route of access to this bluff was a huge iron and stone rampway, which was rigged to collapse by knocking out pins in the major supports.

But even if the enemy managed to reach the top of the plateau and thereby gain a foothold, the third defense waited – the defense that no army had ever broken through. Standing a scant two hundred yards from the edge of the plateau and ringing the entire city in a semicircle, the ends reaching back to the cliff sides protecting the southern approach, was the monstrous Outer Wall. Constructed from great blocks of stone welded together with mortar, the surface had been smoothed down to make scaling by hand virtually impossible. It rose nearly a hundred feet into the air, massive, towering, impregnable. AT the top of the wall, ramparts had been built for the men fighting within the city, with sections cut away to allow concealed bowmen room to shoot down on the unprotected attackers. It was ancient in styling, crude and rough-hewn, but it had repelled invaders for almost a thousand years. No enemy army had penetrated into the inner city since its construction following the First War of the Races.

Just within the great Outer Wall, the Border Legion was quartered in a series of long, sloping barracks interspersed by buildings used for storage of supplies and weapons. Approximately one-third of this great fighting force was kept on duty at any given time, while the other two-thirds remained at home with their families, pursuing their secondary occupations as laborers, craftsmen, or shopkeepers in the city. The barracks were equipped to house the entire army if the need should ever arise, as indeed it had already done on more than one occasion, but at present they were only partially filled. Set back from the barracks, supply housing, and parade grounds was a second wall of stone blocks separating the soldiers' quarters from the city proper. Within this second wall, lining the neat, winding city streets, were the homes and businesses of the urban population of Tyrsis, all carefully constructed and meticulously cared for buildings. The city sprawled over most of the plateau's elevation, running from this second stone wall almost to the cliffs bordering the south approach. At this innermost point of the city, a low third wall had been built which marked the entrance to the government buildings and the royal palace of the King, complete with public forum and landscaped grounds. The tree-shaded parks surrounding the palace provided the only sylvan setting on the otherwise open and sparse flatland of the plateau. The third wall had not been built for defensive purposes, but as a line of demarcation, signifying government-owned property that had been reserved for the King's use and, in the case of the parks, for all the people. Balinor deviated from his description of the city's construction long enough to point out to the Elven brothers that the Kingdom of Callahorn was one of the few remaining enlightened monarchies in the world. While it was technically a monarchy ruled by a King, the government also consisted of a parliamentary body composed of representatives chosen by the people of Callahorn, who helped the ruler hammer out the laws that governed the land. The people took great pride in their government and in the Border Legion in which most either had served at one time or were serving now. It was a country in which they could be free men, and this was something worth fighting for.

Callahorn was a land that reflected both the past and the future. On the one hand its cities had been built primarily as fortresses to withstand the frequent assaults by warlike neighbors. The Border Legion was a carry-over from earlier times when the newly formed nations were constantly at war, when an almost fanatical pride in national sovereignty resulted in a long struggle over jealously guarded land boundaries, when brotherhood between the peoples of the four lands was still only a distant possibility. The rustic, old-fashioned decor and architecture could be found nowhere else in the quickly growing cities of the deep Southland – cities where more enlightened cultures and less warlike policies were beginning to prevail. Yet it was Tyrsis, with, her barbaric walls of stone and warrior men of iron, that had shielded the lower Southland and given it that chance to expand in new directions. There were signs of what was to come in this picturesque land as well, signs that told of another age and time not too far distant. There was a unity of expression in the people that spoke of tolerance and understanding of all races and peoples. In Callahorn, as in no other country in all the sheltered Southland, a man was accepted for what he was and treated accordingly.

Tyrsis was the crossroads of the four lands, and through its walls and lands passed members of all the nations, giving its people an opportunity to see and understand that the differences in face and body that distinguished the races outwardly were negligible. It was the inner person the people had learned to judge. A giant Rock Troll would not be stared at and shunned because of his grotesque appearance by the people of Callahorn; Trools were common in that land. Gnomes, Elves, and Dwarfs of all types and species made regular passages through that country, and if they were friends, they were welcomed. Balinor smiled as he spoke of this new, growing phenomenon that had begun at last to spread to all the lands, and he felt proud that his people were among the first to turn from the old prejudices to look for common grounds of understanding and friendship. Durin and Dayel listened in silent agreement. The Elven people knew what it was like to be alone in a world of people who couldn't see beyond their own limits.

Balinor had finished, and the three comrades swung from the tall grass of the plainland onto a broad road-way. The road wound ahead into the darkness toward the low, squat plateau looming blackly against the horizon. They were close enough now to make out the lights of the sprawling city and the movement of people on the stone ramp. The entrance through the towering Outer Wall was sharply outlined by torch-light, the giant gates standing open on oiled hinges, guarded by a number of dark-garbed sentries. From the courtyard within shone the lights of the barracks, but there was an absence of men's laughter and joking that Balinor found peculiar. The voices that were audible were hushed, even muffled, as if no one wished to be heard. The tall borderman peered ahead watchfully, suddenly concerned that something was amiss, but he could detect nothing out of the ordinary, aside from the unusual silence. He dismissed the matter from his mind.

The Elven brothers followed wordlessly as the determined Balinor mounted the causeway leading to the darkened bluff. Several people passed them as they climbed, and those who looked carefully turned to stare in open shock at the Prince of Callahorn. Balinor failed to acknowledge these strange looks, intent upon the city ahead, but the brothers missed nothing and looked at each other in silent warning. Something was seriously wrong. Moments later, as the three reached the plateau, Balinor, too, stopped in sudden concern. He peered intently toward the gates of the city, then looked about him at the shadowed faces of the people passing, who scattered quickly and wordlessly into the night upon discovering his identity. For a moment the three stood rooted in silence, watching the few remaining passers-by disappear into the darkness, leaving them alone.

'What is it, Balinor?' Durin asked at last.

'I'm not certain,' the Prince replied anxiously. 'Look at the insignia of those guards at the gate. None of them bear the crest of the leopard – the standard of my Border Legion. Instead they wear the sign of a falcon, a mark I do not recognize. The people, too – did you notice their looks?'

The slim Elven faces nodded as one, the keen slanted eyes casting about in undisguised apprehension.

'No matter,' the borderman declared shortly. 'This is still my father's city, and these are my people. We'll get to the bottom of this when we reach the palace.'

Again he started toward the mammoth gates of the Outer Wall, the Elves a step or two behind him. The tall Prince made no effort to hide his face as he approached the four armed guards, and their reaction was the same as that of the astonished passers-by. They made no move to stop the Prince and no words passed between them, yet one hurriedly abandoned his post and disappeared quickly through the gates of the Inner Wall into the streets of the city beyond. Balinor and the Elves passed beneath the shadow of the giant gateway, which seemed to hang in the darkness above them like a monstrous stone arm. They moved past the open gates and the watchful guards into the courtyard beyond, where they could see the low, Spartanlike barracks that housed the famed Border Legion. There were few lights burning, and the barracks appeared to be nearly deserted. A few men scattered about the courtyard wore tunics bearing the insignia of the leopard, but they wore no armor and carried no weapons. One stared momentarily as the three paused in the center of the courtyard, then started in disbelief and cried out sharply to his fellow soldiers. A door burst open from one of the barracks and a grizzled veteran appeared, staring with the others at Balinor and the Elven brothers. He gave a short command, and the soldiers reluctantly turned back to whatever they had been doing, while he hastened over to the three newcomers.

'My Lord Balinor, you've come at last,' the soldier

exclaimed in greeting, his head bowing briefly as he came to attention before his commander.

'Captain Sheelon, it's good to see you.' Balinor clasped the veteran's gnarled hand in his own. 'What's going on in the city? Why do the guards wear the sign of a falcon and not that of our fighting leopard?'

'My Lord, the Border Legion has been ordered to disband! Only a handful of us still remain on duty; the rest are returned to their homes!'

They stared at the man as if he were insane. The Border Legion had been disbanded in the midst of the greatest invasion ever to threaten the Southland? Almost as one they recalled the words of Allanon telling them that the Border Legion was the only hope left to the people of the threatened lands, that the Border Legion must at least temporarily delay the awesome force assembled by the Warlock Lord. Now the army of Callahorn had been mysteriously scattered . . .

'By whose order . . .?' Balinor asked in slow fury.

'It was your brother,' the grizzled Sheelon declared quickly. 'He ordered his own guardsman to assume our duties and commanded the Legion to disband until further notice. The Lords Acton and Messaline went to the palace to beg the King to reconsider, but they did not return. There was nothing more any of us could do but obey . . .'

'Has everyone gone mad?' the infuriated border-man man demanded, clasping the soldier's tunic. 'What of my father, the King? Does he not still rule this land and command the Border Legion? What does he say of this fool's play?'

Sheelon looked away, groping for the words to the answer he was afraid to speak. Balinor jerked him around violently.

'I – I do not know, my Lord,' the man muttered, still trying to turn away. 'We heard the King was ill, and then there was nothing more. Your brother declared himself temporary ruler in the King's absence from the throne. That was three weeks ago.'

Balinor released the man in shocked silence and stared absently at the lights of the distant palace – the home he had come back to with such great hopes. He had left Callahorn because of an intolerable rift between his brother and himself, yet his going had only made matters worse. Now he must face the unpredictable Palance on terms not of his own choosing – face him and persuade him somehow of the folly of his action in disbanding the desperately needed Border Legion.

'We must go at once to the palace and speak with your brother.' The eager, impatient voice of Dayel cut into his thoughts. He looked at the youthful Elf for a moment, reminded suddenly of his own brother's young age. It was going to be so hard to reason with Palance.

'Yes, you're right, of course,' he agreed almost absently. 'We must go to him.'

'No, you mustn't go in there!' The sharp cry of Sheelon held them rooted in place. 'The others who went did not come out again. There are rumors that your brother has declared you a traitor – found you to be in league with the evil Allanon, the black wanderer who serves the dark powers. It has been said that you shall be imprisoned and put to death!'

'That is ridiculous!' exclaimed the tall borderman quickly. 'I am no traitor and even my brother knows this to be true. As for Allanon, he is the best friend and ally the Southland will ever find. I must go to Palance and speak with him. We may disagree, but he would not imprison his own brother. The power is not his!'

'Unless, perhaps, your father is dead, my friend,' Durin cautioned from one side. 'The time to be prudent is now, before we have entered the palace grounds. Hendel believes your brother to be under the influence of the mystic Stenmin, and if he is, you may be in greater danger than you realize.'

Balinor paused, then nodded his agreement. Quickly he explained to Sheelon the threat to Callahorn of an impending Northland invasion, emphasizing his belief that the Border Legion would be vital to the defense of their homeland. Then he gripped the aged soldier's shoulder tightly and bent close to him.

'You will wait four hours for my return or for my personal messenger. If I have not come out or sent word in that time, you will seek out the Lords Ginnisson and Fandwick; the Border Legion is to be reassembled immediately! Then go to the people and demand an open trial of our cause from my brother. He cannot refuse this. You will also send word west and east to the Elf and Dwarf-mations, informing them that we are thus held, both I and the cousins of Eventine. Can you remember all I have said to you?'

'Yes, my Lord.' The soldier nodded eagerly. 'It shall be done as you command. May fortune go with you, Prince of Callahorn.'

He turned and disappeared back into the barracks, while an impatient and angry Balinor moved toward the inner city. Once again, Durin whispered to his younger brother, urging him to remain outside the city walls until he knew what would happen to Balinor and himself, but Dayel stubbornly refused to be left behind. Durin knew it was pointless to argue the matter further, and at last conceded Dayel's right to go along. The slim Elf had not yet reached his twentieth year, and for him life was just beginning. All of the members of the little company that had come from Culhaven had felt a special kind of affection for Dayel, the protective love that close friends always feel for the youngest. His fresh candor and ready friendship were rare qualities in a time when most men lived lives hemmed in by suspicion and distrust. Durin was afraid for him, for he had the most to look ahead to and the fewest years behind. If the boy were harmed in any way, he realized that an irreplaceable part of himself would be lost. Durin watched his brother in silence as the lights of Tyrsis burned through the darkness ahead.

In moments, the three crossed the courtyard and passed through the gates of the Inner Wall to the streets of the city beyond. Once more the guards stared in open amazement, but again they did not move to stop the travelers from entering. Balinor seemed to grow in size as the three proceeded down the Tyrsian Way, the main city thoroughfare, his dark form wrapped ominously in the hunting cloak, the chain mail glinting from exposed fists and neck. He stood taller than before, no longer the weary traveler at his journey's end, but the Prince of Callahorn come home. The people knew him at once, at first stopping and staring like those at the outer gates, then gathering heart from his proud bearing and rushing after him, eager to welcome him home. The crowd swelled from a few dozen to several hundred as the favorite son of Callahorn strode boldly through the city, smiling to those who followed, but hastening to reach the palace. The shouts and cries of the people rose deafeningly, changing from scattered voices to a single rising chant calling the tall borderman's name. A few of the crowd managed to get next to the determined man, whispering ominous warnings. But the Prince would not listen to cautious voices any longer; shaking his head after each warning, he continued on.

The growing crowd passed through the heart of Tyrsis, milling under the giant archways and crosswalks that ran overhead, pushing through the narrow portions of the Tyrsian Way past tall, white-walled buildings and smaller single-family residences to the Bridge of Sendic which spanned the lower levels of the people's parks. At the other end stood the gates of the palace, darkened and closed. At the peak of the bridge's wide arch, the Prince of Callahorn turned abruptly to face the throng still faithfully following him and threw up his hands in a command to halt. They came to an obedient stop, their voices lowering into silence as the tall figure addressed them.

'My friends – my countrymen.' The proud voice rang out in the near darkness, its thundering echoes rolling back. 'I have missed this land and its brave citizens, but I have come home – and I will not leave again! There is no need for fear. This land shall stand eternal! If there be trouble within the monarchy, then it is for me to face it. You must go back now to your homes and wait for morning to show you in a better light that all is well. Please, go now to your homes and I shall go to mine!'

Without waiting to judge the crowd's reaction, Balinor wheeled about and proceeded on across the bridge toward the gates of the palace, the Elven brothers still close at his heels. The voice of the people rose again to call after them, but the crowd did not follow, though many might have wished to do so. Obedient to his command, they turned slowly about, some still shouting his name in defiance at the silent, darkened castle, though others mumbled grim prophecies of what awaited the tall borderman and his two friends within the walls of the imperial home. The three travelers quickly lost sight of the people as they started down the slope of the bridge's high arch in quick, determined strides. In minutes they reached the tall, metal-bound gates of the palace of the Buckhannahs. Balinor never paused, but reached for the huge iron ring fastened to the wood and brought it crashing down against the shuttered gate in thundering knocks. For a moment there was no other sound, as the men stood in the darkness without, listening with mixed feelings of anger and apprehension. Then a low voice from within called for identification. Balinor gave his name and a sharp command to those within to open the gates immediately. In an instant, the heavy bars were drawn back and the gates swung inward to admit the three. Balinor moved into the garden courtyard without a backward glance at the silent guards, his eyes on the magnificent columned building beyond. Its high windows were dark except for those on the ground floor in the left wing. Durin motioned Dayel ahead of him, taking the opportunity to peer into the shadows about them where he quickly discovered a dozen well-armed guards close at hand. All bore the insignia of the falcon.

The watchful Elf knew instantly that they were walking into a trap, just as he had silently anticipated when they had entered the city. His first inclination was to stop Balinor and warn him of what he had seen. But he instinctively knew that the borderman was far too seasoned a fighter not to know what he was getting into. Durin wished once more that his brother had stayed outside the palace walls, but it was too late now. The three crossed the garden walks to the doors of the palace. There were no guards and the doors opened without resistance to Balinor's hurried shove. The halls of the aged building glowed brightly in the torchlight, the flames catching the splendor of the colorful wall murals and paintings that decorated the Buckhannah family home. The wood trimming was old and rich, polished with care and partially covered by fine tapestries and metal plaques of family crests from generations of the famed rulers of the land. As the Elven brothers followed the tall Prince down these silent halls, they recalled darkly another time and place in the recent past – the ancient fortress of Paranor. There, too, a trap had awaited them amid the historic splendor of another age.

They turned left into another hallway, Balinor still in the lead by several strides, his big form filling the high corridor, the long hunting cloak billowing out behind him as he walked. For an instant, he reminded Durin of Allanon, huge, angered, dangerous when he moved catlike as the Prince of Callahorn did now. Durin glanced anxiously at Dayel, but the younger Elf did not seem to notice; his face

171

was flushed with excitement. Durin felt for the handle of his dagger, the cold metal reassuring to his hot palm. If they were to be trapped again, it would not be without a fight.

Then the giant borderman stopped suddenly before an open doorway. The Elven brothers hastened to his side, peering past his broad frame into the lighted room beyond. There was a man standing near the back of the elegantly furnished chamber – a big man, blond and bearded, his broad figure cloaked in a long purple robe with a falcon marking. He was several years younger than Balinor, but held his tall frame erect in the same manner, the hands clasped loosely behind his back. The Elves knew immediately that he was Palance Buckhannah. Balinor moved several steps into the chamber, saying nothing, his eyes riveted on his brother's face. The Elves followed the borderman, looking cautiously about. There were too many doors, too many heavy drapes that could be concealing armed guards. A moment later there was a movement in the hall behind them just out of sight. Dayel turned slightly to face the open doorway. Durin moved a little apart from the others, his long hunting knife drawn, his lean frame bent slightly in a half-crouch.

Balinor made no move, but stood silently before his brother, staring at the familiar face, amazed that the eyes were filled with a strange hatred. He had known it would be a trap, known that his brother would be prepared for them. Yet he had believed all along that they would at least be able to talk as brothers, converse with one another in a frank and reasonable manner despite their differences. But as he looked into those eyes and caught the undisguised glint of burning fury, he realized that his brother was beyond reason, perhaps beyond sanity.

'Where is my father . . .?'

Balinor's abrupt query was cut short by a sudden swishing sound as hidden cords released a large leather and rope net that had hung unnoticed above the intruders, dropping it instantly over all three. The attached weights brought all of them crashing to the floor in staggered dismay, their weapons useless against the toughened cords. Doors flew open from all sides and the heavy drapes whipped back as several dozen armed guards rushed over to subdue the struggling captives. There was never any chance to escape the carefully prepared trap, never even a momentary opportunity to fight back. The captives were relieved of their weapons, their hands bound unceremoniously behind their backs and their eyes blindfolded. They were lifted roughly to their feet and firmly held in place by a dozen unseen hands. There was momentary silence as someone approached and stood before them.

'You were a fool to come back, Balinor,' a chilling voice sounded out of the blackness. 'You knew what would happen to you if I found you again. You are thrice over a traitor and a coward for what you have done – to the people, to my father, and now even to me. What have you done with Shirl? What have you done with her? You will die for this, Balinor, I swear it! Take them below!'

The hands spun them about, shoving and dragging them down the hallway, through one door, down a long flight of stairs to a landing and another hall that wound about in a maze of twists and turns. Their feet thudded heavily on dank stones in a black, unbroken silence. Suddenly they were going down yet another set of stairs and into another passageway. They could smell the stale, chill air and feel the dampness ooze from the stone walls and floor. A set of heavy bolts was drawn slowly back with a screech of aged iron against iron, and the door they held in place ponderously opened. The hands turned them sharply, releasing them without warning as they fell dazed and battered to the stone floor, still bound and blindfolded. The door closed and the bolts slid heavily into place. The three companions listened wordlessly. They heard the sound of footsteps retreating rapidly into the distance until they had faded away altogether. They heard the sounds of clanging metal as doors were barred and shuttered, each farther away than the last, until finally there was only the sound of their own breathing in the deep silence of their prison. Balinor had come home.

CHAPTER

10

It was nearing midnight by the time Allanon had finished disguising the reluctant Flick to his satisfaction. Using a strange lotion produced from a pouch he carried at his waist, the Druid rubbed the skin of the Valeman's face and hands until it was a dark yellow. A piece of soft coal altered the lines in the face and the appearance of the eyes. It was a makeshift job at best, but in the dark he could pass for a large, heavyset Gnome, if not closely examined. It would have been a perilous undertaking even for a seasoned hunter, and for an untrained man to attempt to pass himself off as a Gnome appeared to be suicide. But there was no alternative left. Someone had to get into that giant encampment and attempt to discover what had happened to Eventine, Shea, and the elusive Sword. It was out of the question for Allanon to go down there; he would have been recognized in an instant, even in the best disguise. So the task fell to the frightened Flick, disguised as a Gnome, under cover of darkness, to work his way down the slopes, past the watching guards, into the camp occupied by thousands of Gnomes and Trolls, and there find out if his brother or the missing Elven King were prisoners, in addition to trying to learn something of the whereabouts of the Sword. To complicate matters, the Valeman had to get clear of the enemy camp before daybreak. If he failed to do this, someone would most certainly see through his disguise in the daylight and he would be caught.

Allanon asked Flick to remove his hunting cloak and worked on the material for several minutes, altering the cut slightly and lengthening the hood covering to conceal its wearer better. When he was done, Flick covered himself and found that with the cloak pulled closely about his body, nothing was visible aside from his hands and a shadowed portion of his face. If he stayed away from any true Gnomes and kept moving until dawn, there was an outside chance that he might learn something important and still escape to tell Allanon. He checked to be certain the short hunting dagger was securely fastened to his waist. It was a poor substitute for a weapon, should he have need of one once he was within the encampment, but it gave him a little reassurance that he was not totally without protection. He stood up slowly, his short, heavyset frame wrapped in the cloak as Allanon looked him over carefully and then nodded.

The weather had become threatening during the past hour, the sky a solid bank of rolling, blackened clouds that completely blotted out the moon and stars, leaving the earth in almost complete darkness. The only visible light in any direction came from the blazing fires of the encamped enemy, the flames rushing higher with the sudden appearance of a strong north wind that howled fiercely through the Dragon's Teeth to sweep in rising gusts onto the unprotected plainlands below. A storm was on the way, and it would very likely reach them before morning. The silent Druid was hopeful that the winds and darkness would offer the disguised Valeman a little added cover from the eyes of the sleeping army.

In brief, clipped sentences, the giant mystic offered Flick a few parting words of caution. He explained the manner in which the camp would be arranged, noting the pattern in which guards would be posted about the perimeter of the main army. He told him to look for the standards of the Gnome chieftains and the Maturens, the Troll leaders, which would undoubtedly lie somewhere near the center of the fires. At all costs, he was to avoid speaking to anyone, for the tone of his voice would instantly betray him as a Southlander. Flick listened attentively, his heart pounding wildly as he waited to go, his own mind already made up that he had no chance of escaping detection; but his loyalty to his brother was too great to permit the interference of common sense when Shea's safety was threatened. Allanon closed his brief explanation by promising to see that the youth got safely past the first guard line that had been posted at the base of these slopes. He signaled for complete silence, then motioned for the other to follow.

They moved down out of the rocky shelter of the high boulders, winding their way through the darkness toward the open plain. It was so black that Flick could see almost nothing and had to be led by the hand in order to stay with the surefooted Druid. It seemed to take an interminable length of time for the two to reach an exit point from the twisting maze of boulders, but at last they were able to see once more the fires of the enemy camp burning in the darkness ahead. Flick was bruised and battered from his climb down out of the mountain heights, his limbs aching from the strain, his cloak torn in several places. The darkness of the plain seemed to stand like an unbroken wall between the fires and themselves, and Flick could neither see nor hear the guard lines he knew were there. Allanon said nothing, but crouched back in the shelter of the rocks, his head cocked slightly as he listened. The two remained motionless for long minutes, then suddenly Allanon rose, motioning Flick to remain where he was, and silently disappeared in the night.

When he was gone, the little Valeman looked about anxiously, alone and frightened because he had no idea what was happening. Leaning his heated face against the cool surface of the rock, he went over in his mind what he would do once he reached the encampment. He didn't have much of a plan to rely on. He would avoid speaking with anyone, and if possible, avoid passing close to anyone. He would stay clear of the illuminating firelight which might betray his poor disguise. The prisoners, if in the camp at all, would be held in a guarded tent near the center of the fires, so his first objective would be to find that tent. Once he found it, he would try to get a look inside to see who was there. Then, assuming he got that far, which seemed highly unlikely, he would make his way back to the slopes, where Allanon would be waiting and they would decide their next move.

Flick shook his head in frustration. He knew he would never be able to get away with this disguise – he was neither talented nor clever enough to fool anyone. But ever since losing Shea over the side of the Dragon's Crease days earlier, his attitude had completely altered and the old pessimism and hard-nosed practicality had been replaced by a strange sense of futile desperation. His familiar world had altered so drastically in the past few weeks that he no longer seemed capable of identifying with his old values and sensible practices. Time had become almost meaningless in the punishing, endless days of running and hiding, of fighting creatures that belonged to another world. The years spent living and growing in the peace and solitude of Shady Vale were distant, forgotten days of an early youth. The only constant forces in his upended life of the past weeks had been his companions, particularly his brother. Now they, too, had been scattered one by one until at last Flick stood alone, on the verge of exhaustion and mental collapse, his world a mad, impossible puzzle of nightmares and spirits that chased and haunted him to the brink of despair.

The hulking presence of Allanon had given him little

comfort. The giant Druid had remained from their first meeting both an impenetrable wall of secrecy and a mystical force with powers that defied explanation. Despite the growing camaraderie of the company on the journey to Paranor and beyond, the Druid had remained aloof and secretive. Even what he had told them about his own origin and purposes did little to lighten the dark veil of mystery in which he had wrapped himself.

When the company had been together, the mystic's domination of them had not seemed so overpowering, even though he had remained the undisputed force behind their hazardous search for the Sword of Shannara. But now, with the others gone, leaving the frightened Valeman alone with this unpredictable giant, Flick found himself unable to escape that terrible awesomeness that formed the essence of this strange man. He thought back again on the mysterious tale of the history of the fabled Sword, and again he remembered Allanon's refusal to tell the members of the little company the whole story behind its power. They had risked everything for that elusive talisman, and still no one but Allanon knew how the weapon could be used to defeat the Warlock Lord. Why was it that Allanon knew so much about it?

A sudden noise in the darkness behind him brought the terrified Valeman about in a flash, the short hunting knife drawn and extended in self-defense. There was a sharp whisper and the huge form of Allanon moved silently to Flick's side. A powerful hand gripped his shoulder, guiding him back into the shelter of the rock-covered slope, where the two crouched cautiously in the blackness. Allanon studied the Valeman's face for an instant as if judging his courage, reading his mind to see the nature of his thoughts. Flick could just barely force himself to meet the penetrating gaze, his heart pounding in mingled fear and excitement.

'The guards are disposed of – the way is clear.' The deep

179

voice seemed to rise up out of the depths of the earth. 'Go now, my young friend, and keep your courage and your good sense close at hand.'

Flick nodded shortly and rose, his cloak-shrouded form gliding quickly and stealthily out of the cover of the boulders onto the blackness of the empty plains. His mind ceased to reason, ceased to wonder, as his body took command and his instincts probed the darkness for hidden danger. He moved swiftly toward the distant firelight, running in a half-crouch, pausing occasionally to check his position and listen for the sounds of human movement. The night was an impenetrable shroud all about him, the sky still heavily overcast and wrapped in a huge cloud blanket that shut out even the dim whiteness of the moon and stars. The only light came from the campfires ahead. The plainland was smooth and open, its surface a grassy blanket that muffled the Valeman's footfalls as he raced silently forward. There were few bushes to break the pattern, and it was left to one or two thin, twisted trees to fill the vast emptiness. There was no sign of life anywhere in the darkness and the only sounds were the muffled howl of the rising wind and his own heavy breathing. The campfires that had formerly seemed a low haze of orange light from the base of the mountains spread apart into individual fires as the Valeman drew closer, some burning brightly, their flames well fed on new wood, while others had dimmed and nearly died into coals as the men who tended them slept undisturbed. Flick was close enough now to hear the faint sound of voices in the sleeping camp, but they were not distinct enough to enable him to make out the words.

Almost half an hour passed before Flick reached the outer perimeter of the enemy fires. He paused in a crouch just beyond the light to study the lay of the camp ahead. The cool night wind blowing out of the north fanned the crackling flames of the large wood fires, sending thin clouds of smoke swirling across the open plains toward the

Valeman. There was a second ring of sentries encircling the encampment, but it was only a secondary guard line loosely set at wide intervals. The Northlanders felt there was little need for caution this close to the campsite. The sentries were primarily Gnome hunters, although Flick could distinguish the larger bulks of Troll men scattered about as well.

He paused momentarily to study the strange, unfamiliar features of the Trolls. They were of different sizes, all thick-limbed and covered with a dark, wood-like skin that appeared rough and highly protective. The sentries and the few members of the army that were not asleep, but standing idly about or crouched near the low-burning fires for warmth, had wrapped themselves in heavy cloaks that masked most of their bodies and faces. Flick nodded to himself in satisfaction. It would be easier for him to slip into the camp undetected if everyone remained wrapped in their cloaks, and judging from the increasing coolness of the wind, the temperature would continue to drop until sunrise. It was difficult to see much beyond the outer fires, due to the clouded darkness and the smoke given off by the quick-burning wood.

Somehow the camp seemed smaller from this viewpoint than it had from the heights of the Dragon's Teeth. Flick could not get the same sense of depth from his present position, but he did not try to fool himself. Despite what it appeared to be from where he crouched, he knew that it stretched for over a mile in all directions. Once past the inner sentry line, he would have to pick his way through thousands of sleeping Gnomes and Trolls, past hundreds of fires bright enough to reveal his identity, and all the way avoid contact with the enemy soldiers who were still awake. The first miscalculation the Valeman made would give him away. Even if he managed to avoid discovery, he still had to locate the prisoners and the Sword. He shook his head in doubt and moved forward slowly.

The natural curiosity of the Valeman prompted him to linger near the fringes of the firelight to study further the Gnomes and Trolls still awake, but he resisted the impulse, reminding himself that he didn't have much time as it was. Though he had lived all his life on the same earth with these two foreign races, they were like species from another world to the little Southlander. During his journey to Paranor, he had fought the cunning, savage Gnomes several times, once hand to hand in the labyrinth passages of the Druids' Keep. But he still knew little about them; they were simply an enemy who had tried to kill him. He had learned nothing of the giant Trolls, a habitually reclusive people dwelling principally in the northern mountains and their hidden valleys. In any event, Flick knew that the army was under the leadership of the Warlock Lord, and there was no question as to what *his* goals were!

He waited until the wind carried the smoke from the burning fires between the closest sentry and himself in a series of billowing gusts, then rose and strolled in a casual manner toward the encampment. He had carefully selected an entry point where the soldiers were all sleeping. The smoke and the night masked his bulky form as he moved out of the shadows and into the circle of fires nearest to him. A moment later he stood in the midst of the soundly sleeping forms. The sentry continued to stare blankly into the darkness behind him, unaware of the hurried passage.

Flick wrapped the cloak and head covering closely about his body, making certain that only his hands were immediately visible to anyone passing by. His face was a dim shadow beneath the hood. He glanced about quickly, but there was no movement by anyone close at hand; he had made it this far unnoticed. He breathed deeply of the cool night air to steady himself, then tried to gauge his position in relation to the center of the encampment. He chose a direction which he believed would take him directly toward the hub of the burning fires, glanced about once more to reassure himself, then moved forward with steady, measured steps. Now there could be no turning back.

What he saw, what he heard, what he experienced deep within his mind that night left an indelible print in his memory that would stay with him forever. It was like a strange, somehow elusive nightmare of sights and sounds, creatures and shapes from another time and place – things that never were in and could never belong to his own world, and yet had been cast onto it like so much driftwood from an endless sea. Perhaps it was the night and the wafting smoke from the hundreds of dying fires that clouded his normal senses and created this dreamlike experience. Perhaps, too, it was the aftereffect of a tired, frightened mind that had never conceived of the existence of such creatures, nor imagined their number could be so vast.

The night passed in slow minutes and endless hours as the little Valeman wound his way through the giant encampment, shielding his face from the light of the fires as he moved steadily forward, his eyes searching, studying and always looking further. Cautiously, he picked his tortured way over thousands of sleeping bodies huddled close to the flames, often blocking his progress entirely, each another chance that he might be discovered and killed. There were times when he was certain that he had been discovered, times when his hand moved swiftly, silently to the small hunting knife, his heart dying within him as he prepared to fight for his freedom at the cost of his life. Again and again, men came toward him as if they knew he was an impostor, as if they would stop him and expose him to everyone. But each time they passed by without pausing, without speaking, and Flick would be left alone once again, a forgotten figure in a gathering of thousands.

Several times he passed close to groups of men talking and joking in low tones as they huddled around the fires, rubbing their hands and drawing from the crackling flames what little heat there was to protect them against the growing cold of the night. Twice, perhaps three times, they nodded or waved as he pushed past them, his face lowered, the cloak held close about his body, and he would make some feeble gesture in acknowledgment. Time and again he was afraid he had made a wrong move, failed to speak when he should, walked where he was not permitted – but each time the terrible moment of doubt vanished as he hurried on, and he found himself alone once more.

He wandered through the immense camp for hours without finding any clue to the whereabouts of Shea, Eventine, or the Sword of Shannara. As morning drew near, he began to despair of finding anything. He had passed countless fires, burning low and dying with the close of night, gazed on a sea of sleeping bodies, some with faces turned skyward, some with blankets all around them, all unknown. There had been tents everywhere, marked by the standards of the enemy leaders, both Gnome and Troll, but there had been no guards stationed before them to distinguish them in importance. A few he had checked closely on a chance that he might stumble onto something, but he had found nothing.

He listened to snatches of conversation between the Gnomes and Trolls who were not sleeping, trying to remain inconspicuous and at the same time come close enough to hear what was being said. But the Troll tongue was completely foreign, and what little he understood of the garbled Gnome speech consisted of useless information. It was as if no one knew anything of the two missing men and the Sword – as if they had never been brought to this camp at all. Flick began to wonder if Allanon had been completely mistaken about the trail signs they had followed these past few days.

He glanced apprehensively at the clouded night sky. He could not be certain of the time, but he knew there could be no more than several hours of darkness remaining. For a moment he panicked, abruptly realizing that he might not even have enough time to find his way back to where Allanon was concealed. But shaking off his fear, he quickly reasoned that in the confusion of breaking camp at dawn he would be able to slip quickly back through the sleepy hunters and make the short dash for the slopes of the Dragon's Teeth before the sun found him.

There was a sudden movement in the darkness off to his right, and into the firelight trudged four massive Troll warriors, all fully armed, muttering in low tones among themselves as they moved past the startled Valeman. On impulse more than reason, Flick fell in several yards behind them, curious as to where they might be going dressed in full battle array while it was still night. They were moving at right angles to the course the disguised Flick had chosen to follow into the encampment, and he stayed just behind them in the shadows as they trudged steadily through the sleeping army. Several times they passed darkened tents that Flick believed might be their destination, but they continued on without pausing.

The little Valeman noticed that the style of the encampment was changing rapidly in this particular area. There were more tents than before, some with high, lighted canopies that silhouetted men moving within. There were fewer common soldiers sleeping on the chill earth, but more sentries patrolling between the well-fed fires that lighted the open spaces between tents. Flick found it harder to remain hidden in this new light; to avoid questions and to protect against an increased risk of discovery, he moved right up behind the marching Trolls as if he were one of them. They passed numerous sentries that offered short greetings and watched as they passed, but no one attempted to question the heavily cloaked Gnome who scampered along at the rear of the small procession.

Then abruptly the Trolls turned left and automatically Flick turned with them – only to find himself almost on top of a long, low tent guarded by more armed Trolls. There was no time to turn back or avoid being seen, so when the procession came to a halt before the tent, the fearful Valeman kept right on walking, moving past them as if he were oblivious to what was taking place. The guards evidently failed to think there was anything out of the ordinary, all glancing briefly his way as he shuffled past, the cloak pulled closely about him, and in an instant he was beyond them, alone in the blackness of the shadows.

He halted sharply, sweat running down his body beneath the heavy clothing, his breathing short and labored. There had only been a second to glance through the open front of the lighted tent, between the towering Troll sentries holding the long, iron pikes – only a second to see the crouched, black-winged monster that stood within, surrounded by the lesser forms of both Trolls and Gnomes. But there was no mistaking one of those deadly creatures that had hunted them across the four lands. There was no mistaking the chill feeling of terror that ran through the Valeman's body as he stood breathlessly in the shadows to still his pounding heart.

Something vitally important was taking place inside that heavily guarded tent. Perhaps the missing men and the Sword were there, held by the servants of the Warlock Lord. It was a chilling thought, and Flick knew that he had to get a look inside. His time was up, his luck run out. The guards alone were deterrent enough to anyone trying to pass through the open flaps, and the added presence of the Skull Bearer made the idea suicidal. Flick sat back on his heels in the darkness between the tents and shook his head hopelessly. The enormity of the task utterly discouraged any hope for success, yet what other course lay open? If he returned to Allanon now, they would know nothing more than they had known previously and his arduous night of creeping about the enemy encampment would have been for nothing.

He gazed expectantly at the night sky, as if it might hold some clue to the answer to his problem. The cloud bank remained solidly in position overhead, hanging ominously between the light of the moon and stars and the blackness of the sleeping earth. The night was almost over. Flick rose and pulled the cloak closely about his chilled body once again. Fate may have decided that he should come all these torturous miles only to be killed in a foolish gamble, but Shea depended on him – perhaps Allanon and the others as well. He had to know what was in that tent. Slowly, cautiously, he began to inch his way forward.

The dawn came quickly, a sullen gray lightening of the eastern sky, heavy with mist and silence. The weather had not improved below the Streleheim, south of the persistent wall of darkness that marked the advance of the Warlock Lord. Huge thunder-clouds remained locked overhead like an ominous shroud covering its earthen corpse. Near the base of the western Dragon's Teeth, the enemy sentries had abandoned their night watch to return to the awakening encampment of the Northland army. Allanon sat quietly in the shelter of the boulder-strewn slope, the long, black cloak that was wrapped loosely around his lean, reedlike body offering little protection against either the chill dawn air or the faint drizzle that was rapidly turning into a heavy downpour. He had been there all night, his eyes watching, searching for some sign of Flick, his hopes slowly fading as the sky lightened in the east and the enemy came to life. Still he waited, hoping against the odds that the little Valeman had somehow managed to conceal his identity, somehow managed to slip through the camp undetected and find his missing brother, the Elven King, and the Sword, then somehow managed to work his way clear of the pickets before daylight to reach freedom.

The encampment was breaking up, the tents disassembled and packed as the huge army fell into columns that covered the vast plain like giant black squares. Finally the fighting machine of the Warlock Lord began to march southward in the direction of Kern, and the giant Druid came down out of the rocks where he could be seen by the missing Valeman if he were anywhere close at hand. There was no movement, no sound but the wind blowing softly across the grasslands, and the tall dark figure stood silently. Only the eyes betrayed the keen bitterness he felt.

At last, the Druid turned southward, choosing a course parallel to that of the army marching ahead. Giant strides quickly ate up the distance between them as the rain began to fall in heavy sheets and the vast emptiness of the plains was left behind.

Menion Leah reached the winding Mermidon River immediately north of the island city of Kern only minutes before dawn. Allanon had not been wrong when he had warned the Prince that he would have a difficult time slipping through the enemy lines undetected. The sentry outposts extended beyond the perimeter of the sprawling plain encampment, running west above the Mermidon from the southern edge of the Dragon's Teeth. Everything north of that line belonged to the Warlock Lord. Enemy patrols roamed unchallenged along the southern boundaries of the towering Dragon's Teeth, guarding the few passages that cut through these formidable peaks. Balinor, Hendel, and the Elven brothers had managed to break the security of one of these enemy patrols in the high Kennon Pass. Menion did not have the protective shelter of the mountains in which to conceal himself from the Northlanders. Once he had left Allanon and Flick, he was forced to proceed directly across the flat, open grasslands that stretched south to the Mermidon. But the highlander had two things in his favor. The night remained clouded and completely, impenetrably black, making it nearly impossible to see more than several yards ahead. More important than this, Menion was a tracker and hunter without equal in the Southland. He could move through this shroudlike blackness with speed and stealth, undetected by any but the most sensitive ears.

So it happened that he moved silently from the side of his two companions, still angered that Allanon had forced him to give up the search for Shea in order that he might warn Balinor and the people of Callahorn of the impending invasion. He felt strangely uneasy about leaving Flick alone with the mysterious and unpredictable Druid. He had never completely trusted the giant mystic, knowing that the man was keeping the truth about the Sword of Shannara hidden from them, knowing that there was more to Allanon than he had chosen to tell them. They had done everything the Druid had commanded of them in blind faith, trusting him implicitly each time a crisis had arisen. Each time he had been right – but still they had failed to gain possession of the Sword, and they had lost Shea. Now on top of everything else, it appeared the Northland army would successfully invade the Southland. Only the border kingdom of Callahorn stood ready to resist the assault. Having seen the awesome size of the invader, Menion did not see how even the legendary Border Legion could hope to withstand such a mighty force. His own common sense told him that the only hope was to stall the advancing enemy long enough to unite the Elven and Dwarf armies with the Border Legion and then strike back. He felt certain the missing Sword was lost to them, and that even when they relocated Shea, there would be no further opportunity to search for the strange weapon.

He uttered a low oath as his exposed knee jammed painfully against the sharp edge of a jutting boulder, and he turned his attention to the matter at hand, all further speculation about the future put aside for the time being. Like a lean, black lizard, he skimmed noiselessly down the low slopes of the Dragon's Teeth, winding his torturous way through the maze of knife-edged boulders and rocks that covered the mountainside, the sword of Leah and the long ash bow strapped securely to his back. He reached the base of the slope without encountering anyone, and he peered into the darkness. There was no sign of life. He moved cautiously onto the grass-covered plain-lands, inching forward a few yards at a time, pausing periodically to listen. He knew the sentry lines had to be posted close to this point to be effective, but it was impossible to see anyone.

At last he rose to his feet, as silent as the shadows all about him; hearing nothing, he began to walk slowly southward through the wall of darkness, his hunting knife held loosely in one hand. He walked for long minutes without incident and had just begun to relax in the belief that he had somehow slipped through the enemy lines without either of them knowing it, when he heard a small noise. He froze in midstride, trying to locate the source, and then it came again, a low cough from someone in the darkness directly in front of him. A sentry had given himself away just in time to save the highlander from stumbling into him. One cry would have brought others in an instant.

Menion dropped into a crouch on his hands and knees, the dagger clutched tightly. He began to creep forward toward the source of the cough, his movement soundless. At last his eyes were able to discern the dim outline of someone standing silently before him. From his small size, the sentry was clearly a Gnome. Menion waited a few minutes longer to be certain that the Gnome had his back turned to him, then he crept still closer until he was within several feet. In one fluid motion he rose to tower over the unsuspecting sentry, one steellike arm gripping the fellow's throat, cutting off the cry of warning before it could escape. The butt end of the knife came down sharply on

the exposed head, just back of the ear, and the unconscious Gnome crumpled to the earth. The highlander did
not pause, but slipped ahead into the darkness, knowing
there would be others close at hand, and eager to move
beyond their range of hearing. He held the dagger ready,
anticipating that there might be still another sentry line.
The chill wind blew steadily and the long minutes of the
night crawled on.

Finally he was at the Mermidon, just above the island
city of Kern, its lights faint in the distant south. He paused
at the top of a small rise which dropped off gradually and
sloped downward to form the north bank of the swift river.
He remained in a half-crouch, his long hunting cloak
wrapped about his lean frame to protect himself from the
growing chill of the dawn wind. He was surprised and
relieved that he had reached the river without running into
still other enemy pickets. He suspected that his earlier
assumption had been correct, and that he had passed
through at least one other sentry line without realizing it.

Gazing carefully around, the Prince of Leah assured
himself that no one else was about, then rose and stretched
wearily. He knew he had to cross the Mermidon farther
downriver if he wished to avoid a chilling swim in the icy
waters. Once he reached a point directly across from the
island, he was certain he would find a boat or ferry service to the city. Hitching his weapons higher on his back
and smiling grimly against the cold, he began to walk
southward along the river rise.

He had not gone very far, perhaps no more than a thousand yards, when the rushing of the dawn wind faded for
an instant, and in the sudden stillness he heard an unfamiliar murmur from somewhere ahead. Instantly he
dropped to the ground, his dark form flat against the small
rise. The wind rushed back into his straining ears as he listened in the blackness. The gusting breeze died a second
time and again he heard the low murmur, but this time he

was certain of its origin. It was the muffled sound of human voices carried out of the darkness ahead near the bank of the river. The highlander crawled hurriedly back over the rise to where the terrain again shielded him from the faint lights of the distant city. Then he rose and moved forward in a half crouch, running parallel to the river, his passing noiseless and swift. The voices grew louder and more distinct and at last seemed to come from directly behind the grassy rise. He listened a minute longer, but found it impossible to decipher what was being said. Cautiously, he crawled on his stomach to the top of the rise where he was able to make out a group of dark figures huddled next to the Mermidon.

The first thing that caught his eye was the boat pulled up onto the riverbank and tied to a low bush. There was his transportation if he could get to it, but he discarded the idea almost instantly. Standing in a tight circle next to the moored boat were four very large, armed Trolls, their huge black bulks unmistakable even in this poor light. They were speaking with a fifth figure, smaller and slighter in build, his robes clearly marking him as a Southlander.

Menion studied them a moment with great care, trying to make out their faces, but the dim light gave him only brief glimpses of the man and he didn't appear to be anyone Menion had ever encountered previously. A small, dark beard covered the thin, shallow face of the stranger, and he had a peculiar habit of stroking the little beard in short, nervous pats while he talked.

Then the Prince of Leah saw something else. To one side of the circle of men was a large bundle covered with a heavy cloak and securely tied. Menion studied it dubiously, unable to tell what it was in the darkness. Then to his astonishment, the bundle moved slightly – enough to convince the highlander that there was something alive beneath the heavy coverings. Desperately he tried to think of a way he might move closer to the small party, but already he was too late. The four Trolls and the stranger were parting company. One of the Trolls moved over to the mysterious bundle and, in one effortless heave, threw it over his broad, bulky shoulder. The stranger was returning to the boat, loosening the fastenings and climbing in, the oars lowered to the choppy waters. There were several parting words exchanged, and Menion caught snatches of the brief conversation, including something about having the situation well in hand. The final comment as the boat moved out into the swift waters was a warning from the stranger to wait for further word from him on the Prince.

Menion inched back a bit on the damp grass of the little rise, watching the man and the small boat disappear into the misty darkness of the Mermidon. Dawn was breaking at last, but it came in the form of a dim, hazy grayness that hampered visibility almost as effectively as the night. The sky was still overcast by low-hanging cumulous clouds that threatened to drop to the earth itself should they swell further. A heavy rain would fall before much longer and already the air was coated with a damp, penetrating mist that soaked the highlander's clothing and chilled the exposed skin. The huge Northland army would be on the march toward the island city of Kern within the hour, probably reaching it by midday. There was little time remaining for him to warn its citizens of the impending assault – an onslaught of men and weapons against which the city could not hope to defend itself for long. The people had to be evacuated immediately and taken to Tyrsis or farther south for protection. Balinor had to be warned that time had run out, that the Border Legion must assemble and fight a delaying action until reinforced by the Dwarf and Elven armies.

The Prince of Leah knew there was no time to ponder further the mysterious meeting he had just accidentally witnessed, but he lingered a moment longer as the four

Trolls turned from the riverbank, carrying the struggling bundle, and moved toward the rise to his right. Menion was certain that someone had been taken prisoner by the stranger in the boat and turned over to these soldiers of the Northland army. This night meeting had been pre-arranged by both parties and the exchange made for reasons known only to them. If they had gone to all that trouble, the prisoner must be someone very important to them – and therefore important to the Warlock Lord.

Menion watched the Trolls move away from him into the heavy morning mist, still undecided as to whether he should intervene. Allanon had given him a task to complete – a vital task that might save thousands of lives. There was no time for wild forays in enemy country just to satisfy personal curiosity, even if it meant saving . . . Shea! Suppose it was Shea they had taken prisoner? The thought flashed through the impetuous mind, and instantly the decision had been made. Shea was the key to everything – if there was any chance that he was the captive wrapped in that bundle, Menion had to try to rescue him.

He leaped to his feet and began running swiftly northward, back in the direction from which he had just come, trying to stay on a course parallel to that taken by the Trolls. In the heavy mist, it was difficult to keep his sense of direction, but Menion had no time to be concerned with that. It was going to be extremely difficult to take that prisoner away from four armed Trolls, especially when any one of them was easily a match physically for the slight highlander. There was the added danger that they might at any point pass back through the sentry lines of the Northland outposts. If he failed to stop them before then, he was finished. Any chance of rescue depended on keeping open an escape route to the Mermidon. Menion felt the first rains of the coming storm strike his face as he ran, and the thunder rumbled ominously overhead as the wind began to grow in force. Desperately he searched through the rolling clouds of mist and fog for some sign of his quarry, but there was nothing to be seen. Certain that he had been too slow and had missed them, he raced at breakneck speed across the grasslands, charging like a wild black shadow through the mist, dodging the small trees and clumps of brush, his eyes searching the empty flatlands. The rain beat against his face and ran into his eyes, blinding him, forcing him to slow down momentarily to wipe away the warm haze of mingled rain and perspiration. He shook his head in anger. They had to be somewhere close! He couldn't have lost them!

Abruptly the four Trolls appeared out of the fog behind him and off to the left. Menion had misjudged and completely overtaken and passed them. He dropped into a crouch behind a small clump of bushes and watched a moment as the four moved closer. If they stayed on their present course, they would pass almost next to a large clump of scrub brush farther ahead – still beyond their vision, but within Menion's. The highlander bounded from cover and raced back into the mist until he could no longer see the Trolls. If they had seen him make that quick dash into the fog, he was through. They would be expecting him when they reached the scrub brush. But if not, he would spring his ambush there and make a break for the river. He cut back across the plains to his left until he reached the seclusion of the brush where, panting heavily, he dropped to all fours and peered cautiously through the branches.

For a moment there was nothing but the fog and the rain, and then four bulky figures appeared out of the gray mist, moving steadily toward his place of concealment. He threw off the cumbersome hunting cloak, already soaked through by the morning rains. He would need speed to elude the massive Trolls once he managed to get the prisoner away from them and the cloak would only slow him down. He removed the heavy hunting boots as well. At his side he placed the sword of Leah, its bright blade drawn clear of the leather sheath. Hurriedly, he fitted the loosened string to the great ash bow and withdrew two long, black arrows from their casing. The Trolls were closing quickly on his cover now, their dark forms visible through the leafy branches of the brush. They walked in pairs, one of the foremost carrying the limp form of the bound prisoner. They came carelessly toward the hidden man, obviously at ease in territory they believed entirely under the control of their own forces. Menion rose slowly to one knee, a black arrow fitted to the long bow, and waited silently.

The unsuspecting Trolls were almost on top of the scrub brush when the first arrow flew from out of nowhere with a sharp hum, striking the fleshy calf muscle of the bulky Northlander carrying the prisoner. In a roar of mingled rage and pain, the Troll dropped his burden and fell, clutching the injured leg with both hands. In that instant of shock and confusion, Menion fired the second arrow, scoring a solid hit to the exposed shoulder of the second member of the front pair, spinning the massive form entirely about so that he stumbled wildly into the two behind him.

Without pausing, the agile highlander sprang free of the scrub brush and rushed the amazed Trolls, yelling and swinging the sword of Leah. The Trolls had dropped back a step or two from the momentarily forgotten prisoner, and the quick attacker swept the limp form up onto one shoulder with his free arm before the astonished Northlanders could act. In another instant, he had swept past them, his sword cutting into the forearm of the nearest Troll, who made a vain effort to stop the fleet form. The path to the Mermidon lay open!

Two Trolls, one uninjured and the other slightly wounded, gave immediate chase, lumbering heavily across the rain-covered grasslands in determined silence. Their cumbersome armor and large frames slowed them down considerably, but they moved faster than Menion had expected, and they were refreshed and strong while he was already tiring. Even without the hunting cloak and boots, the lean highlander could not run very fast while carrying the still-bound prisoner. The rain had begun to fall in increasingly heavier sheets, windswept and stinging against his skin as he forced his aching body to run faster still. In leaps and bounds he streaked across the grasslands, twisting past small trees, dodging scrub brush and water-soaked potholes. Even in bare feet, his footing on the wet, slippery grass was unsure. Several times he stumbled and fell to his knees, only to bound immediately to his feet to run again.

There were hidden rocks and thorn-tipped plants scattered through the soft grasses, and soon his feet were cut and bleeding freely. But he didn't feel the pain and he raced onward. The vast plains alone were witness to the strange race between the huge, lumbering hunters and the shadowlike quarry as they labored southward through the driving rains and the chilling wind. They ran without hearing, without seeing, without feeling through the panoramic emptiness, and there was nothing to break the terrible silence but the rush of the gusting wind in the runners' ears. It became a lonely, fearful ordeal of survival – a trial of spirit and stamina that demanded from the youthful Prince of Leah his final, complete reserve of strength.

Time ceased to exist for the fleeing highlander as he forced his legs to move when the muscles had long since passed the normal end of endurance – and still there was no river. He no longer looked back to see if the Trolls were closing. He could sense their presence, hear their labored breathing in his mind; they must be closing the distance rapidly. He had to run faster! He had to reach the river and free Shea . . .

In his near exhaustion, he unconsciously referred to the person wrapped in the bundle as his friend. He had known immediately upon grasping the mysterious prisoner that he was small and slight of build. There was no reason to believe it might not be the missing Valeman. The bundled captive was awake and moving awkwardly as the highlander ran, speaking in muffled phrases to which Menion replied in short, gasping assurances that they were close to safety.

The rain suddenly intensified in force until it was impossible to see more than a few feet in any direction, and the sodden plains turned quickly into a grass-tipped marsh. Then Menion fell over a water-covered root and tumbled headlong into the muddied grass, his precious burden falling in a struggling heap beside him. Bruised and exhausted, the highlander raised himself to his hands and knees, the great sword held ready, and looked back for his pursuers. To his relief, they were nowhere in sight. In the heavy rain and fog, they had momentarily lost him. But even the limited visibility would only slow them down for a few minutes and then . . . Menion shook his head sharply to clear the haze of rain and weariness from his eyes, then crawled quickly to the water-logged heap of clothing that bound the struggling prisoner. Whoever was in that hunting cloak was in good enough shape to run beside him, and Menion's strength was nearly gone. He knew he could carry the added weight no farther.

Awkwardly, hardly aware of what he was doing, the highlander sawed at the tough bonds with his sword. If had to be Shea, his mind told him over and over, it had to be Shea. The Trolls and that stranger had gone to so much trouble not to be seen, had been so secretive . . . The bonds snapped as the sword finally severed them. It had to be Shea! The ropes unwound and the cloak flew back as the person within struggled into the open air.

An astonished Menion Leah wiped the rain from his blinking eyes and stared. He had rescued a woman!

CHAPTER

11

A woman! Why would the Northlanders kidnap a woman? Menion stared through the pouring rain into the clear blue eyes that blinked back at him uncertainly. She was no ordinary woman in any case. She was strikingly beautiful – deeply browned skin covering the finely formed features of the rounded face, a slim graceful figure clothed in a silky material, and her hair . . .! He had never seen anything like it. Even wetted and plastered against her face by the driving rain, falling shoulder length and lower in long, wistful strands, the strange color showed through the grayness of the morning in a deep reddish hue. For a moment he gazed at her in a half-conscious trance, then the throbbing pain from his cut and bleeding feet recalled him to his present situation and the grave danger still facing them.

Quickly he climbed back to his feet, wincing with the pressure on his exposed soles, the weariness flooding through him until he thought he would collapse in total exhaustion. His mind battled fiercely for several long moments as he swayed almost drunkenly, bracing himself on the great sword. The frightened face of the girl – yes, she could still be called a girl, he thought suddenly – peered up at him out of a gray haze. Then she was on her feet next to him, holding him up, talking to him in low, distant tones. He shook his head and nodded stupidly.

'It's all right now, I'm all right.' The words sounded garbled as he spoke. 'Run for the river – we have to reach Kern.'

They began moving again through the mist and the rain, walking rapidly, at times staggering on the uncertain footing of the marshy grasslands. Menion felt his head begin to clear and his strength return as they walked, the girl next to him, her hands locked onto his arm, half holding onto him for her own support, half helping to support him. His keen eyes searched the gloom about them for some sign of the prowling Trolls, certain that they were not too far away. Then abruptly his ears picked up a new sound, the pounding, rushing throb of the Mermidon, its rain-filled waters overflowing the lowland banks as it swept southward toward Kern. The girl heard it, too, and gripped his arm tightly in encouragement.

Moments later they stood on the crest of the small rise that ran parallel with the north bank. The swift river had long since flooded its low banks and was continuing to rise. Menion had no idea where they stood in relation to Kern, but he realized that if they crossed at the wrong point, they would miss the island entirely. The girl seemed to recognize the problem; taking his arm, she began moving downstream along the low rise, peering across the river into the gloom. Menion let her lead him without question, his own eyes casting about anxiously for some sign of the pursuing Trolls. The rain had begun to slacken and the mist was beginning to clear. It would not be long before the storm would end and visibility return, leaving the two revealed to the persistent hunters. They had to chance a crossing quickly.

Menion did not know how long the young woman led him along the river's edge, but at last she halted and indicated in hurried gestures a small skiff drawn up against the grassy embankment. Quickly the highlander strapped the sword of Leah to his back, and together the two pushed off into the swift waters of the Mermidon. The river was icy and the shock of the extreme cold from the spray of the foam-tipped waves jarred Menion to the bone. He rowed fiercely across the swift current as it swept them downriver with terrific force, frequently turning them about completely as they fought to reach the other side. It was a wild, careening battle between river and man that seemed to go on endlessly, and at last everything became hazy and numb in Menion's mind.

What happened in the end was never clear to him. He was vaguely aware of hands reaching to pull him from the skiff to a grassy bank where he collapsed in a breathless stupor. He heard the girl's soft voice speaking to him, and then there was blackness and numbness all about him as he lapsed into unconsciousness. He drifted in and out of darkness and sleep, plagued by an uneasy sense of danger that prodded at his tired mind and demanded that he rise and stand ready. But his body could not respond, and finally he dropped off into a deep slumber.

When he awoke, it was still light out and the rain was falling in a slow, steady drizzle through deep, gray skies. He lay in the warmth and comfort of a bed, dry and rested, his torn feet cleaned and bandaged, and the terrible race to escape the Northlanders behind him. The slow rain beat peacefully on the paned glass windows that let in the daylight through the wood and stone walls. He glanced idly around the finely furnished chamber, realizing quickly that this was not the home of an average citizen, but of royalty. There were insignia and crests on the woodwork that Menion knew to belong to the kings of Callahorn. For a moment the highlander lay quietly and studied the room in silent leisure, allowing the sleep to disperse and his rested mind to awaken fully. He saw a dry set of clothes lying on a chair near the bed, and was just about to rise to dress when the door opened and an elderly serving woman appeared, carrying a tray of steaming food. Nodding politely and smiling, she hastened to the bed with the tray and deposited it on the highlander's lap, propping him up with pillows and urging him to eat it all while it was still hot. Strangely, she reminded Menion of his own mother, a kind, fussy woman who had died when he was twelve. The serving lady lingered until he had taken the first bite, then turned away and went out again, closing the door quietly behind her.

Menion ate slowly, savoring the excellent food, feeling the strength return to his body. It occurred to him only after he had finished almost half the meal that he had not eaten for over twenty-four hours – or perhaps it had been longer. He glanced again through the window to the rain beyond, unable to tell if it was even the same day. It might be the following day . . .

In a flash he recalled his original purpose in coming to Kern – to warn them of the impending invasion by the Northland army. He might already be too late! He was still frozen with the thought, a fork raised halfway to his mouth, when the door opened a second time. It was the young woman he had rescued, refreshed and dry now, dressed in a flowing gown of warm, mixed colors, her long red tresses combed and shining even in the gray light of the rain-clouded day. She was easily the most stunning woman the Prince of Leah had ever encountered. Remembering suddenly the half-raised fork, he lowered it to the tray and smiled in greeting. She closed the door behind her and moved gracefully to his bedside. She was incredibly beautiful, he thought again. Why had she been kidnapped? What would Balinor know about her – what answers could he supply? She stood next to the bedside, looking down at him, studying him with those clear, deep eyes for a moment.

'You look very well, Prince of Leah,' she smiled. 'The rest and the food have made you whole again.'

'How did you know who . . .?'

'Your sword bears the markings of the King of Leah; that much I know. Who else but his son would carry such a weapon? But I don't know you by name.'

'Menion,' the highlander responded, somewhat surprised at the girl's knowledge of his little homeland, a kingdom unfamiliar to most outlanders.

The young woman stretched forth a slim bronzed hand to grasp his own in warm greeting and nodded happily.

'I am Shirl Ravenlock, and this is my home, Menion – the island city of Kern. If not for your courage, I should never have seen it again. For that I shall remain eternally grateful and your friend always. Now finish your meal while we talk.'

She seated herself on the bed next to him and motioned for Menion to continue eating. Again he began to raise his fork; then remembering the invasion, he dropped it to the tray with a noisy clatter.

'You've got to get word to Tyrsis, to Balinor – the invasion from the Northland has begun! There is an army camped just above Kern waiting to . . .'

'I know, it's all right,' Shirl responded quickly, raising her hand to stop him from continuing. 'Even in your sleep, you spoke of the danger – you warned us before you passed out entirely. Word has been sent to Tyrsis. Palance Buckhannah rules in his brother's absence; the King is still very ill. The city of Kern is mobilizing its defenses, but for the moment there is no real danger. The rains have flooded the Mermidon and made any crossing by a large force impossible. We will be safe until help arrives.'

'Balinor should have been in Tyrsis several days ago,' Menion announced with alarm. 'What about the Border Legion? Is it fully mobilized?'

The girl looked at him blankly, indicating that she had no idea what the situation was with regard to either the Legion or Balinor. Abruptly, Menion shoved the tray aside and climbed out of bed, an astonished Shirl rising with him, still trying to calm the excited highlander.

'Shirl, you may think that you're safe on this island, but I can guarantee that time is running out for all of us!' Menion exclaimed, reaching for his clothes. 'I've seen the size of that army, and no amount of flooding is going to slow it down for long – and you can forget about any help short of a miracle.'

He paused at the second button of his nightshirt, suddenly remembering the young woman with him. He pointed meaningfully to the door, but she shook her head negatively and turned away so she couldn't see him changing.

'What about your kidnapping?' Menion asked, dressing himself quickly as he studied her slim back across the room. 'Do you have any idea why you would be so important to the Northlanders – other than the fact that you're a beautiful woman?'

He smiled roguishly, a little of the brashness that Flick distrusted returning. Although he could not see her face, the highlander was certain she was blushing furiously. She was silent a moment before speaking.

'I don't remember exactly what happened,' the answer came at last. 'I was asleep. I was awakened by a noise in the room, then someone grabbed me and I blacked out – I think I was struck or . . . No, I remember now – it was a cloth soaked in some foul liquid that prevented me from breathing. I blacked out and the next thing I remember was lying on the sand near the river – I gather it was the Mermidon. You know how I was tied in that blanket. I couldn't see anything and could hear only a little – but nothing that I could understand. Did you see anything?'

Menion shook his head and shrugged. 'No, nothing much,' he added remembering that the girl was not looking at him. 'One man brought you across in a boat, then turned you over to four Trolls. I couldn't see the man distinctly, but I might recognize him if I saw him again. How about answering my first question – why would anyone kidnap you? Turn around. I'm dressed now.'

The young woman turned obediently and came over next to him, watching curiously as he pulled on the high hunting boots.

'I'm of royal blood, Menion,' she responded quietly. Menion stopped quickly and looked up at her. He had suspected she was no ordinary citizen of Kern when she had recognized the crest of Leah on his sword. Now perhaps he would discover the reason behind her abduction from the city.

'My ancestors were kings of Kern – and for a while of all Callahorn, before the Buckhannahs came to power about one hundred years ago. I am a . . . well, I guess you could say I'm a princess – in absentia.' She laughed at the foolishness of the idea, and Menion smiled back. 'My father is an elder of the council that governs the internal affairs of Kern. The King is the ruler of Callahorn, but this is an enlightened monarchy, as the saying goes, and the King seldom interferes with the governmental workings of this city. His son Palance has been attracted to me for some time, and it is no secret that he plans to marry me. I . . . I believe that, to get to him, an enemy might try to harm me.'

Menion nodded soberly, a sudden premonition springing into his alert mind. Palance was not in line for the throne of Callahorn unless something happened to Balinor. Why would anyone waste time trying to put pressure on the younger son unless they were certain that Balinor would not be around? Again he recalled Shirl's lack of knowledge of the arrival of the Prince of Callahorn, an event that should have taken place days ago and one that all the citizens of the land should have known about.

'Shirl, how long have I been asleep?' he asked apprehensively.

'Nearly an entire day,' she answered. 'You were exhausted

when they pulled us from the Mermidon yesterday morning, and I thought you should sleep. You gave us your warning . . .'

'Twenty-four hours lost!' Menion exclaimed angrily. 'If not for the rain, the city would have already fallen! We've got to act now, but what . . . Shirl, your father and the council! I must speak with them!' He grasped her arms with urgency when she hesitated. 'Don't ask questions now, just do what I say. Where are the council chambers? Quick, take me to them!'

Without waiting for the girl to lead him, Menion took her arm and propelled her through the door to a long hallway beyond. Together they hurried through the empty home and out the front doorway onto a wide, tree-shaded lawn, running to escape the persistent drizzle of the morning rain. The walkways of the buildings beyond were partially sheltered from the rain, and they were spared a second soaking. As they proceeded toward the council hall, Shirl asked him how he happened to be in this part of the country, but Menion responded evasively, still unwilling to tell anyone about Allanon and the Sword of Shannara. He felt he could trust this girl, but Allanon's warning that none of those who journeyed to Paranor should reveal the story behind the missing Sword prevented him from confiding even in her. Instead, he explained that he had come to aid Balinor at his request upon hearing of an impending Northland invasion. She accepted his story without question, and he felt a little guilty for lying to her. Yet Allanon had never told him the complete truth, so perhaps he knew less than he imagined anyway.

They had reached the council hall, its ancient chambers housed within a tall, stone structure surrounded by weathered columns and arched windows laced with metal latticework. The guards that stood leisurely next to the entryway did not question them and they hurried inside, moving down the long, high corridors and up the winding stairways as the walls echoed with the rap of their boots on the worn stone flooring. The council met in chambers situated on the fourth floor of the great building. When at last they were outside its wooden doors, Shirl advised Menion that she would inform her father and the other members of his wish to address them. Reluctantly, the highlander agreed to wait. He stood quietly in the corridor after she had gone inside, listening to the hushed murmur of voices as the seconds ticked slowly away, and the rain continued to beat in a soft, steady rhythm on the glass of the windows that lined the silent hall.

Losing himself for a moment in the peace and solitude of the ancient building, the highlander recalled in brief flashes the faces of the divided company of friends, wondering sadly what had befallen them since Paranor. Perhaps they would never again be together as they had been during those fearful days on the road to the Druids' Keep, but he would never forget their courage and sacrifice and the pride he felt now in recalling the dangers they had faced and overcome. Even the reluctant Flick had displayed a bravery and steadfastness that Menion would not have expected from him.

And what of Shea, his oldest friend? He shook his head as he thought about his missing companion. He missed the Valeman's peculiar mixture of hardheaded practicality and antiquated beliefs. Somehow Shea could not seem to see the change in times even when the sun moved from east to west in the sky above. He did not seem to realize that the land and the people were growing, expanding once more – that the wars of the past were slowly being forgotten. Shea believed that one could turn his back on the past and build a new world with the future, never understanding that the future was inextricably tied to the past, an interwoven tapestry of events and ideas that would never be entirely severed. In his own small way, the little Valeman was a part of the passing age, his convictions a reminder of yesterday rather than a promise of tomorrow. How strange, how incredibly strange it all seemed, Menion thought suddenly, standing in the center of the hall, motionless, his gaze lost in the depths of the weathered stone wall. Shea and the Sword of Shannara – things of an age slowly dying; yet they were the hope of the hour to come. They were the key to life.

The heavy wooden doors to the council hall opened behind the highlander, and his thoughts faded with Shirl's soft voice. She seemed small and vulnerable as she waited beneath the massive beams of the high entryway, her face beautiful and anxious. No wonder Palance Buckhannah wanted this woman for his wife. Menion moved toward her, taking her warm hand in his own, and they entered the council chamber. He noted the ancient austerity of the massive chamber as he moved into the gray light that seemed to slide in tired streaks through the high, iron-webbed windows. The council hall was old and proud, a cornerstone of the island city. Twenty men were seated around a long, burnished wood table, their faces strangely similar as they waited for the highlander to speak – all aged, wise perhaps, and determined. The eyes betrayed the unspoken fear that lingered beneath the calm exteriors – a fear for their city and their people. They knew what the Northland army would do when the rains ceased and the waters of the Mermidon receded in the heat of the open sun. He stopped before them, the girl still next to him, his footfalls dying away into the expectant silence.

He chose his words carefully, describing the massive enemy force that had been assembled under the leadership of the Warlock Lord. He related in part the story of his long journey to Callahorn, speaking of Balinor and the men of the company formed at Culhaven who were now scattered throughout the four lands. He did not tell them about the Sword or about Shea's mysterious origin or even about Allanon. There was no reason for the elders of this council to know anything beyond the fact that the city of Kern stood in danger of being overrun. As he finished, calling upon them to save their people while there was still time, to evacuate the city immediately before all hope of retreat was cut off, he felt a strange sense of satisfaction. He had risked a great deal more than his own life to warn these people. If he had failed to reach them, they might all have perished without ever having had a chance to flee to safety. It was important, really important, to the Prince of Leah that he had carried out his task responsibly.

The questions from the members of the council came with cries of alarm when the highlander had finished, some angry, some frightened. Menion answered quickly, trying to stay calm as he assured them that the size of the North- land army was as awesome as he had described and the threat of attack certain. Eventually the initial furor died away into a more rational deliberation of the possibilities. A few of the elders believed that the city should be defend- ed until Palance Buckhannah could come up from Tyrsis with the Border Legion, but most were of the opinion that once the rains subsided, as they were certain to do with- in a few days, the invading army would easily gain the shores of the island and the city would stand defenseless. Menion listened silently while the council deliberated the matter, weighing in his own mind the courses of action open to them. Finally, the flushed, gray-haired man, whom Shirl had introduced as her father, turned to Menion, drawing him aside in private conference as the council con- tinued its debate.

'Have you seen Balinor, young man? Do you know where he can be found?'

'He should have been in Tyrsis days ago,' Menion respon- ded worriedly. 'He was going there to mobilize the Border Legion in preparation for this invasion. He was in the com- pany of two cousins of Eventine Elessedil.'

The older man frowned and shook his head, conster- nation registering in his lined face.

'Prince of Leah, I must tell you that the situation is more

desperate than it appears. The King of Callahorn, Ruhl Buckhannah, became seriously ill several weeks earlier and his condition does not seem to be improving. Balinor was absent from the city at the time, and so the King's younger son assumed his father's duties. While he has always been a rather unsteady personality, he has of late seemed highly erratic. One of his first acts was to disband the Border Legion, reducing it to a fraction of its former size.'

'Disbanded!' Menion exclaimed in disbelief. 'Why in the name . . .?'

'He found them unnecessary,' the other continued quickly, 'so he replaced them with a small company of his own men. The fact of the matter is that he has always felt overshadowed by his brother, and the Border Legion was under the direct command of Balinor by the King's own order. It's highly probable that Palance felt they would remain loyal to the firstborn son of the King in preference to himself, and he has no intention of returning the throne to Balinor should the King die. He has already made this quite apparent. The commanders of the Border Legion and several close associates of Balinor were seized and imprisoned – all very quietly so that the people would not be outraged by this senseless action. Our new King has taken as his only confidant and adviser a man named Stenmin, a viperous mystic and trickster whose only concern is for his own ambitions, not for the welfare of the people or even Palance Buckhannah. I do not see how we can hope to face this invasion with our own leadership so badly divided and undermined. I'm not even sure we can convince the Prince that the danger exists until the enemy is standing at the open gates!'

'Then Balinor is in grave danger,' Menion said darkly. 'He has gone to Tyrsis, not realizing that his father is ill and that his brother has taken command. We've got to get word to him at once!'

The council members had suddenly risen to their feet,

shouting heatedly, still arguing over what should be done to save the doomed city of Kern. Shirl's father hastened to their midst, but it took several minutes for the few rational members of the distraught council to quiet the others enough to permit the discussion to continue on an orderly basis. Menion listened for a little while, then allowed his attention to drift momentarily to the high, arched windows and the solemn sky beyond. It was not as dark as before, and the rain had begun to slacken further. Unquestionably, it would end by tomorrow, and the enemy force camped beyond the flooded Mermidon would attempt a crossing. Eventual success in attaining a landing was assured, even if the vastly outnumbered soldiers stationed or living in Kern tried to defend the island. Without a large, well-organized army to protect the city, the people would be quickly slain and Kern would fall. He thought back quickly to his parting with Allanon, wondering suddenly what the resourceful Druid would do if he were there. The situation was not promising. Tyrsis was ruled by an irrational, ambitious usurper. Kern was leaderless, its councilmen divided and unsure, debating a course of action that should already have been executed. Menion felt his temper slipping. It was madness to ponder the alternatives further!

'Councilmen! Hear me!' His own voice rose in fury, reverberating back from the ancient stone walls as the voices of the elders of Kern died into whispering silence. 'Not only Callahorn, but all of the Southland, my home and yours, faces certain destruction if we do not act now! By tomorrow night, Kern will be ashes and its people enslaved. Our one chance for survival is escape to Tyrsis; our one hope for victory over this mighty Northland army is the Border Legion, reassembled under Balinor. The Elven armies stand ready to fight with us. Eventine will lead them. The Dwarf people, engaged for years in fighting the Gnomes, have promised to aid us. But we must

211

stand fast separately until all are united against this monstrous threat to our existence!'

'Your plea is well spoken, Prince of Leah,' Shirl's father responded quickly as the flushed highlander paused. 'But give us a solution to our immediate problem so that our people can reach Tyrsis. The enemy is camped directly across the Mermidon, and we stand virtually defenseless. We must evacuate almost forty thousand people from this island and then guide them safely to Tyrsis, which is miles to the south. Undoubtedly the enemy has already posted sentries all around our shores to prevent any attempt to cross the Mermidon before the assault on Kern. How can we overcome such obstacles?'

A fleeting smile crossed Menion's lips.

'We'll attack,' he stated simply.

For a moment there was shocked silence as they all stared in utter disbelief at the deceptively passive face. The words of astonished reply were still forming on their lips as he held up one hand.

'An attack is exactly what they will not be expecting – particularly if it comes in the night. A quick strike against a flank position of their main encampment, if executed properly, will confuse them, cause them to think that it's an assault by a heavily armed force. The darkness and the confusion will hide our true size. Such an attack is certain to draw in their outlying sentry lines around the island. A small command can make a great amount of noise, set a few fires, and pin them down for at least an hour – perhaps longer. While that's going on – evacuate the city!'

One of the elders shook his head negatively.

'Even an hour would not be sufficient time, though your plan may be daring enough to catch the Northlanders off guard, young man. Even if we managed to ferry all forty thousand people from the island to the southern shore, it would still be necessary to march them southward to Tyrsis – almost fifty miles. The women and children would require days to travel that distance under normal conditions, and once the enemy finds Kern has been abandoned, they'll follow its people southward. We cannot hope to outrun them. Why should we even attempt it?'

'You will not have to outrun them,' Menion declared quickly. 'You won't be taking these people south by land – you will take them down the Mermidon! Put them in small boats, rafts, anything that you now have or can build by tonight that will float. The Mermidon flows southward deep into Callahorn, within ten miles of Tyrsis. Disembark at that point, and all can easily reach the safety of the city by daybreak, long before the cumbersome Northland army can mobilize and follow!'

The council rose to its feet, shouting their approval, caught up in the fire and determination of the highlander's spirit. If there was any way that the people of Kern could be saved, even though the island city itself must fall to the enemy hordes, it must be tried. The council adjourned after a short discussion to mobilize the working people of the city. Between this time and sunset, every citizen who was able to assist would be expected to aid in the construction of large wooden rafts capable of transporting several hundred people. There were already hundreds of small boats scattered about the island which individual citizens used to navigate the river in order to reach the mainland. In addition, there were a number of larger ferries for mass transportation which could be pressed into service. Menion suggested that the council order all armed soldiers in the city to begin a vigilant patrol of the coastline, permitting no one to leave the island. All details of the planned escape would be carefully concealed from everyone but the council members for as long as possible. The highlander's greatest concern was that someone might betray them to the enemy, cutting off their escape route before they had a chance to act. Someone had seized Shirl in her own home, whisked her out of the heavily populated city, and ferried her across into the hands of the Trolls – a chore that could not have been accomplished by anyone unfamiliar with the island. Whoever he was, he remained free and hidden, perhaps still safe within the city. If he learned the exact details of the evacuation plan, he would undoubtedly attempt to warn the Northlanders. Secrecy was absolutely necessary if this dangerous venture was to be successful.

The remainder of the day passed quickly for Menion. Forgotten for the moment were Shea and his companions of the past few weeks. For the first time since Shea had come to him in the highlands, the Prince of Leah was faced with a problem that he fully understood, requiring skills he knew how to employ. The enemy was no longer the Skull King or the spirit creatures that served him. The enemy was flesh and blood – creatures that lived and died according to the same rules as other men, and their threat was one the highlander could appreciate and analyze. Time was the greatest single factor in his plan to outwit the waiting army, and so he threw himself into the most important undertaking of his life, the saving of an entire city.

Together with the members of the council, he directed the building of the giant wooden rafts which would be utilized to convey the majority of the besieged citizens of Kern down the still-flooded Mermidon to the safety of Tyrsis. The point of embarkation was to be the southwest coastline immediately below the city proper. There was a broad but well-concealed inlet from which the rafts and smaller boats would be launched under cover of darkness. Directly across the river from the inlet stood a series of low bluffs that ran to the edge of the embankment. Menion thought that a handful of men could ford the river when the main attack on the enemy encampment began later that night; once across, they could subdue the small guard post that would be keeping watch. After the sentries were dispatched, the boats and rafts would be launched, flowing downriver with the current, following the south branch of the Mermidon to Tyrsis. There was nothing to assure them that the vessels would not be spotted instantly, but it was the only possible course of action. Menion believed that if the sky remained clouded, the sentry commands were withdrawn upriver to defend against the fake assault on the main encampment, and the people of the city kept silent on the rafts, then the evacuation might be successful.

But toward late afternoon, the rain started to slacken off altogether and the clouds began to thin out, permitting small strips of blue to seep through the rolling grayness. The storm was drawing to an end, and it appeared the night sky would be cloudless and the land exposed to the revealing light of the new moon and a thousand winking stars. Menion was seated in one of the smaller rooms of the council hall when he saw these first signs of a clearing, his attention momentarily diverted from the huge map spread out on the table before him. At his side were two members of the disbanded Border Legion, Janus Senpre, a lieutenant commander of the Legion and the highest ranking officer on the island, and a grizzled veteran named Fandrez. The latter knew the country around Kern better than anyone and had been called in to advise the attack squad in its strike against the giant Northland army. Senpre, his superior, was surprisingly young for his rank, but a sharp and determined soldier with a dozen years of field duty already behind him. He was a devoted follower of Balinor, and like Menion, he was considerably upset to learn that nothing had been heard from Tyrsis concerning the Prince's arrival. Earlier that afternoon, he had selected two hundred seasoned soldiers from the disbanded Border Legion to form the strike force that would be directed against the enemy camp.

Menion had offered his aid and it had been eagerly accepted. The highlander was still cut and bruised about the feet and lower legs from his arduous flight after rescuing Shirl Ravenlock, but he refused to stay behind with the evacuation party when the feint by the small attack squad had been his idea. Flick would have written off his insistence as a foolish mixture of stubbornness and pride, but Menion Leah would not be left in comparative safety on the island while a battle was being fought across the river. It had taken him years to find something worthwhile to fight for, something more than personal satisfaction and the irresistible lure of one more adventure. He was not about to be a passive spectator while the most awesome threat in centuries decimated the race of Man.

'This point – over here by the Spinn Barr – that's the landing point to take,' the slow, grating voice of Fandrez cut into his thoughts, drawing his attention back to the carefully detailed map. Janus Senpre agreed, looking at Menion to be certain he was taking careful note. The highlander nodded quickly.

'They will have sentries posted all along that grassland just above the bar,' he said in reply. 'If we don't dispose of them immediately, they could cut off any retreat.'

'Your job will be to keep them out of there – keep the way open,' the Legion commander stated.

Menion opened his mouth in objection, but was cut short.

'I appreciate your desire to come with us, Menion, but we still have to move much faster than the enemy, and your feet are in poor condition for any prolonged running. You know that as well as I. So the shore patrol is yours. Keep our path to the boats open, and you will be doing us a much greater service than by coming with us.'

Menion quietly nodded his agreement, though he was keenly disappointed. He had wanted to be in the forefront of the assault. Deep in the back of his mind, he still maintained hope of finding Shea a prisoner in the enemy camp. His thoughts drifted to Allanon and Flick. Perhaps they had found the missing Valeman, as the Druid had promised they would try to do. He shook his head sadly. Shea, Shea, why did it have to happen to someone like you – someone who just wanted to be left alone? There was a madness in the scheme of life that men were forced to accept either with resigned fury or blunt indifference. There could be no final resolution – except, perhaps, in death.

The meeting ended shortly thereafter, and a despondent and bitter Menion Leah wandered aimlessly out of the council chamber still lost in thought. Almost without realizing it, he walked down the stone stairway of the huge building to the street and from there made his way back toward Shirl's home, keeping close to the covered walks and building walls. Where was it all leading? The threat of the Warlock Lord loomed before them like a towering, unscalable wall. How could they possibly hope to defeat a creature that had no soul – a creature that lived according to laws of nature completely foreign to the world into which they had been born? Why should a simple young man from an obscure hamlet be the only mortal entity with the ability to destroy such an indescribably powerful being? Menion desperately needed to understand something of what was happening to him and to his absent friends – even if it was only one small piece in a thousand comprising the puzzle of the Warlock Lord and the Sword of Shannara.

Suddenly he found himself in front of the Ravenlock home, the heavy doors standing closed, their metal latches looking cold and frosted in the graying mist that hung in wisps with the cooling of the late afternoon air. He turned quickly from the entryway, not wishing to go in or to be with people for the moment, but preferring the solitude of the empty veranda. Slowly he moved along its stone path into the little garden at the side of the house, the leaves and flowers dripping softly with the rain of several days, the grounds beyond damp and green. He stood quietly, his own thoughts as hazy and wistful as the setting

217

in which he paused, giving way for one brief moment to the sinking despair that seized him when he thought of how much he had lost. He had never felt alone like this before, even in the dark emptiness of the highlands of Leah when he had hunted far from his own home and friends. Something deep within hinted with dread persistence that he would never go back to what had been, that he would never go back to his friends, his home, his old life. Somewhere in the days behind, he had lost it all. He shook his head, the unwanted tears building on the edge of his lids as the dampness closed in about him and the chill of the rain slipped deep into his chest.

There were sudden footsteps on the stone behind him and a small, lithe form came to a silent halt at his elbow, the rust-red locks shadowing wide eyes that looked up at him momentarily and then strayed to the garden beyond. The two stood without speaking for a long time, the rest of the world shut away. In the sky above, heavy clouds were rolling in, covering the last faint traces of blue as the darkness of early twilight began to deepen. Rain was falling again in steady sheets on the besieged land of Callahorn, and Menion noted with absent relief that it would be a black and moonless night on the island of Kern.

It was well after midnight, the rain still falling in a soggy drizzle, the night sky still impenetrably black and ominous, when an exhausted Menion Leah stumbled heavily onto a small, crudely constructed raft moored in a peaceful inlet on the southwestern coast of the island. Two slim arms reached out to catch him as he collapsed, and he stared wonderingly into the dark eyes of Shirl Ravenlock. She had waited for him as she said she would, even though he had begged her to go with the others when the mass evacuation began. Cut and bruised, his clothing torn and his skin wet from the rain and his own blood, he let her wrap him in a cloak still somehow dry and warm and pull him against her shoulder as they crouched in the night shadows and waited.

There had been some who had returned with Menion, and a few more who boarded now, all battle weary, but fiercely proud of the courage and sacrifice they had displayed that night on the plains north of Kern. Never had the Prince of Leah seen such bravery in the face of such impossible odds. Those few men of the fabled Border Legion had so utterly disrupted the enemy camp that even now, some four hours after the initial strike, the confusion was still continuing. The enemy numbers had been unbelievable – thousands after thousands milling about, striking out at anyone within reach, inflicting injury and death upon even their own companions. They had been driven by more than mortal fear or hatred. They had been driven by the inhuman power of the Warlock Lord, his incredible fury thrusting them into battle like crazed beings with no purpose but to destroy. Yet the men of the Legion had held them at bay, repeatedly thrown back only to regroup and strike once more. Many had died. Menion did not know what had preserved his own meager life, but it bordered on a miracle.

The mooring ropes were loosened, and he felt the raft begin to drift away from the shore, the current catching it and pulling it into the center of the flooded Mermidon. Moments later they were in the main channel, moving silently downriver toward the walled city of Tyrsis, where the people of Kern had fled several hours earlier in a perfectly executed mass evacuation. Forty thousand people, huddled on giant rafts, small boats, even two-man dinghies, had slipped undetected from the besieged city as the enemy sentry posts guarding the western bank of the Mermidon hastily returned to the main encampment, where it appeared a full-scale attack by the armies of Callahorn was in progress. The beating of the rain, the rushing of the river, and the cries of the distant camp had blotted out the muffled sounds of the people on the rafts and boats, crowded and jammed together in a desperate, fearful bid for freedom. The darkness of the clouded sky had hidden them well, and their collective courage had sustained them. For the time being at least, they had eluded the Warlock Lord.

Menion dozed off for a time, aware of nothing but a gentle rocking sensation as the river bore the raft steadily southward. Strange dreams flashed through his restless mind as time drifted away in long moments of peaceful silence. Then voices reached through to him, jostling his subconscious, forcing him to wake abruptly, and his eyes were seared by a vast red glare that filled the damp air about him. Squinting sharply, he raised himself from Shirl's arms, uncertainty registering on his lean face as he saw the northern sky filled with a reddish glow that matched the brightness of the dawn's gold. Shirl was speaking softly in his ear, the words faint and poignant.

'They have burned the city, Menion. They have burned my home!'

Menion lowered his eyes and gripped the girl's slim arm with one hand. Though its people had been able to escape, the city of Kern had seen the end of its days and, with terrible grandness, was passing into ashes.

12

The hours slipped silently away in the entombed blackness of the little cell. Even after the eyes of the captives had grown used to the impenetrable dark, there remained a solitude that numbed the senses and destroyed their ability to discern the passage of time. Beyond the empty darkness of the room and their own muffled breathing, the three captives could hear nothing save the infrequent scurrying of a small rodent and the steady drip of icy water on worn stone. Finally their own ears began to lie to them, to hear sounds where there was only silence. Their own movement was meaningless, because they could expect it, identify it, and dismiss it as insignificant and hopeless. An interminable length of time lingered and faded, and still no one came.

Somewhere in the light and air above, amid the sounds of the people and the city, Palance Buckhannah was deciding their fate and indirectly the fate of the Southland. Time was running out for the land of Callahorn; the Warlock Lord moved closer with each passing hour. But here, in the silent blackness of this small prison, in a world shut away from the pulse beat of the human world, time had no meaning and tomorrow would be the same as today. Eventually they would be discovered, but would they emerge again into the sun's friendly light, or would it be a transfer from one darkness into yet another? Would they find only the terrible gloom of the Skull King, his power extended not only into Callahorn, but into the farthest reaches of all the provinces of the Southland?

Balinor and the Elven brothers had freed themselves within a short time after their captors had departed. The ropes binding them had not been secured with the intention of preventing any chance of escape once they were safely locked within that dungeon room, and the three had lost no time in working the knots loose. Huddled together in the darkness, the ropes and blindfolds cast aside, they discussed what would become of them. The dank, rotting smell of the ancient cellar almost stifled their breathing as they crouched close to one another, and the air was chill and biting even through their heavy cloaks. The floor was earthen, the walls stone and iron, the room barren and empty.

Balinor was familiar with the cellar beneath the palace but he did not recognize the room in which they had been imprisoned. The cellar was used primarily for storage, and while there had always been a number of walled rooms in which wine barrels had been placed to age, this was not one of them. Then, with chilling certainty, he realized that they had been imprisoned in the ancient dungeon constructed centuries ago beneath the cellar and later sealed off and forgotten. Palance must have discovered its existence and reopened the cells for his own use. Quite probably, he had imprisoned Balinor's friends somewhere in this maze when they had come to the palace to object to the disbanding of the Border Legion. It was a well-concealed prison, and Balinor doubted that anyone searching for them would ever find it.

The discussion was completed quickly. There was little to say. Balinor had left his instructions with Captain Sheelon. Should they fail to return, he was to seek out Ginnisson and Fandwick, two of Balinor's most dependable commanders, and order them to reassemble the Border Legion to defend against any assault by the Warlock Lord and his invading army. Sheelon had also been told to send word to the Elf and Dwarf nations, warning them of the situation and calling for their immediate support. Eventine would not permit his cousins to remain the prisoners of Callahorn for very long, and Allanon would come as soon as he heard of their misfortune. Four hours must have passed long ago, he thought, so it should only be a matter of time. But time was precious, and with Palance determined to gain the throne of Callahorn, their own lives were in grave danger. The borderman began to wish silently that he had listened to Durin's advice and avoided a confrontation with his brother until he had been certain of the outcome.

He had never imagined that matters would go this far awry. Palance had been like a wild man, his hatred so consuming that he had not even waited to hear what Balinor would say. Yet there was little mystery to this irrational behavior. It was more than personal differences between the two brothers that had prompted the youth's savage action. It was more than the illness of his father, an illness Palance somehow believed his brother was responsible for. It had something to do with Shirl Ravenlock, the alluring woman Palance had fallen in love with months before and had vowed to marry despite her own reticence toward the match. Something had happened to the young Kern girl, and Balinor had received the blame. Palance would do anything to get her back safely, if she was indeed missing, as his brother's few words immediately before they had been brought to this dungeon had indicated.

The borderman explained the situation to the Elven brothers. He felt certain Palance would come to them soon and demand information concerning the young woman. But he would not believe them when they said they knew nothing . . .

More than twenty-four hours passed, and still no one

came. There was nothing to eat. Even after their eyes gradually grew accustomed to the blackness, there was nothing to view but their own shadowy forms and the walls about them. They took turns sleeping, trying to conserve their strength for whatever lay ahead, but the abnormal silence prevented any real sleep, and they resigned themselves to a light, restless slumber that did little to refresh their bodies or their spirits. At first they attempted to find a weak spot on the hinges of the bulky iron door, but it was securely fastened in place. Without tools of any sort, they found it impossible to dig very far into the chill, iron-hard surface of the dirt flooring. The stone walls were aged, but still firm and solid, without any sign of a weak or crumbling layer in the mortar. Eventually they abandoned their attempts to escape and sat back in silence.

Finally, after endless hours of waiting in the chill darkness, they heard the distant sound of clanging metal as an ancient iron door somewhere above swung ponderously open. There were voices, muffled and soft, and then footsteps on stone as someone began to descend the worn stairs to the lower dungeon where the three were imprisoned. Quickly they rose to their feet and crowded close to the cell door, listening expectantly as the footsteps and the voices drew closer. Balinor could distinguish the voice of his brother above the rest, strangely hesitant and broken. Then the heavy latches were drawn back, the sudden grating of metal piercing to the ears of the three captives, who had become accustomed now to the deathlike silence of their prison, and they moved back from the massive cell door as it swung slowly inward. Blazing streaks of torchlight flashed into the darkened room, forcing the prisoners to shield their weakened eyes. As they slowly adjusted to this new light, several figures entered the room and came to a halt just within the entryway.

The younger son of the ailing King of Callahorn stood foremost of four figures, his broad face relaxed and his lips pursed. His eyes alone betrayed the hatred that burned within, and there was a maddened, almost desperate way that they moved from one captive to the next as he clenched his hands tightly behind him. He was clearly Balinor's brother, possessing the same facial construction, the same wide mouth and prominent nose, and the same big, rugged build. Next to him stood a man that even the Elven brothers recognized instantly, though they had never met him. He was the mystic Stenmin, a gaunt, slightly stooped figure, lean and sharp in his features, and clothed in reddish robes and trappings. His eyes were strangely shadowed, reflecting an undisguisable evil in the man who had gained the complete confidence of the new, self-proclaimed King. His hands moved over his body nervously, raising almost mechanically from time to time to stroke the small, pointed black beard that shaded the angular face. Behind him stood two armed guards, dressed in black and bearing the insignia of the falcon. Beyond them, just outside the doorway, stood two more. All held wicked-looking pikes. For a moment no one spoke; no one even moved as the two parties scrutinized each other in the torchlit gloom of the little cell. Then Palance made a quick motion toward the open door.

'I will speak with my brother alone. Take these other two out.'

The guards silently complied, leading the reluctant Elven brothers from the room. The tall Prince waited until they had left, then turned questioningly to the scarlet-robed figure still at his side.

'I thought that perhaps you might have need of me . . .?' The lean, calculating face stared steadily at the impassive Balinor.

'Leave us, Stenmin. I will speak with my brother alone.'

His tone of voice bordered on anger, and the mystic nodded obediently, quickly backing out of the cell. The heavy door closed with an ominous thud, leaving the two brothers alone in a silence broken only by the hissing of the torch flame as it consumed the dry wood and flashed into gleaming sparks. Balinor did not move, but stood waiting expectantly, his eyes trying to probe his brother's young face, trying to reach the old feelings of love and friendship they had shared as children. But they were missing, or at least carefully submerged in some dark corner of the heart, and in their place was a strange, restless anger that seemed to rise as much from dissatisfaction with the situation as from dislike of the captive brother. An instant later the fury and the contempt were gone, replaced by a calm detachment that Balinor found both irrational and false, as if Palance were playing a role without any real understanding of the character.

'Why did you come back, Balinor?' The words came out slowly, sadly. 'Why did you do it?'

The tall borderman did not reply, unable to comprehend this sudden change of mood. Before, his brother had been willing to have him torn to pieces in order to learn the whereabouts of the beautiful Shirl Ravenlock, yet now he seemed to have completely dismissed the matter from his mind.

'No matter, no matter I suppose.' The reply came before Balinor had recovered from his astonishment at the abrupt change. 'You could have stayed away after . . . after all the . . . after your treachery. I hoped you would, you know, because we were so close as children and you are, after all, my only brother. I will be King of Callahorn . . . I should have been firstborn anyway . . .'

He trailed off into a whisper, his mind suddenly lost in some unspoken thought. He had gone mad, Balinor thought in desperation, and could no longer be reached!

'Palance, listen to me – just listen to me. I have done nothing to you or to Shirl. I've been in Paranor since I left here weeks before, and I returned only to warm our people that the Skull King has assembled an army of such awesome proportions that it will sweep through the entire Southland unchallenged unless we stop it here! For the sake of all these people, please listen to me . . .'

His brother's voice pierced the air in shrill command. 'I will hear no more of this foolish talk of invasion! My scouts have checked the country's borders and report no enemy armies anywhere. Besides, no enemy would dare to attack Callahorn – to attack me. . . . Our people are safe here. What do I care for the rest of the Southland? What do I owe them? They have always left us to fight alone, to guard these borderlands alone. I owe them nothing!'

He took a step toward Balinor and pointed menacingly at him, the strange hatred flaming anew as the young face contorted savagely.

'You turned against me, brother, when you knew that I was to be king. You tried to poison me as you poisoned my father – you wanted me as sick and helpless as he is now . . . dying alone, forgotten, alone. You thought you had found an ally that could gain the throne for you when you left with that traitor Allanon. How I hate that man – no, not a man, but an evil thing! He must be destroyed! But *you* will remain in this cell, alone and forgotten, Balinor, until you die – the fate you had planned for me!'

He turned away suddenly, breaking his tirade off with a sharp laugh as he paced to the closed door. Balinor thought he was about to open it, when the hulking youth paused and looked back at him. Slowly he came around, the eyes sad again.

'You could have stayed away from this land and been safe,' he muttered as if confused by this fact. 'Stenmin said you would come back even when I assured him you would not. He was right again. He is always right. Why did you come back?'

Balinor thought quickly. He had to keep his brother's attention long enough to find out what had happened to his father and his friends.

227

'I . . . I discovered I had been mistaken – that I was wrong,' he answered slowly. 'I came home to see our father and to see you, Palance.'

'Father.' The word came out like an unfamiliar name as the Prince moved a step closer. 'He is beyond our help, lying like one already dead in that room in the south wing. Stenmin looks after him, as I do, but nothing can be done. He does not seem to want to live . . .'

'But what is wrong with him?' Balinor's impatience burst free, and he moved toward the other threateningly.

'Keep your distance, Balinor.' Palance backed away hastily, drawing a long dagger and holding it protectively before him. Balinor hesitated a moment. It would be easy to seize the dagger, hold the Prince captive until he was released. Yet something restrained him, something deep inside that warned against such a move. Quickly he stopped, holding up his hands and backing away to the far wall.

'You must remember you are my prisoner.' Palance nodded in satisfaction, his voice unsteady. 'You poisoned the King and you tried to poison me. I could have you put to death. Stenmin advised me to have you executed immediately, but I am not the coward that he is. I was a commander in the Border Legion, too, before . . . But they're gone now – disbanded and sent home to their families. My reign shall be a time of peace. You don't understand that, Balinor, do you?'

The borderman shook his head negatively, desperately trying to hold his brother's attention for a few minutes longer. Palance had apparently gone mad, whether from a latent congenital defect of the mind or from the strain of whatever it was that had been happening since Balinor had left Tyrsis with Allanon; it was impossible to tell. In any event, he was no longer the brother that Balinor had grown to manhood with and had loved as he had loved no one else. It was a stranger living in the physical shell that was his brother's body – a stranger obsessed with the need to be King of Callahorn. Stenmin was behind this; Balinor knew it. The mystic had somehow twisted the mind of his maddened brother, bending it to his own uses, filling it with promises of his destiny as King. Palance had always wanted to rule Callahorn. Even when Balinor had left the city, he knew Palance felt certain he would one day be King. Stenmin had been there all the time, counseling and advising in the manner of a close friend, poisoning his mind against his brother. But Palance had been strong-willed and independent, a sane and healthy man who would not be broken easily. Yet he was changed. Hendel had been wrong about Palance, but apparently Balinor had been wrong as well. Neither could have foreseen this, and now it was too late.

'Shirl – what of Shril?' the tall borderman asked quickly.

Again the anger faded from his brother's darting eyes and a slow smile crept over his lips, relaxing the anguished face for an instant.

'She is so beautiful . . . so beautiful.' He sighed foolishly, the dagger falling harmlessly to the cell floor as the Prince opened his hands to emphasize the feeling. 'You took her from me, Balinor – tried to keep her from me. But she is safe now. She was saved by a Southlander, a Prince like myself. No, I am King of Tyrsis now, and he is only a Prince. It's just a little kingdom; I had never heard of it myself. He and I will be good friends, Balinor, the way you and I once were. But Stenmin . . . says I can trust no one. I even had to lock away Messaline and Acton. They came to me when the Border Legion was sent home, trying to persuade me to . . . well, I guess to give up my plans for peace. They didn't understand . . . why . . .'

He stopped suddenly, his lowered eyes falling on the momentarily forgotten dagger. He picked it up quickly, placing it back in its belted sheath with a sly smile at his brother, looking strikingly like a clever child that has just avoided a scolding. There was no longer any doubt in Balinor's mind that his brother was totally incapable of making rational decisions. He was suddenly struck with his earlier premonition that while he could easily seize the dagger and hold his brother prisoner, it would be a serious mistake. Now he knew why that innate sense of warning had been generated. Stenmin fully realized Palance's condition and had purposely left the brothers alone in that cell. If Balinor had attempted to disarm Palance and to escape while holding him prisoner, the evil mystic could have accomplished his obvious goal in one bold stroke by killing both brothers. Who would question him when he explained that Palance had met his death by accident while his brother was attempting to flee his prison confinement? With both brothers dead and their father incapable of governing, the mystic might be able to seize control of the government of Callahorn. Then he alone would determine the fate of the Southland.

'Palance, listen to me, I beg of you,' Balinor pleaded quietly. 'We were so close once. We were more than just brothers by bloodline. We were friends, companions. We trusted each other, loved each other, and we could always work our problems out by understanding each other. You can't have forgotten all that. Listen to me! Even a king must try to understand his people – even when they don't agree on the way things are to be handled. You agree with that, don't you?'

Palance nodded soberly, the eyes vacant and detached as he tried to fight the haze that blocked his thought processes. There was a glimmer of understanding, and Balinor was determined to reach the memory that lay locked somewhere deep within.

'Stenmin is using you – he is an evil man.' His brother started abruptly, taking a step backward as if to avoid hearing more. 'You've got to understand, Palance. I am not your enemy, nor am I the enemy of this country. I did not poison our father. I did not harm Shirl in any way. I only want to help . . .'

His plea was suddenly cut short as the ponderous cell door swung open with a sharp rasp, and the angular features of the wily Stenmin appeared. Bowing condescendingly, he entered the cell, his cruel eyes fastened intently on Balinor.

'I thought I heard you call me, my King,' he smiled quickly. 'You've been in here alone so long, I thought something might have happened . . .'

Palance stared at him uncomprehendingly for a moment, then shook his head negatively and turned to leave. In that instant Balinor considered leaping upon the evil mystic and crushing the life from him before the absent guards could act. But he hesitated for that single brief moment, uncertain that even this would save him or aid his brother, and so the opportunity was lost. The guards came back into the cell, leading the Elven brothers, who looked about dubiously, then rejoined their comrade on the far side of the little room. Suddenly Balinor recalled something Palance had said when he was talking about Shirl. He had mentioned a Prince from a tiny Southland kingdom – a Prince who had rescued the young girl. Menion Leah! But how could he be in Callahorn . . .?

The guards were turning to leave now and with them the silent Palance and his evil consort, a red-clad arm guiding the mindless Prince from the room. Then abruptly, the lean figure turned to look once more on the three captives, a thin smile spreading over the pursed lips as the bowed head cocked carefully to one side.

'In the event my King should have failed to mention it, Balinor . . .' The words sounded with a slow, burning hatred. 'The guards at the Outer Wall saw you speaking with a certain Captain Sheelon, formerly of the Border Legion. He was trying to speak with others about your . . . predicament, when he was seized and imprisoned. I don't believe he will have much chance to cause us any further trouble. The matter is quite ended now, and within time even you will be forgotten.'

Balinor's heart sank suddenly at this final piece of news. If Sheelon had been seized and confined before he had been able to reach Ginnisson and Fandwick, then there would be no one to assemble the Border Legion and no one to appeal to the people on his behalf. His absent companions would not know of his imprisonment upon reaching Tyrsis, and even if they suspected what had happened, what hope would they have of ever finding out what had become of him? This lower level of the ancient palace was unknown to all but a very few, and its entrance was well concealed. The three despondent captives watched in bitter silence as the guards placed a small tray of bread and a jug of water just inside the open door, then moved back into the hallway, carrying with them all of the burning torches but one. The grimly smiling Stenmin held this last light as he waited for the stooped form of Palance to follow the burly guards. But Palance paused uncertainly, unable to take his eyes from his brother's proud, resigned face; the faint torchlight illuminated the broad features in reddish streaks and the long, deep-rutted scar emerged dark and cruel in the half shadow. The brothers faced each other in silence for several long moments, and then Palance started back toward Balinor with slow, measured steps, shaking off Stenmin's hand as it tried to restrain him. He came to a halt only inches away from his brother, the dazed, searching eyes still fastened on that granite-hewn countenance as if trying to absorb from it the determination mirrored there. An uncertain hand raised itself quickly, pausing for an instant, then resting firmly on Balinor's shoulder, the fingers gripping tightly.

'I want to . . . know.' The words were a whisper in the near darkness. 'I want to understand . . . You must help me . . .'

Balinor nodded silently, his own great hand reaching up to take his brother's in a brief clasp of love. For a moment they remained locked together, as if the friendship and love of childhood had never faded. Then Palance turned away and moved quickly out of the cell, hastily followed by a disturbed Stenmin. The heavy door closed with the grating of iron fastenings and metal clasps, shutting in the three friends and the impenetrable darkness once more. The departing footsteps died slowly into silence. The waiting began anew, but any real hope of rescue seemed irretrievably lost.

A shadowy form detached itself from the blackness of the night-shrouded trees in the deserted park beneath the high span of the Sendic Bridge and darted silently toward the palace of the Buckhannahs. In quick, surefooted leaps, the powerful, compact form cleared the low hedges and shrubs, weaving between the stately elms, a pair of watchful eyes studying the wall enclosing the royal grounds, searching carefully for any sign of the night watch. Near the iron-wrought gates above the park, where the bridge opened onto the high ground, several guards patrolled, the falcon insignia visible in the torchlight of the gate entrance. Slowly the dark form climbed the gently sloping embankment toward the moss- and ivy-covered walls above; upon gaining the higher ground, it melted instantly into the shadows of the stone.

For long moments, it remained completely invisible as it moved steadily away from the main gate and the feeble torchlight. Then the intruder was visible once more, a dark blur against the faintly moonlit west wall as strong arms clung tenaciously to the sturdy vines, pulling the bulky form silently to the rim of the stone. There the head raised itself cautiously, and the keen eyes peered down into the empty palace gardens, making certain there were no guards close at hand. With a mighty heave of the powerful shoulders, the intruder gained the lip of the wall and, springing lightly over, landed with a soft thud amid the garden flowers.

Running in a half-crouch, the mysterious figure sprinted for the shadowy cover of a huge spreading willow. Pausing breathlessly within the giant tree's protective limbs, the intruder heard the approaching sound of voices. Listening carefully for a few moments, he concluded it was nothing more than the idle conversation of several palace guards making their appointed rounds. He waited confidently, his compact frame blending so closely with the squat trunk of the tree that he was totally invisible from more than a few feet away. The guards appeared seconds later, still conversing in relaxed voices as they passed through the silent gardens and were gone. Resting furtively for a few minutes longer, the stranger studied the dark bulk that occupied the center of these tree-shaded gardens – the tall, ancient palace of the Kings of Callahorn. A few lighted windows broke the misty blackness of the massive stone structure, casting bright streamers into the deserted gardens. There were faint, distant voices within, but their owners remained anonymous.

In a quick dash, the intruder crossed to the shadows of the building, pausing briefly beneath a small, darkened window in a recessed alcove. His strong hands worked frantically at the ancient catch, pushing at it and loosening the fastening. At last, with an audible snap that seemed to penetrate the entire palace grounds, the catch broke and the window swung silently inward. Without waiting to see if the patrolling guards had heard the sounds of his forced entry, the intruder slipped hastily through the small opening. As the window closed behind him, the faint light of a clouded moon caught for just an instant the broad, determined face of the redoubtable Hendel.

Stenmin had made one serious miscalculation when he

had imprisoned Balinor and the cousins of Eventine. His original plan had been a simple one. The aged Sheelon had been secured almost the moment after he left Balinor's side, preventing him from carrying out the Prince's instructions for warning his friends of his own imprisonment. With Balinor and the Elven brothers, his only companions when he had entered the city of Tyrsis, safely locked away beneath the palace, and with the Prince's close friends, Acton and Messaline, imprisoned as well, it seemed safe to assume that no one else in the city would cause any real difficulty. The word had already been spread that Balinor had come for a brief visit and gone on his way, returning to the company of the mystic Allanon, the man whom Stenmin had convinced Palance Buckhannah and most of the people of Tyrsis was an enemy and a threat to the land of Callahorn. Should any other friends of Balinor's appear and question the story of the borderman's abrupt departure, they would come first to the palace to speak with his brother, now the King, and it would be a simple matter to have them quietly disposed of. Undoubtedly this would have been exactly the situation with just about anyone except Hendel. But the taciturn Dwarf was already familiar with Stenmin's treacherous ways and suspected that he had gained an unshakable hold over the disturbed Palance. Hendel knew better than to reveal his presence before finding out what had actually happened to his missing companions.

It was a peculiar turn of events that brought him back to Tyrsis. When he left Balinor and the Elven brothers near the woodlands north of the fortress, he fully intended to travel straight to the western city of Varfleet and from there proceed back to Culhaven. Once in his own land, he would assist in mobilizing the Dwarf armies to defend the southern territories of the Anar against the expected invasion of the Warlock Lord. He traveled all night through the forests north of Varfleet and by morning entered the city, where he immediately called on old friends and, after a brief greeting, went directly to sleep. It was afternoon by the time he was awakened, and after washing and eating, he prepared to depart for his homeland. He had not yet reached the gates of the city when a ragged band of Dwarfs staggered through the streets and demanded to be taken before the council. Hendel hurried along with them, questioning one he recognized as they were escorted to the council chambers. To his dismay he learned that a massive force of Trolls and Gnomes was marching directly for the city of Varfleet from out of the Dragon's Teeth and would strike within the next day or two. The Dwarfs were part of a patrol that had spotted the huge army and tried to slip past it to warn the Southlanders. Unfortunately they were seen and most were killed in a pitched battle. Only this small handful had managed to reach the unsuspecting city.

Hendel knew that if an armed force were moving toward Varfleet, there was in all probability a second, much larger force moving against Tyrsis. He was certain that the Spirit Lord planned to destroy the cities of Callahorn quickly and thoroughly, leaving the gateway to all the Southland open and undefended. His first duty was to warn his own people, but it was a long, two-day march to Culhaven and two more days back again.

He quickly discovered that Balinor had been mistaken in his belief that his father was still the King. If Balinor were killed or imprisoned by his insanely jealous brother or the treacherous mystic Stenmin before he could secure the throne and gain command of the Border Legion, then Callahorn was doomed. Someone had to reach the borderman before it was too late. There was nobody available for the job but Hendel. Allanon was still searching the Northland for the missing Shea, accompanied by Flick and Menion Leah. He made his decision quickly, ordering one of the battered Dwarfs in the ragged patrol to leave that very night for Culhaven. Whatever else happened, word would have to be brought to the Dwarf elders that the invasion of the Southland had begun through Callahorn and that the Dwarf armies must march to the aid of Varfleet. The cities of Callahorn must not fall or the lands would be divided and the very thing Allanon feared most would come to pass. With the Southland conquered, the Dwarf armies and the Elven armies would be divided and the Warlock Lord would be assured his eventual victory over all the lands. The ragged Dwarf gave his solemn promise to Hendel that he would not fail – that they would all leave at once for the Anar.

It took Hendel many hours to get back to Tyrsis, since this time travel was slow and dangerous. The forests had been penetrated by Gnome hunters whose mission it was to prevent any communication between the cities of Callahorn. More than once Hendel was forced to hide himself until a large patrol had passed, and time and again he was compelled to go far out of his way to avoid crossing heavily guarded sentry lines. The network of sentry posts was far tighter than it had been in the Dragon's Teeth, an indication to the seasoned border fighter that the attack was close at hand. If the Northlanders planned to strike Varfleet within the next day or so, then Tyrsis would be assaulted at the same time. The smaller island city of Kern might have already fallen. It was daylight when the Dwarf succeeded in penetrating the last of the sentry lines and was approaching the plains above Tyrsis, the danger of detection by the Gnomes behind and the threat of discovery by the evil Stenmin and the misguided Palance just ahead. He had met Palance several times, but it was unlikely the prince would remember him, and he had encountered Stenmin only once. Nevertheless, it would be wise to avoid attracting anyone's attention.

He entered the waking city of Tyrsis, concealed in the midst of dozens of traders and travelers. Once within the great Outer Wall, he wandered for several hours through the nearly deserted barracks of the Border Legion, speaking with the soldiers there and searching for some clue concerning his friends. Finally he was able to learn that they had arrived in the city at sunset two days ago and gone directly to the palace. They had not been seen again, but there was good reason to believe that Balinor had visited briefly with his father and then left. Hendel knew what this meant, and for the remainder of the daylight hours he posted himself close to the palace grounds, watching for any sign of his missing friends.

He noticed that the palace was well-guarded by soldiers wearing the crest of a falcon, a sign he didn't recognize. There were soldiers stationed at the main gates and throughout the city, all bearing the same insignia, and these were apparently the only activated units in all of Tyrsis. Even if he found Balinor alive and managed to free him, it would not be a simple task to regain control of the city and reactivate the Border Legion. The Dwarf heard no mention of the invasion from the north, and it appeared the people were totally ignorant of the danger facing them. It was incredible to Hendel that even someone as disturbed and misguided as Palance Buckhannah would refuse to prepare the city against a threat as awesome as that posed by the Warlock Lord. If Tyrsis fell, the younger son of Ruhl Buckhannah would have no throne left him. Hendel silently studied the terrain composing the People's Park that stretched beneath the wide span of the Bridge of Sendic. When it was dark, he began his assault on the guarded palace.

Now he paused momentarily within the darkened room, closing the window tightly behind him. He was in a small study, the walls lined with shelves of books carefully marked and labeled. It was the personal library of the Buckhannah family, a luxury in these times when so few books were written and dissemination was considerably limited. The Great Wars had nearly obliterated literature

238

from the face of the earth, and little had been written in the embattled, desperate years since. To have a private library and to be able to sit and read any of several hundred books at leisure were privileges shared by very few, even in the most enlightened societies of the four lands.

But Hendel scarcely gave the room more than a passing thought as he moved on catlike feet for the door at the far end, his keen eyes detecting a dim light along the crack near the floor. Cautiously the Dwarf peered into the lighted hallway. There was no one in sight, but he suddenly realized that he had not yet decided what his next step would be. Balinor and the Elven brothers could be anywhere in the palace. After rapid consideration of the alternatives, he concluded that they would be imprisoned in the cellar beneath the palace if they were alive. He would search there first. Listening for a long moment to the silence, the Dwarf took a deep breath and stepped calmly into the hallway.

Hendel was familiar with the palace, having visited Balinor on more than one occasion. He did not recall where specific rooms were situated, but he knew the halls and stairways, and he had been taken to the cellar where the wines and food were stored. At the end of the hall, he turned left at the cross passage, certain the cellar stairs were just ahead. He reached the massive door that shut out the chill of the lower passages when he heard voices in the hall behind him. Hastily he tugged at the door, but to his dismay it would not open. He pulled again with his powerful shoulders hunched down and knotted, and still the door did not move. The voices were almost on top of him now, and in desperation he moved to reach another place of concealment. At that instant his eyes fell on a safety catch close to the floor which he had missed. With the voices just beyond the corner of the hall and the footsteps of several men echoing on the polished stone flooring, the Dwarf coolly drew back this second latch, swung open the heavy door, and darted inside. The door closed behind him just as three sentries rounded the corner on their way to relieve the guards stationed at the south gate.

Hendel did not wait to find out whether he had been seen, but darted down the stone-hewn stairs into the blackness of the deserted storage cellar. Pausing at the bottom of the stairway, the Dwarf groped along the cold stone of the wall for an iron torch rack. After several long minutes he found it, wresting the torch quickly from its setting and lighting it with the aid of flint and iron.

Then, with slow, painstaking care he searched the entire cellar, room by room, corner to corner. Time passed quickly, and still he found nothing. At last he had searched everywhere without any success, and it began to appear his friends were not being held captive in that part of the palace. Reluctantly Hendel forced himself to admit that they might have been imprisoned in one of the upper rooms. It seemed strange that either Palance or his evil adviser would risk having the captives seen by people visiting. Still, Hendel considered, perhaps Balinor had indeed left the city of Tyrsis and gone in search of Allanon. But he knew that guess was wrong even before the thought was completed. Balinor was not the kind of man who would seek anyone's help with this kind of problem – he would face his brother, not run. Desperately, Hendel tried to imagine where the borderman and the brothers might have been secured, where in the ancient building prisoners could be safely concealed from everyone. The logical place was beneath the palace in the dark, windowless depths he had just . . .

Suddenly Hendel remembered that there were ancient dungeons that lay beneath even this cellar. Balinor had mentioned them in passing, remarking briefly on their history, noting that they had been abandoned and the entry sealed over. Excitedly, the Dwarf peered around the shadowed chamber, trying to recall where the ancient passage had been built. He was certain that this was where his

240

friends had been taken – it was the one place a man could be hidden and never found. Almost no one knew of its existence outside of the royal family and their close associates. It had been sealed over and forgotten for so many years that even the eldest citizens of Tyrsis might not recall its existence.

Ignoring the small adjoining rooms and passages, the determined Hendel carefully studied the walls and flooring of the central chamber, certain that it had been here he had viewed the sealed opening. If it had indeed been reopened, it should not be difficult to find. Yet he could see it nowhere. The walls appeared solid and the molding unbroken as he probed and tapped along the base. Once again his search proved fruitless, and once again he felt that he might have been mistaken. Despondently, he collapsed against one of the wine casings resting in the center of the floor, his eyes scouring the walls desperately as he tried to remember. Time was running out for Hendel. If he did not escape before daylight, he would probably join his friends in captivity. He knew he was missing something, overlooking something that was so obvious it had managed to escape him. Cursing silently, he rose from the wine barrel and walked slowly about the large chamber, thinking, trying to recall. It was something about the walls . . . something about the walls . . .

Then he had it. The passageway was not through the walls, but through the center of the floor! Suppressing a wild shout of glee, the Dwarf rushed over to the wine casings against which he had twice that evening so casually rested. Straining his powerful muscles to almost superhuman limits, he managed to roll aside several of the unwieldy barrels so that the stone slab which covered the hidden entryway was revealed. Grasping an iron ring hinged at one end of the slab, the sweating Dwarf pulled upward with an audible groan. Slowly, the stone grating in protest, the giant slab swung upward and fell back heavily on the flooring. Hendel peered cautiously into the black hole before him, extending the feeble torchlight into the musty depths. There was an ancient stone stairway, wet and covered with a greenish moss, that disappeared into the blackness. Holding the light before him, the little man descended into the forgotten dungeon, silently praying that he was not making another mistake.

Almost immediately he felt the biting chill of the stale, imprisoned air cutting through his clothing to cling maliciously to the warm skin beneath. The musty, barely breathable atmosphere caused him to wrinkle his nose in distaste and move down the steps more quickly. Such confining, tomblike holes frightened him more than anything, and he began to question his wisdom in deciding to venture into the ancient prison. But if Balinor were truly a captive in this terrible place, the risk was worth taking. Hendel would not abandon his friends. He reached the bottom of the stairs and could see a single corridor leading directly ahead. As he moved slowly forward, trying to peer through the damp gloom that defied even the light of the slow-burning torch, he could make out iron doors cut into the solid stone of either wall at regular intervals. These ancient, rusted slabs of iron were windowless and fastened securely in place by huge metal clasps. This was a dungeon that would terrify any human being – a windowless, lightless row of cubicles where lives could be shuttered away and forgotten as surely as the dead.

For untold years the Dwarfs had lived like this following the devastating Great Wars in order to stay alive and had emerged half-blind into a nearly forgotten world of light. That terrible memory had imbedded itself in generations of Dwarfs, leaving them with an instinctive fear of unlighted, confined places that they would never completely overcome. Hendel felt it now, as nagging and hateful as the clammy chill of the earth's depths into which this ancient grave had been carved.

Forcing down the rising knot of terror that hung in his throat, the determined hunter studied the first several doors. The bolts were still rusted in place and the metal covered with layers of dust and unbroken cobwebs. As he passed slowly down the line of grim iron portals, he could see that none of them had been opened in many years. He lost count of the number of doors he checked and the dim corridor seemed to continue on endlessly into the blackness. He was tempted to call out, but the sound might carry back through the open entryway to the chambers above. Glancing apprehensively behind him, he realized that he could no longer see the opening or the stairs. The darkness looked exactly the same behind as it did ahead. Gritting his teeth and muttering softly to himself to bolster his waning confidence, he moved forward, carefully scrutinizing each door he passed for signs of recent use. Then, to his astonishment, he heard the vague whisper of human voices through the heavy silence.

Freezing into a motionless statue, he listened intently, afraid that his senses were deceiving him. Yet there they were again, faint, but clearly human. Moving ahead quickly, the Dwarf tried to follow the sound. But as suddenly as they had appeared, the voices were gone. Desperately, Hendel glanced at the doors to either side. One was rusted shut, but the other bore fresh scratches in the metal, and the dust and cobwebs had been brushed away. The latch was oiled and had been recently used! With one quick tug, the Dwarf pulled back the metal fastening and yanked open the massive door, thrusting the torch before him, the light falling sharply on three astonished, half-blinded figures who rose hesitantly to face this new intruder.

There were warm cries of recognition, a rushing together with outstretched hands, and the four friends were reunited. The rough visage of Balinor, towering above the drawn faces of the smiling Elven brothers, appeared relaxed and confident, and only the blue eyes betrayed the borderman's deep sense of relief. Once again, the resourceful Dwarf had saved their lives. But this was no time for words or feelings, and Hendel quickly motioned them back down the darkened passage toward the stairway leading up from this frightening dungeon. If daybreak found them still wandering beneath the palace, the chance of discovery and recapture would be a near certainty. They had to escape immediately into the city. In hurried steps they moved down the corridor, the dying torchlight held before them like the probing cane of a blind man seeking the way.

Then came the sudden grating of stone on stone and a heavy thudding noise as if a tomb had closed. Horrified, Hendel charged ahead, reaching the damp stone steps and stopping short. Above, the huge stone slab had been closed, the fastenings secured, and the exit to freedom barred. The Dwarf stood helplessly beside his three friends, shaking his head in stunned disbelief. His attempt to save them had failed; he had only succeeded in becoming a captive himself. The torch in his gnarled hand was almost burned out. Soon, they would be left in total blackness, and the waiting would begin again.

To be continued . . .

Look out for . . .

THE SECRET OF THE SWORD

by Terry Brooks

Can the Prince of Leah rally the southern forces to stall the advancing armies of doom? Is there any hope for Balinor and his allies, trapped in the dungeons of his own castle? And can Shea Ohmsford, against all the odds, recover the fabled Sword of Shannara and fulfil the prophecy of defeating the Dark Lord and his deadly Skull Bearers . . .?

Find out in *The Secret of the Sword*, the final volume of Terry Brooks' classic fantasy trilogy *The Sword of Shannara*, available from all good bookshops.

www.atombooks.co.uk

FROM THE TWO RIVERS

Part One of The Eye of the World

by *Robert Jordan*

Life in Emond's Field has been pretty boring for Rand Al'Thor and his friends until a strange young woman arrives in their village. Moraine is an Aes Sedai, a magician with the ability to wield the One Power, and she brings warnings of a terrible evil awakening in the world. That very night, the village is attacked by bloodthirsty Trollocs – a fearsome tribe of beast-men thought to be no more than a myth. As Emond's Field burns, Moraine and her warrior-guardian help Rand and his companions to escape. But it is only the beginning of their troubles. For Moraine believes Rand Al'Thor is the Dragon Reborn, and that he is fated to unite the world against the rising darkness and lead the fight against a being so powerful and evil it is known simply as *the Dark One*.

www.atombooks.co.uk

WWW.ATOMBOOKS.CO.UK